"You specifically wanted to kiss a stranger?"

Max tilted his head as he asked the question. The moonlight touched the mellow honey of his eyes and glistened against the white teeth as he smiled again.

He sounded curious, not shocked. Penny had been turning over various half-truths, wondering how she could explain her eccentric behavior without revealing too much. But to her surprise it suddenly seemed oddly easy to just tell the truth.

"Actually, yes." She sighed. "It was on my list."

His smile broadened. "Really."

"Yes. I have a list. Not a bucket list, exactly. But a—" She couldn't bring herself to say *risk-it list,* which suddenly sounded too cute and sophomoric. "Just a list of all the things I have always wanted to do but never got the chance."

But that wasn't really true. Any female who could walk on her own two feet could have done the absurd thing she did this morning. It wasn't as if she'd asked for his permission or cooperation.

Still, when she caught the interested gleam in his eye, she couldn't stop the feeling of pride in herself, in her boldness.

I could kiss him again!

Dear Reader,

Are you a risk taker? Do you dance on the cliff edge, laugh at the rain?

If so, you're lucky! Some people—like me—were born more timid. We're peacemakers, rule followers, boat steadiers. We have to work to be brave.

So when it came time to create Penny Wright's story, I could easily empathize with her struggle to live a bolder life. At least Penny has a good excuse! The youngest of the three Wright sisters of Bell River Ranch, she was only eleven when her father killed her mother. It's taken her sixteen years to emerge from that shadow.

For inspiration, Penny creates a risk-it list—a catalogue of little things she's always wanted to try, but never had the nerve. She starts small, hoping to gather courage as she goes along.

But funny thing about life...it has a way of setting its own pace. Right at the stumbling start, she meets dynamic Max Thorpe and his motherless ten-year-old daughter. The two may hide it better, but underneath they are every bit as wounded as Penny herself. Suddenly she's facing the biggest risk of all: the risk of losing her heart.

I hope you enjoy watching Penny find the courage, love and freedom she deserves. I hope, too, that your own risk-it list is full of exciting adventures. May every one make you stronger!

Warmly,

Kathleen O'Brien

P.S.—Visit me at my website www.kathleenobrien.com, or come by and say hi on Facebook or Twitter!

KATHLEEN O'BRIEN

The Ranch She Left Behind

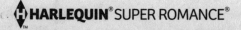

HARLEQUIN® SUPER ROMANCE®

Recycling programs
for this product may
not exist in your area.

ISBN-13: 978-0-373-71892-4

THE RANCH SHE LEFT BEHIND

Copyright © 2013 by Kathleen O'Brien

This edition published by arrangement with Harlequin Books S.A.

For questions and comments about the quality of this book, please contact us at CustomerService@Harlequin.com.

Printed in U.S.A.

ABOUT THE AUTHOR

Kathleen O'Brien was a feature writer and TV critic before marrying a fellow journalist. Motherhood, which followed soon after, was so marvelous she turned to writing novels, which could be done at home. A rule follower who still hears the terrifying voice of Sister Alice in her head whenever she contemplates stepping over the line, she's so glad she discovered romance writing. On the page, she can indulge her secret love of grand drama, goofy escapades and emotional whirlwinds without even getting her knuckles rapped.

Books by Kathleen O'Brien

HARLEQUIN SUPERROMANCE

1015—WINTER BABY*
1047—BABES IN ARMS*
1086—THE REDEMPTION OF MATTHEW QUINN*
1146—THE ONE SAFE PLACE*
1176—THE HOMECOMING BABY
1231—THE SAINT†
1249—THE SINNER†
1266—THE STRANGER†
1382—CHRISTMAS IN HAWTHORN BAY
1411—EVERYTHING BUT THE BABY
1441—TEXAS BABY
1572—TEXAS WEDDING
1590—FOR THE LOVE OF FAMILY
1632—TEXAS TROUBLE
1668—THAT CHRISTMAS FEELING
    "We Need a Little Christmas"
1737—FOR THEIR BABY
1746—THE COST OF SILENCE
1766—THE VINEYARD OF HOPES AND DREAMS
1830—WILD FOR THE SHERIFF#
1860—BETTING ON THE COWBOY#

*Four Seasons in Firefly Glen
†The Heroes of Heyday
#The Sisters of Bell River Ranch

HARLEQUIN SINGLE TITLE

MYSTERIES OF LOST ANGEL INN
    "The Edge of Memory"

Other titles by this author available in ebook format.

To Nancy Robards Thompson and Lori L. Harris, who always find a way to make the story come right—and keep me laughing even when I don't sleep or eat.

And, of course, to Ann Evans, whose wisdom guides every word, just as it always did.

CHAPTER ONE

PENNY WRIGHT JERKED awake, her heart pounding so hard it seemed to beat against her eardrums. What had happened? What was wrong? There'd been a sound…something big….

Oh, no… She sat up, tossing aside the covers, and swung her bare legs toward the floor. "Coming, Ruth!" She fumbled for the lamp switch. Had her aunt fallen again? "Don't move, Ruth. I'll be right th—"

But the act of sitting up was enough to start clearing the cobwebs out of her mind, and she knew there was no point in finishing the sentence. Ruth hadn't fallen. Ruth couldn't hear her.

Ruth had died two months ago.

The town house was silent around her. So silent she could hear the gears of the banjo clock move, preparing to sound the hour in the downstairs parlor…

So what noise had she heard just now?

It must have been something major, to wake her up like that, to make her heart hammer so hard. Or had it been just a dream noise? She dreamed a lot these days—dreams of flying, of dancing, of climbing mountains and riding wild palominos. Freedom dreams. It was as if her subconscious was trying to tell her to get out of this town house and do something.

But she just kept on staying. She was comfortable here. She was used to the quiet, the shadows, the isolation. Even if she sometimes felt like Sleeping Beauty inside her castle tower, at least she always felt safe.

The clock began to bong. *One. Two. Three. Four.* Then it fell silent again, leaving nothing but the eerie after-vibrations that pulsed invisibly up the stairs and made the air in Penny's bedroom hum.

Instinctively, she glanced at her cell phone. More like four-thirty, really. The clock had kept perfect time while Ruth had been alive, but ever since her death it had fallen further and further behind, as if time had begun to slow and stretch, like warm molasses. Just a minute here, a minute there… But it added up.

Soon, the clock would perpetually be living in yesterday.

Oh, well. Too tired to worry, Penny fell back against her pillow. The larger noise she had imagined, it must have been a dream.

But then, with a cold shiver, she registered the sound of another noise—registered it more with her nerve endings than her eardrums.

A much smaller noise this time. A sneaky sound, a muffled creak… She gasped softly, recognizing it. The fifth stair from the top, the one that couldn't be fixed. She'd always had to step over it on her way to bed at night, so she wouldn't wake Ruth.

Someone who didn't know about that little creak was, even now, tiptoeing up the stairs.

Her heart began to pound again. Someone was in the house.

Without hesitation, she slid open the nightstand drawer. Ruth, a practical woman to the core, had insisted that Penny keep protection beside her at all times, especially once the neighborhood began to deteriorate. A gun would have been out of the question—neither Ruth nor Penny liked weapons, or had any confidence that they could prevent a bad guy from getting hold of it.

Therefore, Penny kept a can of wasp spray beside her. Effective from a safe distance, nonlethal, and carrying the added benefit of surprise. Penny had found the idea almost funny and had bought it more for Ruth's peace of mind than her own.

But now, as she saw the shadowy figure appear in her doorway, she sent a fervent thank-you to her practical aunt, who apparently was going to save her one more time—even from the grave.

Ben Hackney, their next door neighbor and a retired policeman, had warned them that, if they ever had to use the can, they shouldn't holler out a warning, but should spray first and ask questions later. So Penny inhaled quickly, put her finger on the trigger, aimed and shot.

A man's voice cried out. "What the fu—?"

She could see the figure a little better now—a man, definitely, dressed in black, his face covered. Her breath hitched. Covered! His eyes, too? If his eyes were covered, would the wasp spray have any effect?

But then the man's hands shot to his face. A guttural growl burst out of him, a sound of both pain and rage. With every fraction of a second, the growl grew louder.

"Goddamn it—"

The voice was deep, middle-aged, furious. She didn't recognize it.

Absurdly, even as she shot the spray again, she felt a shimmer of relief. What if it had been someone she knew? Someone like…

It could have been poor Ben. The man was eighty and had spent a quarter of a century nursing an unrequited love for Aunt Ruth. He'd been good to Penny, too, through the years.

Thank God she hadn't attacked some well-meaning friend like that.

But the relief was brief. The calculations flashed through her mind in a fraction of a second, and then she was left with one awful truth—this was a real intruder. She was left with a *stranger,* who had, without question, come to harm her.

And a can of wasp spray that wasn't bottomless.

For one horrible second, the man lurched forward, and Penny backed up instinctively, though she had nowhere to go. Her spine hit the headboard with an electric bang that exploded every nerve ending in her brain. Somehow, she kept her finger on the trigger and held her numb arm steady enough to keep the spray aimed toward his face.

"You *bitch!*" He dropped to his knees, shaking his head violently. With a cold determination she hadn't known she possessed, she lowered her aim and found him where he had hit the floor.

The spray connected again. Crying out, he roiled backward, a crablike monster, and the sight of his confusion gave her courage. She stood. She was about to follow him, still spraying, when she realized he was trying to reach the stairs.

"No! Wait!" she called out, though warning him made no sense. As long as he was leaving, what did she care what happened to him? But…the staircase!

An irrational panic seized her, freezing all logical thought. He might be a thief, or a rapist, or a murderer. And yet, she couldn't let him just fall backward, helplessly, down that steep, uncarpeted walnut spiral of stairs.

A picture of her mother's body flashed into her mind. The green eyes staring blindly at the ceiling. The black hair glistening as a red pool spread on the floor around her…

"No!" Penny cried out again, louder. She dropped the

wasp spray onto the bed and moved toward the door. "No... the stairs!"

But either the intruder didn't hear her or he couldn't think straight over the pain. He kept scrambling backward, kept bumping and lurching, his shadowy body hurtling toward the point of no return.

And then, just as she reached the hall, he fell.

"No!" The word was a whisper that came out on an exhale of horror. "No...no..."

The sound of his body hitting the steps, one after another, cracked like gunfire. It ricocheted through the house, through the empty rooms and the high ceilings, and, it seemed, through every muscle in Penny's body.

Oh, God. Frozen, she peered over the banister. She wondered if she was going to be sick. If his body lay there, arms and legs at crazed angles like an abandoned rag doll...

If his head rested hideously on a red satin pillow of blood...

She squeezed the wooden rail, squinting. But it was too dark to be sure of anything. He could have been a pile of black laundry at the foot of the stairs. An inanimate object.

No, no, no... Her mind was like one of her father's unbroken horses, running away faster than she could follow. "Please, not again."

But then, as if in answer to a prayer, the shadows seemed to shift, then jerk, then fall still again. Another groan.

Not dead, then. Not dead. As relief swept through her, she heard the jagged gasps of her own lungs, as if she'd been unable to breathe until she was sure he lived.

He lived.

The crumpled shadow shifted. The man stood, moving oddly, but moving. Then he ran to the front door, dragging one leg behind him, and, in a sudden rectangle of moonlight, disappeared into the night.

The minute she couldn't see him anymore, she sank to her knees, right there on the upper landing. It was a complete collapse, as if the batteries that had locked her legs into the upright position had been abruptly switched off.

As she went down, she grabbed for the phone on the marble table. It clattered to the floor. She couldn't feel her fingers, but she found the lighted numbers somehow and punched them in.

9...1...1...

LATER, AS A PINK DAWN light began to seep into the edges of the black clouds, Penny started to shiver. She grabbed her upper arms with her hands and rubbed vigorously.

And only then did she finally realize why, as they interviewed her and took her statement, the police officers kept giving her such strange looks and asking whether she might like to finish the interview inside.

She'd said no because she couldn't bear the thought. She couldn't go in there. Not yet. Not until she stopped reliving the moment the man fell down the stairs. Even then, she wondered if she'd be able to enter by the front door. At Bell River, where her mother had died, Penny hadn't entered by the front in seventeen years.

But these officers didn't know any of that. All they knew was how inappropriately dressed she was for a cold June San Francisco dawn. She was wearing only a thin cotton T-shirt. Dingy, shapeless, with sparkly multicolored letters across the chest that read Keep Calm and Paint Something.

It was too big—she'd lost weight since Ruth's death—so it hit her midthigh, thank goodness. The letters were peeling because she'd washed it so often. But it had been a gift from Ruth, and Penny had worn it almost every night since her aunt's death.

The officer taking her statement was young. Though

Penny was only twenty-seven, she felt aeons older than Officer McGregor. Even the name seemed too big for someone who looked more boy than man, not old enough to be out of high school.

He frowned as she rubbed her arms, and he made a small, worried sound. Then, with a jerky motion, he darted up the steps and into the town house. When he emerged seconds later, he held her running shoes, which she kept by the door, and one of Ruth's sweaters, which had hung on the coat tree for years.

He extended them awkwardly. "I just thought, if you really don't want to go inside…"

"Yes. Thank you." Smiling, she took the shoes gratefully, and wobbled on first one foot, then the other, to tug them on without even unlacing them. His arm twitched, as if he wanted to help steady her, but that was one impulse he did resist.

He held out the sweater so that she could insert her arms, but even that made him blush.

"Thank you," she said again, warmly enough, she hoped, to make him feel more at ease about whether his gesture had been too personal. "I guess I was numb at first, but the chill started to get to me. I feel much better now."

He nodded, obviously tongue-tied, pretending to read over his notes from their interview. She closed the sweater over her chest, wrapped her arms there to hold it shut, and watched him without speaking.

She was sorry he felt embarrassed. But it was soothing, somehow, to witness this gallant innocence. It was like…a chaser. Something sweet to wash away the bitter aftertaste of the shadowy, hulking threat, who had, in such a surreal way, appeared at her bedroom door.

"Pea! Are you mad, girl? It's freezing out here!"

She turned at the sound of Ben Hackney's voice. *Oh, no.*

The first police vehicle had arrived with blue lights flashing, and they must have woken him. He probably had been alarmed, wondering what had happened next door.

"I'm fine, Ben," she said. As he drew closer, she saw that he carried one of his big wool overcoats, which he draped over her shoulders without preamble.

"You *will* be fine—when you get inside. Which you're going to do right now." He glared at McGregor. "If you have more questions, you'll have to ask them another time. I just spoke to your boss over there, and he agreed that I should take Miss Wright in and get her warm."

McGregor lifted his square chin—a Dudley Do Right movement. "Miss Wright has indicated that she doesn't want to go into the house, sir."

"Not that house, you foolish pup. *My* house."

McGregor turned to Penny. "Is this what you'd prefer, Miss Wright? Is this gentleman a friend?"

Penny put her hand on Ben's arm. "Yes, a good friend," she began, but Ben had started to laugh.

"I'm going to take care of her, son. Not serve her up in a pie." His voice was oddly sympathetic. "I know how you're feeling. You want to slay dragons, shoot bad guys, swim oceans in her name."

McGregor's eyebrows drew together, and he started to protest, but he was already blushing again.

"Nothing to be ashamed of," Ben assured him, slapping him on the shoulder. "She has that effect on everyone. Give her your card. That way, if she ever decides she wants to, she can call you."

"Ben, for heaven's sake." He had been trying to match her up with a boyfriend for the past ten years. She had to credit him with good instincts, though—he'd never liked Curt.

She turned to McGregor. "He's teasing," she said. "He thinks it'll make me feel better, after—"

To her surprise, the officer was holding out his business card. "Oh." She accepted it, looked at it—which was stupid, because what did she expect it to say, other than what it did? James McGregor, SFPD, and a telephone number. She wished she had pockets.

For one thing, having pockets would mean she had pants. "Thank you."

Then Ben shepherded her away, across the dewy grass, up his stairs—the mirror image of the ones on Ruth's town house—and hustled her to the kitchen, where she could smell coffee brewing.

The kitchen was toasty warm, but she kept on the overcoat, realizing that the shivering wasn't entirely a result of temperature. He scraped out a chair at the breakfast nook, then began to bustle about, pouring coffee and scrambling eggs with a quiet calm as she recounted what had happened.

When the facts had been exchanged, and the immediate questions answered, he seemed to realize she needed to stop talking. He kept bustling, while she sat, staring out at the brightening emerald of the grass and the gorgeous tulips he grew with his magical green thumbs.

She liked the small sounds of him working. The clink of a spoon against a cup, the quick swish of water dampening a dishcloth, the squeak of his tennis shoes.

The simple sounds of another human being. Suddenly she realized how completely alone she'd been the past two months.

Finally, the internal shivering ceased. With a small sigh of relief, she shrugged off his coat. Glancing at the clock over the stove, she realized it was almost seven.

She must have been here an hour or more. She should go home and let him get on with his day.

"Thank you, Ben," she began, standing. "I should go ho—" All of a sudden she felt tears pushing at her throat, behind her eyes, and she sat back down, frowning hard at her cup. "I—I should…"

"You should *move,*" Ben said matter-of-factly. He had his cup in one hand and a dish towel in the other, drying the china in methodical circular motions, as if he were polishing silver.

"Move?" She glanced up, wondering if she'd misheard. "Move out of the town house?"

He nodded.

"Just because of what happened this morning?"

"No. Not *just* that. You should move because you shouldn't be living there in the first place. For Ruth, maybe it was right. She liked quiet. For you…"

He shook his head slowly, but with utter conviction. "I always knew it was wrong of her to keep you there. Like a prison. You're too young. You're too alive."

"That's not fair," she interjected quickly. Criticism of Ruth always made her uncomfortable. Where would she have been if Ruth hadn't agreed to take her in? "Ruth knew I needed—a safe harbor."

"At first, yes." Ben sighed, and his gaze shifted to the bay window overlooking the gardens. His deep-set blue eyes softened, as if he could see them as they'd been fifteen years ago, an old man and a little girl, with twin easels set up, twin paint palettes smudged with blue and red and yellow, each trying to capture the beauty of the flowers.

"At first, you did need a quiet home. Like a hospital. You were a broken little thing."

He transferred his troubled gaze to her. Then he cleared his throat and turned to the sink.

Ben knew about the tragedy that had exiled Penny from Bell River, of course. Everyone knew, but Ruth hadn't allowed anyone to speak of it to Penny. She thought it would be too traumatic. Having a mother die tragically was bad enough for any child. But having your mother killed by your father…and your father hauled away to prison…

And then being ripped from the only home you'd ever known, split from your sisters and asked to live in another state, with a woman you barely knew…

Traumatic was an understatement. But, though Ruth had meant well, never being allowed to talk about what had happened—that might have been the hardest of all. Never to be given the chance to sort her emotions into words, to put the events into some larger perspective. Never to let them lose power through familiarity.

Sometimes Penny thought it was a miracle she hadn't suffered a psychotic break.

"Sweet pea, I'm sorry. But I need to say this." Ben still held the cup and dishrag, and was still rubbing the surface in circles, as if it were a worry stone.

"Of course," she said. "It's okay, Ben. Whatever it is."

"Good." He put down the cup and rag, then cleared his throat. "Ruth did mean well. I know that. You needed to heal, and at first it was probably better to heal quietly, in private. But you've been ready to move on for a long time."

"How could I? Ruth was so sick, and—"

"I know. It was loyal of you to stay, to take care of her when she needed you. But she doesn't need you anymore, honey. It's time to move on."

At first Penny didn't answer. She recognized a disturbing truth in his words. That truth made her so uncomfortable she wanted to run away. But she respected him too much to brush him off. They'd been friends a long time. He was as close to a father as she'd ever had.

"I know," she admitted finally. "But moving on…it's not that easy, Ben."

"Of course it is!" With a grin, he stomped to the refrigerator and yanked down the piece of paper that always hung there, attached by a magnet shaped like Betty Boop. "Just do it! Walk out the door! Grab your bucket list and start checking things off!"

She laughed. "I don't have a bucket list."

"You don't?" Ben looked shocked. He stared at his own. "Not even in your head? In your heart of hearts? You don't have a list of things you want to do before you die?"

She shook her head.

"Why? You think bucket lists are just for geezers like me?"

"Of course not. I've never had any reason to—"

"Well, you do now. You can't hide forever, Pea. For better or worse, you aren't like the nun in Ruth's parlor. You were never meant for that."

Ruth's parlor overflowed with lace doilies and antimacassars, Edwardian furniture and Meissen shepherdesses. Ruth had covered every inch of wall space with framed, elaborate cross-stitch samplers offering snippets of poetry, advice and warnings—so many it was hard to tell where one maxim ended and the next one began.

Penny had loved them all, but her favorite had been a picture of a woman putting on a white veil. When Penny moved in, at eleven, she'd assumed the woman was getting married, but Ruth had explained that the poem was really about a woman preparing to become a nun.

The line of poetry beneath the veil read, "And I have asked to be where no storms come." Penny had adored the quote—especially the way it began with *and,* as if it picked up the story in the middle. As if the woman had already explained the troubles that had driven her to seek safety in a convent.

"My father murdered my mother," Penny always imagined the poem might have begun. "And so I have asked to be where no storms come."

She'd mentioned it to Ben only one time. He gave her a camera for her twelfth birthday, and she took a picture of the sampler, among her other favorite things. When she showed it to him, he had frowned, as if it displeased him to see how much she liked it.

He was frowning now, too. "I hope you're not still toying with the idea of taking the veil."

Penny chuckled. "Of course not." She remembered what Ruth had said when Penny had asked if she was too young to become a nun.

"Far too young," Ruth had responded with a grim smile, "and far too Methodist."

"Good." Ben waved his hand, chasing the idea away like a gnat. "You'd make a horrible nun. You were made for marriage, and children, and love."

"No." She shook her head instinctively. No, she definitely wasn't.

"Of course you are. How could you not know it? The men know it. Every male who sees you falls in love with you on the spot. You make them want to be heroes. Think of poor Officer McGregor out there."

It was her turn to blush. Penny knew she wasn't glamorous. She had two beautiful sisters, one as dark and dramatic as a stormy midnight, the other as pale and cool as a snow queen. Penny was the boring one. And if she hadn't been boring to begin with, these years with Ruth, who didn't believe in wearing bright clothing or making loud noises, had certainly washed her out to a faded, sepia watercolor of a woman.

The only beauty she had any claim to showed up in her art.

Ben's affection made him partial. As if to offset Ruth's

crisp, undemonstrative manner, he had always handed out extravagant compliments like candy.

"Don't be silly, Ben."

"I'm not. You are. You've got that quiet, innocent kind of beauty, which, believe me, is the most dangerous. Plus, you're talented, and you're smart, and you're far too gutsy to spend the rest of your life hiding in that town house."

She had to smile. She was the typical youngest child— meek, a pleaser, bossed around by everyone, always trying to broker peace. "Come on. *Gutsy?*"

"Absolutely. You've conquered more demons at your young age than most people face in a lifetime. Starting with your devil of a father, and going up through tonight."

"I haven't been brave. I've simply endured. I've done whatever I had to do."

"Well, what do you think courage is?" He smiled. "It's surviving, kiddo. It's doing what you must. It's grabbing a can of wasp spray and aiming it at the monster's ugly face."

She laughed, and shook her head. "And then shaking like a leaf for four hours straight?"

"Sure. For a while you'll shake. But trust me, by tomorrow, you'll realize tonight taught you two very important things. One, you can't hide from trouble—not in a nunnery, and certainly not in a San Francisco town house."

The truth of that sizzled in the pit of her stomach. She might want to be where no storms come—but was there any such place?

She nodded slowly. "And two?"

"And two…" He took her hand in his and squeezed. "Two…so trouble finds you. So what? You're a warrior, Penelope Wright. There's no trouble out there that you can't handle."

MAX THORPE HADN'T been on a date in ten months, not since his wife died. Apparently, ten months wasn't long enough.

Everything about the woman he'd taken to dinner annoyed him, from her perfume to her conversation.

Even the way she ate salad irritated him. So odd, this intensely negative reaction. She'd seemed pretty good on paper—just-turned-thirty to his thirty-four, a widow herself. A professional, some kind of charity arts work on the weekends. His friends, who had been aware that divorce had been in the air long before Lydia's aneurysm, had started trying to set him up with their single friends about six months after her death, but this was the first time he'd said yes.

Obviously he'd surrendered too soon—which actually surprised him. Given the state of his marriage, he wouldn't have thought he'd have this much trouble getting over Lydia.

But the attempt to reenter the dating world had gone so staggeringly wrong from the get-go that he'd almost been glad to see his daughter's cell phone number pop up on his caller ID.

Until he realized she was calling from the security guard's station at the outlet mall.

Ellen and her friends, who had supposedly been safe at a friend's sleepover, had been caught shoplifting. The store would release her with only a warning, but he had to talk to them in person.

Shoplifting? He almost couldn't believe his ears. But he arranged a cab for his date, with apologies, then hightailed it to the mall, listened to the guard's lecture, and now was driving his stony-faced eleven-year-old daughter home in total silence.

A lipstick. Good God. The surprisingly understanding guard had said it all—how wrong it was morally, how stupid it was intellectually, how much damage it could do to her life, long-term. But Max could tell Ellen wasn't listening.

And he had no idea how he would get through to her, either.

Ellen had turned eleven a couple of weeks ago. She wasn't allowed to wear lipstick. But even if she was going to defy him about that, why steal it? She always had enough money to buy whatever she wanted, and he didn't make her account for every penny.

In fact, he almost never said no to her—never had. At first, he'd been overindulgent because he felt guilty for traveling so much, and for even *thinking* the D word. Then, after Lydia's death, he'd indulged his daughter because she'd seemed so broken and lost.

Great. He hadn't just flunked Marriage 101, he'd flunked Parenting, too.

"Ellen, I need to understand what happened tonight. First of all, what were you and Stephanie doing at the mall without Stephanie's parents?"

Ellen gave him a look that stopped just shy of being rude. She knew he didn't allow overt disrespect, but she'd found a hundred and one ways to get the same message across, covertly.

"They let her go to the mall with friends all the time. I guess her parents *trust* her."

He made a sound that might have been a chuckle if he hadn't been so angry. "Guess *that's* a mistake."

Ellen folded her arms across her chest and faced the window.

The traffic was terrible—Friday night in downtown Chicago. It would be forty minutes before they got home. Forty very long minutes. He realized, with a sudden chagrin, that he'd really rather let it go, and make the drive in angry silence. Though he'd adored Ellen as a baby and a toddler, something had changed through the years. He didn't speak her language anymore.

He didn't know how to couch things so that she'd listen, so that she'd care. He didn't know what metaphors she thought in, or what incentives she valued.

The awkward, one-sided sessions of family therapy, which they'd endured together for six months to help her deal with her grief, hadn't exactly prepared him for real-life conversations.

Even before that, everything had come together in a perfect storm of bad parenting. His job had started sending him on longer and longer trips. Mexico had happened. When he returned from that, he was different—and not in a good way. His wife didn't like the new, less-patient Max, and he didn't like her much, either. She seemed, after his ordeal, to be shockingly superficial, oblivious to anything that really mattered in life.

And she had taken their daughter with her to that world of jewelry, supermodels, clothes, diets. When they chattered together, Max tuned out. If he hadn't, he would have walked out.

He hadn't blamed Lydia. He knew she clung to her daughter because she needed an ally, and because she needed an unconditional admiration he couldn't give her. But as the gulf widened between Max and Lydia, it had widened between Max and Ellen, too.

He might not travel that much anymore, but he'd been absent nonetheless.

"Ellen." He resisted the urge to give up. "You're going to have to talk to me. Stealing is serious. I have no idea why you'd even consider doing something you know is wrong. You have enough money for whatever you need, don't you?"

She made a tsking sound through her teeth. "You don't understand. It's not always *about* money."

"Well, then, help me to understand. What is it about?"

"Why do you even care? I'm sorry I caused you trouble. I'm sorry I interrupted you on your *date*."

He frowned. Could his dating already be what had prompted this? He'd talked to her about the dinner ahead of time, and she'd professed herself completely indifferent to when, or whom, he chose to date.

But he should have known. Ellen rarely admitted she cared about anything. Especially anything to do with Max.

"I don't care about the date," he said. "It wasn't going well, anyhow. Right now, all I want is to be here. I want to sort this out with you."

She laughed, a short bark that wasn't openly rude, but again, barely. "Right."

"If you want me to understand, you have to explain. If it's not about money, what is it about? Are you angry that I went on a date?"

"No. Why should I be? It's not like Mom will mind."

He flinched. "Okay, then, what is it?" He took a breath. "Ellen, I'm not letting this go, so you might as well tell me. Why would you do such a thing?"

She unwound her arms so that she could fiddle with her seat belt, as if it were too tight. "You won't understand."

"I already don't understand."

"It's like an initiation."

He had to make a conscious effort not to do a double take. But what the hell? What kind of initiation did eleven-year-olds have to go through?

"Initiation into what?"

"The group. Stephanie's group."

"Why on earth would you want to be part of any group that would ask you to commit a crime?"

"Are you kidding?" Finally, Ellen turned, and her face was slack with shock. "Stephanie's the prettiest girl in school, and the coolest. If you're not part of her group, you might as well wear a sign around your neck that says Loser."

A flare of anger went through him like something shot from a rocket. How could this be his daughter? He'd been brought up on a North Carolina farm, by grandparents who taught him that nothing seen by the naked eye mattered. The worth of land wasn't in its beauty, but in what lay beneath, in the soil. The sweetest-looking land sometimes was so starved for nutrients that it wouldn't grow a single stick of celery, or was so riddled with stones that it would break your hoe on the first pass.

People, they told him, were the same as the land. Only what they had inside mattered, and finding that out took time and care. Money just confused things, allowing an empty shell to deck out like a king.

For a moment, he wanted to blame Lydia. But wasn't that the kind of lie that his grandfather would have hated? All lies, according to his grandfather, were ugly. But what he called "chicken lies" were the worst. Those were the ones you told to yourself, to keep from having to look an ugly truth in the eye.

So, no. He couldn't blame Lydia. First of all, where did Lydia come from? From Max's own foolish, lusty youth. From his inability to tell the empty shell from the decked-out facade.

And, even more important, why should Lydia's influence have prevailed over his?

Because he'd abdicated, that's why. He'd opted out. He'd failed.

But not anymore. He looked at his little girl, at her brown hair that used to feel like angel silk beneath his hands. He remembered the dreams he'd built in his head, as he walked the floor with her at night. He remembered the love, that knee-weakening, heart-humbling rush of pure adoration....

"We're going to have to make some serious changes," he said. His tone was somber—so somber it seemed to startle her, her eyes wide and alarmed.

"What does that mean?"

"I'm not sure yet," he said. "But you should brace yourself, because they're going to be big changes. We've gotten off track somewhere. Not just you. Me, too. We have to find our way back."

She swallowed, as if the look on his face made her nervous. But she didn't ask any further questions.

Which was good, because he didn't have many answers. Only one thing he knew, instinctively. He couldn't do it here, in Chicago, with the traffic and the malls and the Stephanies. And the memories of Lydia around every corner.

He had no idea how, but he was going to fix this. He was going to stop giving her money, stop assuaging his guilt with presents and indulgence. He was going spend time with her, get to know her and teach her those hard but wonderful life lessons his grandparents had taught him.

And maybe, along the way, he'd relearn some of those lessons himself.

CHAPTER TWO

Two months later

SILVERDELL, COLORADO, HADN'T changed much in seventeen years. Penny had noticed that last year, when she came back as the dude ranch idea was first being considered, and then again when her sister Rowena got married.

But on this visit, she was particularly struck by the snow-globe effect—perhaps because her own world had changed so dramatically. She drove slowly down Elk Avenue, noting how many stores remained from her childhood, and how many of the replacement shops had maintained the feel of their predecessors.

August. Early fall in Silverdell. She remembered it so well. And here it all was. Same big tubs of orange and gold chrysanthemums on the sidewalk, same colorful awnings over shovel- and ski-jacket-filled windows that warned of the winter to come.

Same park square, roiling with what might easily have been the same laughing children.

She slowed now, watching them kick piles of leaves into tiny yellow storms and chase each other, squealing, until someone fell, then got up, giggling, with grass stains on elbows and chin.

She and her sisters, Rowena and Bree, had rarely been part of all that. In fact, she used to watch those mischievous kids and wonder where they got the courage to be so naughty. Didn't their fathers have tempers, too?

Their fathers...

She knew she ought to go to the ranch. Or at least by her new duplex.

But she knew she wasn't ready. It didn't make any sense, but she needed more time to come to terms with being in Silverdell again—and with the big changes that were coming.

It didn't help to remind herself that they were changes she'd wanted. Changes she'd *chosen.* Suddenly the changes seemed more than "big." They seemed crazy. Risky. Terrifying.

Annoyed with herself, but unable to break through the emotional paralysis, she found a parking space and headed into the ice-cream shop. She was hungry and nervous. Even before she had grown a full set of teeth she'd learned that a banana split could make everything better.

Her father and Ruth would both have been horrified— ice cream before lunch? *Instead* of lunch? But they weren't here. And she wasn't a child. Surely this one tiny act of independent thinking wasn't too much for her, even today.

Baby steps.

"Hey!" The string-bean-shaped young man behind the counter tossed down his magazine and stood at attention, apparently delighted to see her. The shop was empty, so maybe he really was. "What can I get you?"

She glanced at the calligraphy on the menu over his head. "I'd love a banana split. Double whipped cream."

"Awesome!" He grinned as if she'd said the magic words and began pulling out ingredients. "It's getting nippy out, and we don't get much business once it turns cold. We sell hot chocolate, but it takes a lot of hot chocolates to pay the rent, you know?"

She smiled, thinking how close her calculations had been when she decided how much rent she'd need to ask for the other side of her new duplex.

"Yeah," she said. "I know."

"About a hundred million," the young man said, inserting his knife into a banana as carefully as if he were performing surgery. "Plus, there's no art to making a cup of cocoa. Not like a good banana split." He arranged the slices into the curved boat, tossing away a couple of bruised bits. "Now this is something you can get creative with."

A warmhearted ice-cream artist who worried about making the rent but couldn't force himself to serve a bruised banana. She made a mental note to come in as often as she could. Her sweet tooth didn't know seasons.

She smiled. See? She hadn't taken a single bite, and she was already feeling better.

"Go ahead and grab a seat," he said. "I'm Danny. This is my shop. I'll make you something special, and bring it to you."

She arranged herself by the window, dropped her purse on the other side of the table and pulled out her legal pad and pen. Maybe if she worked on her list, she would retrieve her courage, and she could head to Bell River.

She flipped over a couple of pages, filled to the margins with practical information about who to call if the water wasn't hooked up, or the electricity went wonky. All that was important, but not right now.

The third page… That's the one that mattered. She tapped her pen against her lips and read what she'd written so far.

The Risk-it List.

The very words looked good, in her favorite turquoise ink, against the yellow lined paper. Last night, when she'd stopped—not wanting to arrive in Silverdell after dark—

she had worked on the list. Right before she fell asleep, she'd doodled a small bluebird in the upper right corner of her paper.

The bluebird of happiness. That's what Ro used to call it. Ro and Bree used to take Penny "hunting" in the woods, with butterfly nets that supposedly were magical, nets that could catch the bluebird that would make everything at Bell River right.

Obviously, they'd never captured one. But Penny had drawn birds, photographed them, been fascinated by them, ever since. This one was fat and contented, and smiled at the list below him.

The Risk-it List. She'd decided it should be twelve items long. She had six entries so far, and two check marks.

Sell town house. Check.

Buy place in Silverdell— Don't let Bree and Ro overrule. Don't tell Bree and Ro until purchase complete! Check.

Host a party...wearing a costume.

Learn to juggle.

Learn to dance.

Cut hair.

Seven...Seven...

Penny chewed on the end of her pen—a habit she'd never been able to break—and tried to make up her mind what number seven should be.

Ben had been right, of course. When the shock of the wasp spray incident had worn off, a strange pride took its place. She felt empowered. Why shouldn't she? She'd prevailed over a big, hulking intruder. She might have been terrified, but she hadn't panicked. She'd kept her head, and she'd driven him away—without anyone getting seriously hurt.

She'd decided that very day to start the list. And before any doubt could set in, she'd accomplished numbers one and two. Sell the town house—almost frighteningly easy. And buy a small house in Silverdell—much scarier, as she didn't have time to see it for herself but had to trust Jenny Gladiola, Silverdell's longtime real estate agent.

But she'd accomplished both, and now here she was, less than three miles from Bell River Ranch. Here to stay. Here to call Silverdell home again, after all these years.

A shiver passed through her. Thanks to Jenny's discretion, no one in the family yet knew she was in town. Jenny had been a Dellian real estate agent forever, and she'd kept her career flourishing, through good markets and bad, by knowing how to keep her mouth shut.

For now Penny was safe. However, telling Bree and Rowena absolutely had to be next.

Her sisters had been begging her for months to come live at the dude ranch with them. They could use the help, they said. They needed an art teacher, they said. But she knew the truth—they were worried about her. They wanted to slip her into their nest, straight from the nest Ruth had kept her in.

No one wanted her to learn to fly.

But, by golly, she was going to learn anyhow.

So…back to the Risk-it List. What should number seven be? She had to pick very carefully. After the two big jolts of selling the town house and buying the duplex, she wanted the rest of the list to be relatively easy. She'd tackle a few of her phobias—but she wouldn't set herself up for failure. No wrestling pythons in the rain forest or taking a commercial shuttle to the space station.

Just juggling, costumes, kissing…

Ben would laugh. He was much more the space station type. She'd decided not to call hers a bucket list. It sounded too ambitious. That might come later, after she'd accomplished everything on this one. After she'd learned a little bit about who Penny Wright really was.

Instead, she'd called it the Risk-it List. A list of things she'd never had the nerve to do—though she'd always envied others who did. Things that looked daring, or exciting, or just plain fun. Things that might be mistakes. Things that might make her look silly. Things she had phobias about...

Aha! Phobias!

So seven would be: *Ride in a hot air balloon. (fear of heights)*

Take a picture of someone famous. (shyness)
Get a beautiful tattoo. (fear of disapproval)
Kiss a total stranger. (fear of...everything)
Go white-water rafting (fear of dying ☺*)*
Make love in a sailboat.

Number Eleven, the white-water rafting, would probably be the scariest. She really, really found the rapids terrifying. So obviously she'd left that till toward the end of the list.

But where had that crazy Number Twelve come from? Was it from some movie she'd seen? Some couple she'd spotted setting off into San Francisco Bay...with her imagination supplying the rest?

"What's so funny?"

Danny, the ice-cream artist, was at her table, holding a bowl so laden with beautifully arranged sweets that she knew she'd never be able to finish it.

He looked for a safe place to set it down. Flushing, she tilted her legal pad toward her chest to hide it, then felt ridiculous. Why did she care whether he saw it?

"Nothing, really," she said awkwardly. "I just wrote the wrong thing... You know... I mean I spelled it all wrong."

Argh. Why did she always feel nervous if she did anything remotely unconventional? She *was* unconventional, darn it. She was an artist at heart, not a banker. She wanted to dress in flamboyant colors and patterns, and laugh loudly, and lie down on the sidewalk to get the best angle on a snail. She wanted to sing and dance and go to parties—and make love in a sailboat.

Ruth wasn't here to reproach her. Her father wasn't here to mock. No one cared. No one.

She could simply have laughed and said, "I wrote 'sex on a sailboat' on my wish list, though until this very minute I had no idea it was a fantasy of mine."

Danny was probably no more than twenty-three, fresh out of college—he'd probably be a lot more embarrassed than she was.

New Number One: Stop Being Such a Doormat.

Oh, well. Baby steps, remember? She gave him a warm smile to offset any insult he might have taken from the snatched-away list. She complimented his gorgeous creation, stuck a finger—*sorry, Ruth*—into the whipped cream, then stuck the finger into her mouth and sighed. Real whipped cream. Sinfully delicious.

"It's fantastic," she said. "I've moved back to town, and you can be sure I'll be a regular customer!"

But it was too late. Obviously offended, he'd dialed his friendliness down about three notches. He wandered toward the ice-cream cases and began stacking and restacking prepackaged tubs—though they'd been perfectly aligned already.

Darn it. She sighed, annoyed with herself all over again. That was three strikes. Afraid to pull into Bell River. Afraid to pull into her own new duplex. Afraid to let this nice man see that she was making a list of dreams.

She'd better stiffen up, and fast, or the ego boost of banishing her intruder would disappear into a cloud of self-doubt. Her life might slide right back into the gray, conformist soup of the past seventeen years.

No. Darn it. No.

She couldn't stand that. She wouldn't let it happen. One way or another, she'd find the courage to—

The bell rang out as the door opened. She kept her legal pad against her chest as two people walked in. A little girl, maybe ten? Sulky, angry about something.

As she did with everyone she saw, Penny mentally began to sketch the child. A duckling still, but with definite traces of swan showing up around the edges. Her chubby cheeks were out of proportion to her longish, narrow chin. Someday, in the next year or two, her contours would lengthen, and she'd have the sweetest heart-shaped face....

Her hair was a glorious mess—shining, thick, brown, glossy curls that she had no idea what to do with now. And her figure obviously was hard to fit. A thick waist over too-long, too-skinny legs that made her look a little like a candy apple on toothpicks today. But when she got her teenage growth spurt, and that torso stretched out to match the limbs....well, watch out, Dad.

Ohhhh. When Penny's gaze finally shifted to Dad, she felt a small kick beneath her ribs. What a wonderful face... and the rest of him wasn't bad, either.

His coloring wasn't dramatic—the daughter must have inherited that from Mom. He was brown-haired, with hints of honey in the strands, and a similar honeyed stubble on his cheeks and chin. His eyes, too, were brown—they caught the light through the window, and glowed amber, rich, a lot like the caramel sliding down her ice cream right now.

But he didn't need to be painted with bold colors to be memorable. He oozed power—it was in the jut of his cheekbones, the knife-edge of his jaw, the full sensuality of his lips. And in that body. If he didn't work outdoors, he must work out *indoors*...about twenty hours a day.

Something else made her lower her legal pad, uncap

her pen and start to sketch, though. Not the power. She wasn't impressed by power—in fact, it repelled her. No, what her pen flew across the page trying to capture was something less easily defined. Something in the curve of his neck, or maybe it was the elegant slide of light across his cheek, twinkling like a hint of magic in those tiny, un-shaven shadows.

She bit her lower lip, frustrated. The pen wasn't subtle enough; she needed charcoals, or watercolor. Or was wa-tercolor too insipid? Pen and ink, maybe, would find the tightrope balance between sweetness and strength.

Suddenly, the sweetness took the upper hand. Oh, he was smiling, and that changed everything! A hint of rascal in the slight overbite, but a rush of kindness and harmony in the open lips, a torrent of sensuality in the wide expanse of...

Her pen froze. He wasn't just smiling. He was smil-ing at *her*.

He was watching her watch him.

Which, she realized as she stared at her pad, she must have been doing for quite a while. The drawing was tak-ing shape, filling in with detail. It wouldn't be mistaken for anyone or anything but him.

Her cheeks burned as she realized his daughter was watching her, too. How long had she been in her trance, drawing while the rest of the world disappeared? Father and daughter had already ordered, and the little girl was even now sucking absently on the straw of an ice-cream float while she stared at Penny.

Nervously, Penny set down the pad and pulled the top pages over to cover her sketch. She tried to make the move-ment look natural, but she knew it was hopeless.

"Why were you drawing my dad?" The girl frowned, pointing her float toward the notebook, as if to prevent Penny from denying it.

"Ellen. Don't be rude," the man said, still smiling. He reached out to pull back his daughter's outthrust glass, but she made a petulant sound and lurched clear of him in one willful, rebellious motion.

Her father's grip had obviously been gentle, so the force was twice what she needed to break free. The results were disastrous. Ice cream and root beer and whipped cream flew everywhere.

Everywhere. Across the girl's hand, onto the floor, onto her shoes—and even onto her dad's crisp white shirt and golden suede jacket.

Her cheeks flamed red. "Now look what you did," the girl said, obviously covering her embarrassment with aggression.

Oh, no, don't make him look a fool—especially not with strangers to witness the disrespect! Penny's chest tightened, and her stomach did a dizzy swooping thing. She didn't dare look at the father. Though the girl was bratty, Penny's heart ached for her, and she wished she could prevent what must be coming.

But several seconds passed, and she heard nothing. No yelling, no curses, not even a cold, scathing reprimand. Penny glanced up. To her surprise the child was disappearing into the ladies' room, and the father calmly tugged napkins out of the dispenser.

"Ah, man, I'm sorry," Danny said, running a dishrag under some water. "I'll make her another one. No charge."

Yeah, right. Penny tightened again, thinking how unlikely it was that the father would reward such rudeness with a second chance at ice cream.

"Don't be silly," the man said in a pleasant tone, surprising Penny so completely she felt her lower jaw sag. "Of course we'll pay for it. But make it a double, okay? And what the heck. I'll have one, too."

And just like that, Penny's tension drained away, as if someone had pulled the stopper out. She felt a wave of irrational happiness wash in after it. The happiness was irrational because logically, just one nice man, one patient father—that didn't change anything, not for her. She had grown up with a terrifying father, and she still had the emotional scars to prove it.

This man was no one to her—she didn't even know his name. But he was…well, right now he felt like hope personified. He was the rainbow after the storm, the unicorn emerging from the forest, the olive branch that proved land still existed, land that an exhausted sailor might someday reach.

Right now, she absolutely loved this beautiful, beautiful man.

Impulsively, she stood. He'd run out of napkins, and he still had whipped cream flecked across his neck and under his chin. He probably didn't even realize it. She extracted a dozen napkins from the dispenser on her table and moved toward him.

Danny was absorbed in making the new floats.

"Here," she said as she reached the counter. "Let me help with that. You've still got a spot, here—" She stood on tiptoe. He was tall. "And here."

She leaned in.

Number Ten. Kiss a total stranger.

This was perfect. Not an artificial check mark on an arbitrary list. She *wanted* to kiss him. For daughters everywhere, including the angry kid in the bathroom, and the terrified little girl she herself once had been, Penny wanted to give him a heartfelt thank-you kiss.

On the cheek, of course. She shut her eyes. Her lips tingled, anticipating the soft bristles of his stubble. He smelled sweet, as if he'd been traveling in a perfume-filled car. But

not a grown woman's perfume. A pink-cotton-candy perfume—the kind a ten-year-old would wear.

Cotton candy and honey bristles… Something fluttered
in her belly. How could such a combination be sensual?

But as she moved in, he must have shifted his face toward her, because her impetuous kiss landed not on soft
bristles, but on the warm, ridged flesh of his lips.

She inhaled sharply, opening her eyes—and found herself staring into the deep pools of his. She had connected
with the edge of his mouth, not the center, where the sharply
drawn bow formed. But still…she felt the warmth of the
stiff rim around the velvet flesh. She felt the minty heat of
his surprised breath.

For a minute, she couldn't pull away.

He didn't, either. For a second, a few seconds—it was
hard to tell, because time seemed as sticky and easily
stretched as the caramel on her sundae—they stood there,
joined by shocked eyes and warm, half-open mouths.

He made a low sound, a primitive sound that could be
identified in any country, on any planet, as pleasure. But he
didn't dive in, snatching the opportunity lewdly, as some
men might have done. Instead, he slowly, almost imper-
ceptibly, tilted his head to the right…then delicately drew
it back again to the left.

The subtle movement caused his lips to brush hers with
an excruciating tingle. All through her body, nerve endings
reacted, as if he'd put a match to her mouth. Her cheeks
flamed. Her chest radiated heat like a sunburst. Her heart
couldn't remember exactly what to do, and thumped around
in her chest, confused.

Surely the whole thing didn't last more than two or three
seconds. Danny hadn't even finished churning ice cream
into the floats. Two or three seconds, and then—it might
have been prearranged—they both pulled back at the same

moment. She had to work hard to steady her breathing, as if she'd been jogging, and she felt the strangest urge to adjust her untouched clothes and smooth her unruffled hair.

In contrast, he looked surprised but utterly calm. His caramel eyes were smiling. The outside corners tilted up, managing to look quizzical and delighted at the same time.

"I'm not sure what I did to deserve that," he said in low, pleasant tones. "But I hope you'll tell me…so that I can do it again."

"It isn't what you did," she said awkwardly, backing up a step. "It's what you didn't do."

"What I didn't do?"

She tried to laugh, tried to match his composure, though she suddenly felt utterly ridiculous. He'd never understand. He probably had no idea what some fathers were capable of doing to a daughter who got mouthy and rude.

She let her gaze drift to the hallway where his daughter had disappeared only two or three minutes before. "I guess I wanted to thank you, on behalf of all the clumsy, fussy little girls out there, for not losing your temper."

For a minute he looked truly confused. His brows drew together a fraction of an inch, and he tilted his head one degree. "Over ice cream?"

"Partly ice cream." She raised her eyebrows. "But mostly…attitude."

"Ah. The attitude." He sobered slightly. "Well, we've got kind of a special case, because—"

"Dad, let's *go*."

The little girl had emerged, still scowling, clearly not happy to see her father talking to Penny. At the same moment Danny came around the counter, big silver containers in both hands, whipped cream oozing in snowy rivers down the sides.

"Here you go!" He beamed. "Extra whipped cream, extra cherries, I even threw in some jimmies."

He tilted one of the floats, eager to show off the happy face he'd made with cherries and sprinkles—and he almost lost his grip on the slippery vessel. For a few laughing, chaotic seconds, both father and daughter were absorbed in trying to make the transfer without upsetting another drink.

Penny took advantage of that moment to slip out, her legal pad tucked safely under her arm.

Yes, she was running away. But it didn't feel like the same kind of cowardice she'd hated in herself earlier. It was more…preservation of something inexplicably special.

She simply couldn't bear to let the girl start quizzing her again about why she'd been drawing Dad. And, for whatever reason, she didn't want the frozen-time beauty of their accidental kiss to become…ordinary.

She moved quickly, let the door fall shut on the chimes behind her, and then turned left, making her way toward her car.

Time to go to Bell River. She could handle it now. She felt, in fact, as if she could handle anything.

Still hugging her legal pad, she took a deep breath of the crisp August afternoon air. She felt so buoyant she had to make a conscious effort not to skip, or break into song.

She might have made a fool of herself in there, but looking foolish hadn't killed her.

In fact, it had made her sizzle and pop inside. As if Danny had put her under the soda water spigot and injected her with fizzy carbonation. She felt free.

The idea of freedom was so new, and at the same time so old, that she laughed out loud. A saleslady who had been arranging flowers in front of a store looked up with a cautious smile.

"May I help you?"

"No, thanks," Penny said, smiling. "I'm fine. I know exactly what I want."

And, for the first time in years, that was true. She did know what she wanted.

She wanted to be herself.

MAX TWIRLED THE rusted pressure relief valve at the top of the cottage's water heater carefully. Ellen had tried to grab a quick shower earlier, but turning the spigot had triggered a series of banging, popping noises. Sounded like sediment buildup to Max.

Since they'd arrived in town almost a week early, he couldn't blame their landlady for the problem. And since it was Saturday, he couldn't expect a plumber to come out on a moment's notice—not without charging a fortune in overtime.

"Dad, call the plumber. It's not like we're *poor*," Ellen had whined, disgusted. She took after Lydia that way. She didn't mind how long he sat at the drafting table sketching blueprints for his newest office complex or luxury resort. In fact, at those times, she'd brag to her friends about her father, the Important Architect.

But work that left him dirty, or smelly, or disheveled? That was embarrassing. Just one of the things they were in Silverdell to unlearn.

"We would *get* poor in a hurry if we never did anything for ourselves," he had responded calmly, though he'd known it would make her roll her eyes.

It had. But he couldn't continue catering to her quirks simply to avoid an eye roll. Nor could he keep indulging her whims, as he wanted to, just because she was angry, lonely and motherless.

He'd finally accepted that his job was harder than that.

Nothing let him off the hook when it came to responsible parenting.

Responsible parenting. Even his grandfather wouldn't ever have used such a stupid expression. It sounded like the stuffiest, most judgmental jackassery....

He groaned. No wonder Ellen thought he was boring. In her estimation, thirty-four was already ancient, and his endless talk of work ethic and responsibility and self-control clearly made her want to puke.

For a moment, his thoughts returned to the woman at the ice-cream store. Wonder what Ellen would have thought, if she'd seen the woman come right up and kiss boring old dad, right out of nowhere?

She probably would have puked.

But Max's reaction had been very different—and a little unnerving. This eccentric young woman wasn't really his type. She was the "little girl lost" type—and he'd been around long enough to be fairly cynical about that particular female style. In his experience, it was usually either a sign of dysfunction, or pure sham.

She was clearly in her early twenties, and she had a shy but stunning beauty, as if she were something magical that was accustomed to living in the forest. A swinging, colorful dress over playful cowgirl boots. Long, brown hair pulled back by a simple tortoiseshell headband, falling down her slim back, as glossy and healthy as a child's.

No, Flower Child doll wasn't his type. He was thirty-four, not fourteen.

And yet, when she kissed him, every atom in his body had leaped to attention, as turned on as if he actually were that breathless fourteen-year-old. For about three incredible seconds, time had stood still in a glittering pool of sexual awareness.

And then she was gone. Just as well. Ellen hadn't seen

the kiss, but she was an eagle-eyed little thing, and she was always spoiling for a fight, always looking for proof that she wasn't important to Max. If the kiss had gone on much longer...

He couldn't help wondering whether he'd see the woman again. Silverdell was a small town, so unless she'd been passing through, another meeting seemed inevitable. And awkward.

It might be better if she was merely a tourist stopping for a respite from driving. It would be oddly disappointing to meet her and discover she was a fake, or a fool, or a mother of four.

He'd far rather remember their encounter as a rare, mystical moment when his cynicism had evaporated, his "responsibility" had dropped away, and he'd kissed a fairy forest creature.

"Are you done yet?"

Ellen's voice, impatient, wafted into the basement. He snapped back to reality.

"Not yet. A couple more minutes."

He refocused, though he hated to mentally return to this shadowy, dirty basement where the water heater stood, its silver cylinder winking oddly, picking up whatever light broke through. He hated basements. He always had, even before Mexico. But *responsible parenting* meant he couldn't succumb to his aversion.

And, in the end, the basement was just a big, dusty rectangle of concrete. He could leave anytime he wanted. Funny how often he reminded himself of that when he entered tight spaces or underground rooms. The doors were open. His hands and legs were free.

He could leave anytime he wanted.

He double-checked the garden hose connection on the drain valve one more time before letting the hot water through. He hoped to heaven Ellen continued to obey him, staying inside the house while he worked. The water probably wasn't hot enough to hurt anyone—the timer had been set to *off* when they arrived an hour ago—but he refused to take any chances. If she stood downhill from the draining water…

She could be burned. Not likely, but it could happen. And these days he didn't take the slightest of chances. Ever since Lydia's death… No, even before that. Ever since Mexico, really.

No wonder he drove Ellen crazy. He didn't understand anything that mattered to her. He didn't watch reality TV, where people voted away those who annoyed them, instead of learning to coexist. He could listen only so long to whether stripes or prints were "in" this year, or which of her friends would have to buy a bra first.

And that boy singer she idolized… The girlie little princess made Max want to laugh, frankly. As did Ellen's fixation with getting her ears pierced and wearing eyeliner. At eleven? *Hell, no.*

But Lydia would have let her wear it. Buy it. Watch it. Listen to it.

So not only was he stuffy and dense about why "people like them" didn't fix their own water heaters, he was a traitor to Lydia's memory.

"Mom said I could." "Mom promised, as soon as I turned eleven." *Mom said. Mom said. Mom said…*

But Mom was gone. And that, of course, was Max's real sin. He wasn't Lydia. He never would be. And he couldn't bring Lydia back. Just as he hadn't been able to save her.

He gave the valve a final twist, watching the hose hiccup as the water surged through it. A few drops glistened around the fitting, where the metal didn't quite meet, and pooled in the dust.

The basement hadn't been used, obviously, in months. It smelled of dead bugs, and grime, and something oily— a leaking lawn mower, an unwashed chain saw, a toppled can of WD-40....

A tremor shimmered down his arm, and he slammed a mental door on the memory. All basements smelled the same. Mexican basements, Colorado basements, probably even Parisian basements.

Out of nowhere, the banging started again, the fire-cracker pops echoing around him like gunshots. It was just the heater, complaining, but it was too late to tell himself that. His body was already reacting, before his mind could catch up.

Pop. Bang.

The tremor flared to life, and his arm began to shake. Then his legs softened. His knee joints grew soupy. The sounds reverberated hollowly, as if they'd been caught inside his skull, and bounced off every cranial wall.

His heart knocked frantically, demanding his ribs to open and let it free. He fell to his knees, his elbows over his ears, his hands locked behind his head. It was dark. He smelled the oil-gas mixture of dirty power tools....

Oh, God...

Then, suddenly, a rectangle of silver light tilted across the floor.

"Dad?"

He squeezed his elbows together, somehow silencing the tremors. He took a deep breath.

"Yes. I'll be right up. What is it?"

His voice sounded almost normal. She would probably assume that the edge of thin tension was merely annoyance.

"I wanted to tell you I'm going out back. There is, like, a little orchard, over by the school. Just beyond the fence."

"Okay." He took another deep breath. Her voice, even

crabby and unfriendly as it always was these days, pulled him to shore, as surely as if it were a bowline tied to a dock.

And the light helped, too. There had never been light, before....

One muscle at a time, the trembling subsided. His heart calmed, accepting that it must stay in his body.

"Okay," he repeated. "Be careful, though. Stay away from the water I just drained. And don't go so far that you can't hear me if I call."

"I have my cell," she observed sourly, as though he were being deliberately dense. But when he didn't respond to that, she surrendered. "Okay, I'll stay nearby. Remember, though, if you get distracted later by work or something, I *did* tell you where I was going."

"Yeah." He stood, though he felt the need to touch the wall for balance. His head finally began to clear. "Thank you for that, Ellie. I'm really glad you did."

CHAPTER THREE

BELL RIVER RANCH was only two miles out of downtown Silverdell proper—which luckily didn't leave enough driving time for doubt or insecurity to set in. Penny rolled down the windows of the rental car and let the cool early-fall breeze blow through her hair. The air smelled sweet, like Russian sage, rose and cosmos, all of which had been planted along the fringes of the Bell River property years ago. It was, to Penny, the defining scent of Home.

And, as always, it triggered a dozen contradictory emotions inside her. Excitement. Fear. Loss. Hope.

Home.

When she spotted the big, two-story timber-and-brick main house rising up around the bend, she slowed the car to a crawl. She needed to let her emotions move through her, giving the intensity time to subside.

The place looked wonderful, new roof gleaming in the morning sun, grass as green as finger paint rolling out in all directions. The trees burned gold and orange and red, but were still full and leafy—the best of both summer and fall, as if the seasons had decided to share this one overlapping month of August.

But…oh, look at all those cars. So many people! Penny had received regular updates from her sisters, so she knew that business was good, but she hadn't quite absorbed what that meant. There would be guests everywhere. No real privacy, for explaining. And Bree's new guy—Grayson

Harper—he'd be there, too, and Penny would meet him for the first time.

Worst of all, once Bree and Ro heard that Penny intended to stay in Silverdell, but not with them…that she'd bought her own house…

Explaining why without hurting anyone's feelings could take hours.

Was she ready for all that? She glanced into the rearview mirror, into her own wide, expectant eyes, which looked abnormally bright and alive. Partly it was the reflected color from the vivid turquoise-navy-and-pink-flowered pattern of her dress. This dress had been her only new purchase since Ruth's death.

The "Russian doll" dress was so unlike anything she'd worn—at least since she was a child. The people at the ice-cream store didn't know her, so they didn't know how out of character it was. But Bree and Ro hadn't seen her look like this in years.

Was it too much? Too conspicuous? She remembered Ruth's voice, pronouncing flatly that "flamboyant" clothes made her look cheap, or foolish.

Ruth had insisted on neutrals—white shirts, gray slacks, khaki skirts and brown or black shoes. For someone who loved color and pattern as much as Penny did—and had ever since she was a little girl gathering flowers to make garlands for her ponies—such a drab palette was torture.

She smiled at her reflection, and the flicker of doubt soon disappeared. She loved Ruth—but the old lady had been wrong. This brightly colored dress, with its long, belled sleeves and gathered empire waist, might not look like a nun's habit, but it suited Penny. It put pink in her cheeks and blue in her eyes.

Or had that impulsive ice-cream kiss done those things?

It didn't matter. She was happy, and she was comfortable

in her own skin, her own clothes, for the first time in a long time. She didn't even care that she had worn no makeup— she rarely did—or that her ponytail had been torn to shreds by the wind through the windows.

She was ready.

She pulled into Bell River and drove around back, to the little parking lot. But that was full, so she rounded the house on the other side, till she reached the front. She parked near the new fountain, and then, without thinking much about it, walked all the way to the back again, so that she could enter by the kitchen door.

Her aversion to the front foyer hadn't ever subsided, and she wasn't going to add that to today's list of hurdles she needed to clear.

"Penny?"

She had climbed halfway up toward the back porch steps when she heard Rowena's voice, equal parts shock and delight. "Pea, is it really you?"

Penny smiled as Ro came rushing through the door, her arms still full of linens she'd obviously been folding. Rowena had always been an uncorked bottle of raw emotion. The difference, now that she'd found true love here in Bell River, was that the emotion bubbling out of her was happiness, not anger.

"What on earth are you doing here? Why didn't you call?" She draped an unfolded sheet across her shoulder like a toga, freeing her arms for hugging. The sheet was warm, straight from the dryer, and smelled sweet and clean.

"I'm sorry," Penny said. "I wanted to surprise you, so—"

"I'm surprised, all right!" Rowena laughed. "Look at you! You look fantastic!" She smoothed the sleeve of Penny's dress affectionately, with that big-sister pride, and Penny grinned as if she'd just gotten an A on something important. "But darn it. We've got every single room rented out through September. If I'd known you were coming…"

Rowena frowned, her green eyes fiercely focused on solving the problem immediately. "Let's see—"

"It's okay, Ro." Penny took a breath. "You see, I'm not—"

"Naw, don't worry." Rowena grinned, tucked her hand under Penny's elbow and led her toward the house. "We'll think of something. We'll kick Alec out of his room if we have to. He's in the doghouse anyhow, for sneaking out last night, and—"

"I did not sneak out! I left a note!" As if out of nowhere, Alec suddenly bounded up the stairs behind them. "Hi, Penny! You can have my room if you want, but I did *not* sneak out!"

Penny turned, hardly recognizing the mud ball she saw rushing toward her. Rowena's new stepson, ten-year-old Alec Garwood, was ordinarily a twinkling, ridiculously handsome four-foot-three hunk of pure mischief. Today, though…

Today Alec's clothes and cowboy boots were black, his hands were silver, and his face and hair were gray. At first glance he looked like a statue, but Penny realized quickly that he was covered in mud from head to toe—his thick blond thatch sticking out like a witch's broom, and his white teeth and blue eyes gleaming from his gray face like jewels embedded in a cave wall.

He hugged Penny as if everything were perfectly normal, though, and seemed shocked when Rowena cried out in a mixture of laughter and horror. "What do you think you're doing? You're going to ruin Pea's pretty dress!"

"Why?" Alec reared back, insulted. Then he glanced down at his hands. "Oh. Yeah. Sorry. Trouble was chasing a duck. I had to stop him. He's even dirtier than I am."

"Great." Rowena rolled her eyes—but there was no real anger in her voice. From the start, Rowena had doted on this rascally little boy. "That dog's not coming in the house until he's clean. And neither are you." She poked the tip of her index finger onto the center of Alec's head, and twirled it to signal that he should turn around. "Barn hose. Now."

Alec smiled, showing those diamond teeth and cracking the drying mud around his lips. He never minded being scolded, which was a good thing, since he seemed chronically to be in trouble.

"See you later, Penny," he said, waving a filthy hand, dislodging gobbets of mud, which then rained onto the porch. "If you use my room, be careful. Definitely don't open the jar under the bed, okay?"

"Oh, my dear Lord." Rowena laughed out loud. "Scat, you disgusting creature!"

They both watched the boy trot away, whistling merrily and calling for his dog. He passed Barton James, the general manager Ro had hired last year, and the two high-fived each other. Barton never so much as blinked at the mud that caked the boy.

"Penny!" Barton bounded up the stairs, apparently as delighted to see Penny as if they were best buddies, when actually she'd met him only a couple of times.

But everyone loved Barton, and Barton loved everyone. She accepted his hug without reservation—laughing when he had to slip his guitar around to his back to make room. How he managed to get so much accomplished, and yet always be strumming some tune on that old thing, no one could ever understand.

"Good thing you're here," he said merrily. "I've just about got the older two Wright gals married off, and I was wondering who I'd matchmake next."

Penny laughed. "Not me," she assured him. "I've sworn off men for an entire year."

He frowned, as if she'd said she ate little green Martians for lunch. "Poppycock," he said. "A year? At your age? Can't be done."

"Barton, not everyone is as romantic as you are." Rowena shook her head. "Hey, see if you can find Bree, okay? Let her know Penny's come home!"

"Done," he said. He kissed Penny one more time, then held her at arm's length, appraising her. "I'm thinking an older man. Not old like me. *I wish.* But a few years older than you, maybe. Seen the world. Would know how to treat a lady."

"Barton." Rowena gave him The Look.

"Okay, okay," he said, grinning, and then he sauntered off, swinging his guitar back to the front.

Rowena turned to Penny with a smile. "Sorry about that. He really is such a darling old man. But he can be a bit much sometimes."

"I love him," Penny said honestly. Barton was obviously a treasure—the perfect general manager for the ranch. Not only was he a charmer who immediately won over every female guest, he was also a former dude ranch owner himself and knew everything. More than once, he'd kept the neophyte Wright women from making terrible mistakes.

As he told it, he'd tried retirement for a couple of years and hated it. He was born to work, and the harder he worked the happier he was. There wasn't a chore too lowly, or a responsibility too heavy for him to take on with a smile. He sawed and painted, cooked and cleaned, ran financial programs and mocked up publicity flyers. He sang and danced, played the guitar and chess and horseshoes and generally made sure no man, woman or child left Bell River Dude Ranch feeling disappointed.

"Sorry about Alec, too," Rowena said. "We've got a lot of crazy males around here, apparently. I'll move the jar, whatever it is." She shuddered dramatically.

"Ro, it's okay. You don't need to kick Alec out. I'm not staying at the ranch."

Rowena stopped abruptly at the threshold and turned. "You're not?"

"No."

"Aw, Penny. You don't have to go back to San Francisco tonight, surely? Dallas would be so disappointed. You haven't even met Gray yet. You can't go back tonight!"

"No, but—"

"Penny!" Bree appeared in the great room suddenly, balancing a tray of coffee cups and flatware. Obviously Barton hadn't found her, because her face lit up with delighted surprise, and she instantly began searching for a clear space on which to deposit the tray.

Once free, Bree enveloped Penny in a hug so tight she temporarily had to give up all thought of breathing.

"Why didn't you call?" Bree frowned at Rowena. "You didn't forget to tell me, did you, Ro? You're so caught up in planning the winter schedule—"

"I didn't forget. She just showed up out of nowhere. I'm still trying to figure out what's going on." Ro turned back to Penny. "So, if you're not going back tonight, of course you'll stay here. We wouldn't hear of your staying anywhere else."

"Ro, I—"

"No foolishness about imposing. It's your house. Rats— I shouldn't ever have rented the sister suite. But we'll think of something. Where are your things?"

Ro moved to the window to scan the yard. "I'll get Barton back. Or somebody. Who's not leading a class right now, Bree? We've got tons of strapping college kids. One of them will bring your suitcases in."

But Bree was staring at Penny thoughtfully. Her cool, observant control had always spotted things Rowena's passionate fire either overlooked or tried to will away.

"Hang on a minute, Ro." Bree's blue eyes had darkened slightly, and her cameo-pale forehead furrowed. "Everything's okay, isn't it, Pea?"

"Everything's fine." Eventually, Penny would have to tell them about the intruder. But one thing at a time.

"Good." Rowena scraped her black hair away from her face impatiently. She was an old hand at rejecting any little reality that annoyed her. "Then of course you won't go back to San Francisco tonight, so let's find one of the kids to—"

"Ro, let Penny talk." Bree put her hand on their older sister's arm.

Penny smiled, grateful. Rowena was a steamroller when she got going, and Penny would find herself ensconced in one of the cottages by nightfall, with a pet parakeet and a Silverdell voter's ID, if she didn't slow things down.

Bree's voice was gentle. "Tell us what's going on, Penny. Did you really come all this way just for one day? Are you really going back tonight?"

Penny took a breath. "No. In fact, I'm not going back to San Francisco at all. I sold the town house."

"You *what?*" Both her sisters spoke at once.

"I sold the town house. You know Ruth left it to me, for a nest egg. She expected me to sell, and luckily it moved very quickly. So I've come back to Silverdell."

"Then…but that's fantastic!" Rowena frowned, tugging the sheet from her shoulder and glancing around the porch, her gaze again calculating, sorting. "Okay, so we'll have to free up something more permanent. They're almost finished with the four new cottages, but they won't be move-in ready until—"

"Rowena!" Penny squared her shoulders. "Bree. I know this is going to be a shock, and that's why I didn't call ahead. Or write. I wanted to tell you in person, face-to-face. The thing is…I'm not going to be living at the ranch."

"Don't be silly," Rowena repeated, almost absently. "It's no imposition. It's what we've all been hoping for. You know we've been begging you to come ever since Ruth died. Since before Ruth died. Of course you'll live here."

"No. I won't." Penny took Ro's right hand and Bree's left into her own. "I love you for wanting to take care of me. But I won't be moving into the ranch."

Rowena opened her mouth, obviously prepared to protest reflexively, but a glare from Bree made her shut it again.

"Damn it, Ro. *Let her explain.*"

But could she? Could she ever make them understand how, up until today, she'd always been a stranger to herself, a guest in her own life? Their love, Ruth's love, the exile to San Francisco, the quiet, hermit life with her great-aunt… where no storms came…

No storms. And nothing else, either.

Everyone had tried to shield her from the ugliness of the Wright family history. Maybe they thought that, since she'd been only eleven at the time of the tragedy, she had a chance of growing up unscarred if they wrapped her in cotton and tucked her away.

But in the end, they'd only managed to create a ghost of a girl, who had no idea who she was or what she wanted out of life.

"I've bought a house. A duplex. I'm renting one side out for now, but eventually I hope to open a studio. Give lessons, maybe. Definitely paint and take pictures, and anything else that will help me earn a living."

The news wounded them. She could see it in the speechless shock that wiped their eyes and smiles clear of emotion.

"I'm sorry," she said, though she'd vowed to herself that she wouldn't apologize. She had nothing to apologize for. She had a right to make her own decisions, to live wherever she pleased. And yet she hated to hurt them.

"Rowena, Bree...please try to understand. I love you both more than I can say. But it's time I created a life of my own."

THE DUPLEX MAX had rented was newly refurnished, which was one of the reasons he'd chosen it. He'd come out twice to look at various possible rentals. He'd seen plenty of houses much grander than this little cottage, but grand didn't suit his agenda. Simple suited him. Simple and clean, with structural integrity and enough charm to please the soul.

Even Ellen hadn't been able to say the duplex was ugly. Small, yes. But delightful in a quaint, historic-cottage way. A pale butter-yellow with blue trim around the windows and doors, the one-story wooden structure looked neat and friendly, glowing under autumn sunshine filtered through half a dozen gorgeous aspens.

And *furnished* made it even better. For the next nine months, he could leave all the big pieces in Chicago, which was a relief. Back home, every stick of furniture seemed saturated with memories of Lydia. That was her chair at the dinner table. That was where she sat while they watched TV. Even the pencil marks on the woodwork measuring Ellen's growth had been made by Lydia.

Which was probably more proof that Max had been a hopelessly absentee father. But he couldn't change the past. All he could do was rededicate himself to his daughter from now on. No do-overs in this life—but luckily you did occasionally get to *start* over.

And it would be easier to start over without Lydia's ghost everywhere they turned.

He had put away his clothes and books and set up his drafting table. Later, he'd have to go buy supplies, but for now the landlady had been thoughtful, providing everything from magazines on the coffee table to knives and forks in the pantry.

Maybe he'd wait for Ellen to come back from exploring, and then they'd make a grocery run. He wasn't very good at cooking yet, but he'd mastered the red rice with tuna horror she seemed to love best. She'd probably had it twice a week in the months since Lydia died.

He walked out to the car one more time, clearing out the last of the loose items—Ellen's paper cup from the fast-food lunch they'd grabbed as they neared Silverdell, her tangled earbuds and the cherry-flavored lip balm she'd bought at a gas station. He dug out a paperback book about a vampire high school, which had gotten wedged between the seats. He was finally extricating himself from the SUV when he heard another car drive up beside his.

He straightened, smiling, wondering if it might be his landlady, who would also be his next-door neighbor. The agent had explained that the owner, someone named Penelope Wright, would live on the other side, though so far he'd seen no signs of her. For some reason, he'd assumed she was a retiree—maybe the old-fashioned name did that. But perhaps she wasn't retired, and had merely been at work all day.

Reflections of aspen leaves dappled her car's windshield, so he couldn't see anything except the hint of a bright blue coat or dress.

He waited, still smiling a welcome, ready to start off on

the right foot. But, oddly, the person in the car didn't open
the door. Maybe she was on the phone, tying up some final
details before she hung up.

He turned back to the SUV, checking under the seats
one last time, not wanting to look impatient. He had just
collected a stray French fry when he heard the woman get
out of her car and clear her throat.

"I…I…" She started over. "You…"

Poor thing. She sounded as if she might struggle with
a stammer.

"Hi," he began, turning with a smile. The rest of his
greeting died on his lips. Standing in front of him was the
woman from the ice-cream store.

It couldn't be. But…

It also couldn't be anyone else. Even without the same
cute dress, silly boots, shining hair…he would never forget that face.

For a split second, the shock left him mildly uncomfortable. The encounter earlier had been so random, so
strange. It had been over in less than a minute, and she'd
disappeared suddenly, without a word, as if embarrassed
by her boldness.

So how had she found him again? She didn't know his
name—he didn't know hers. He hadn't told the soda jerk
anything about his plans. And yet, out of nowhere, this
same woman pulled up in his driveway a few hours later?

How was it possible? Silverdell wasn't *that* small.

Was there any chance this sweet-faced young woman
was…

Stalking him?

"Wow. This is so awkward I honestly don't know what
to say." The woman shook her head and squeezed her
eyes shut, as if she hoped that when she opened them, he
wouldn't be standing there.

But of course he was.

"Okay. So I guess you have to be Mr. Thorpe. You're here early. I mean, that's fine. It's just that…I wasn't even considering the possibility that my tenant might already be in Silverdell. Before, I mean. Earlier, I mean. When I…"

She took a deep breath, held out her hand and managed a smile. "I guess I should properly introduce myself, even if it's a little late. I'm Penny Wright. I'm your…your…."

He took her hand. "My landlady?"

She nodded. "I cannot tell you what an idiot I feel. If I had considered, even for a second, that you…that we…"

She flushed, starting at the neck, which wasn't very helpful, because it caused Max to focus on the graceful column of her throat. His gaze followed the pink stain up, as it spread across the delicate jawline, and then her cheeks.

And, just like that, there it was again—the hot, helpless, fourteen-year-old feeling. He wanted to kiss that pulsing spot where her throat met her chin—and at the same time he wanted to be the white knight who knew exactly what to say to make her feel better.

But he couldn't do either one, because he was too busy hoping she couldn't tell what she did to him…physically. He realized he still held her hand, and he let it go as nonchalantly as he could.

He fought down the sensation. This was ridiculous. The both of them, grown adults, standing here temporarily reduced to blithering idiots—all over a casual kiss. A quick, closed-mouth kiss between total strangers that had meant absolutely nothing.

Get a grip, Thorpe.

"You shouldn't feel foolish," he said, smiling. "It was very sweet, and I didn't mind a bit. But if you'd rather, we could agree that it never happened."

She nodded eagerly. "If we could, if you would…I mean,

that would be terrific. I'd appreciate it. So much. That's not really me. I mean, I don't do things like that, ordinarily. It was just—just this silly thing I did because…you see, I was making this crazy list, and—"

He was loving the stumbling explanation, and wondering whether he might have grown *too* cynical, through the years. This innocent honesty didn't look like a sham. This looked like the real thing. An adorable, awkward naïveté.

But her cascade of half sentences was cut off by the arrival of more vehicles, which pulled up in a caravan and jockeyed one at a time for parking space in the street just outside the duplex. Max looked first at the newcomers—a late-model pickup truck, a hybrid SUV and a wildly expensive sports car. Then he looked at Penny, whose expressive face was registering both surprise and annoyance.

"Oh, my goodness, they are *impossible!* I should never have told them the address!" She glanced at Max apologetically. "My family. I told them not to come, but they're… well, they hover. They mean well, but—"

"Hey! Penny!" A tall blond man in a suit hopped out of the truck, strode over and scooped Penny into his embrace. "What a surprise, kiddo! Ro called and she said we needed to get over here ASAP to help."

"Dallas!" Penny's annoyance seemed to fade as she accepted his hug. Max watched curiously, trying to sort out the relationships. Whoever this was, she liked him. Brother, maybe? But there wasn't much resemblance.

"I'm sorry you had to come," she said. "I'm perfectly fine on my own. There's really nothing to be done. My furniture won't arrive until tomorrow."

"Ah, but that seems to be the problem. They can't stand the idea of you camping out on a sleeping bag. Ro and Bree are mobilizing a small army to make this place homey. The SUV is loaded with food, supplies, blow-up mattress, books, shampoos, and there may even be a lawn mower back there. You'll be lucky if they don't start hanging wallpaper before it gets dark."

Penny groaned. But then she seemed to remember her manners. She stepped back from the hug, and, putting her hand on the man's arm, included Max in her smile.

"Dallas, this is my tenant, Max Thorpe. We've just met, this very minute. Max, this is my brother-in-law, Dallas Garwood."

Max shook Dallas's hand, noting the sharp scrutiny the blue-eyed man gave him and meeting it with a bland smile and a slightly raised brow. Dallas Garwood was the distrustful type? But what about Max made him suspicious in the first place?

"Nice to meet you, Dallas," he said politely.

Another man had stepped out of the jazzy sports car and was making his way over. His greeting was warm, but a bit more restrained, as if he weren't quite as close to Penny as Dallas was.

"Hey, Penny. I'm Gray, and—"

"Gray!" Dallas thumped the newcomer on the shoulder. "Penny, it's hard to believe you haven't met Gray. He's been underfoot for months now. He's been dying to meet you, because somehow he's decided you're the only one who can persuade Bree to set a wedding date."

Penny accepted a hug from the second man, and then rather stiltedly attempted to introduce him to Max, too.

"Grayson Harper, this is Max Thorpe, my tenant. Max, Gray is my sister Bree's—"

"Fiancé," Gray said, stepping forward to help smooth over Penny's uncertainty about the label. He shook Max's hand, and again Max was aware of getting a steely-eyed, mildly threatening appraisal.

You'd better be a good guy, the stare said. *You'd better not mess with our Penny.*

Damn. Max wondered whether he had picked up some kind of scary stain that looked like blood while he was in the basement. Surely he didn't give off a serial killer vibe, did he? He was just a road-weary dad in jeans and a suede jacket, holding his daughter's *Vampire High* pulp novel, and a bubblegum-blue Slurpee cup. How dangerous could he possibly look?

"Nice to meet you, Gray," he said with a deliberately cool tone. He met the aggressive gaze without blinking.

Commotion over by the cars drew their gazes. Two women were emerging from the hybrid SUV—one blonde, one black-haired, both stunning. They laughed as they stumbled over each other and tried to extricate large casserole dishes. Their hands were covered in large blue oven mitts that said the dishes were still hot.

The sisters, no doubt. Though where the family resemblance was, Max had no idea. Obviously they were bringing dinner—and everything else under the sun. The SUV was packed to the gills with random paraphernalia. In addition to the unwieldy casserole dish she carried, the brunette sister had a potted flower tucked under one elbow. The blonde had wedged a framed picture under each arm. They were so encumbered they could hardly walk.

For a second, Max understood why Penny had looked annoyed. *Hover* might be an understatement.

He needed to get out of the way and let her deal with this. "I'd better go find Ellen," he said. "We've had a long day."

She frowned. "But we…" She met his gaze with an apologetic smile, as if to say she knew they needed to talk more. But then her glance angled toward the approaching women, and she shut her eyes in something that looked like exhaustion.

"We'll talk tomorrow?" She made it a question. "About... about the lease and everything. If there's anything the agent didn't provide—"

"Everything seems perfect," he assured her. It was strange—especially given that she clearly already had an army poised to protect her—but he still had the urge to put her at ease. "We're going to turn in early, I'm sure."

He lifted one eyebrow playfully. "Most of it is already a bit of a blur. For instance, I can hardly remember this morning."

She gave him a grateful smile. But the sisters had reached the driveway, so she launched one more time into a rote introduction. Max said the polite phrases, shaking hands with the two beauties who stared at him as if he were Jack the Ripper. They talked about having plenty of food to share, but he insisted on heading back into his own side of the duplex.

He almost got away. Just as he reached his own door, he saw a shadow fall behind him. He turned, and wasn't surprised to see Gray Harper standing on the front porch.

Max had figured out, finally, what must have happened. Small-town grapevines being what they were—someone must have reported the kiss.

"Look," he said, "I don't know what's bugging you guys. I'm here to do a construction project, a resort just outside town called Silverdell Hills. You can look me up, if you'd like. I'm a paying tenant. I have no intention of annoying your sister-in-law in any way."

Gray tilted his head. "Well, apparently there's a story going around—"

"I'm sure there is. I'm not sure exactly what the story said by the time it reached you, but *she* kissed *me,* not vice versa."

The other man grinned. Though he was irritated, Max

had to admire that Gray didn't try to deny it, or to pretend that Max had imagined the unanimous, wordless antagonism.

"Fair enough," Gray said. "That *is* what we heard, actually. That she kissed you. But Ro and Bree couldn't believe it—and it does sound a bit out of character."

"I wouldn't have a clue." Max shrugged. "I hadn't ever met her—I mean, met her by name—until ten minutes ago. When I was told I had a landlady named Penelope Wright, I pictured some blue-haired grandmother who would grow delphiniums and make cookies for my daughter."

"She does make a mean cookie, I hear." Gray smiled. "Look, I don't blame you for being ticked off. But you know how sisters can be. Or you will, if you live here long. These sisters, in particular. They worry about Penny as if it were their full-time job."

Max raised his eyebrows. "Gray. I don't know what Penny's problems are. But I know what mine are. I came here for some quiet time to focus on my daughter, who lost her mother last year. I'm not a con man or a pervert. But I am tired, and I need to get my daughter home, fed and put to bed."

"Okay." Gray nodded. "But there's just one last thing. No offense intended, honestly. But Bree won't sleep if I don't tell you. See, Penny's the baby of the family, and she's been through a lot. When they heard the story about this morning, they about flipped."

"Just say it, Harper," Max said, trying not to sound as impatient as he felt. "Whatever it is, no offense taken, I guarantee."

"Well." Gray shifted, clearly uncomfortable. "They want you to know that Penny...well, her brother-in-law, Dallas... The thing is...he's the sheriff."

The sheriff? So?

Then Max understood, and, finally, he started to laugh. This was about as unsubtle a warning as he could possibly imagine. He began to wonder whether Penny might be more than merely charmingly naive. Maybe she was a little barmy. Why else would her whole family feel so frantic to caution him that she was protected?

Or…on second thought…maybe the *whole family* was nuts. Maybe, by renting this duplex in a hurry, he'd just stepped into the biggest nest of crazy in all of Colorado.

"Fantastic." He let his laugh die off to a dark chuckle. "The sheriff of Silverdell. *Got it.* You can report that I am sufficiently intimidated by the badge. But listen. I'm going to say this one more time, and then I really think you should let it go. Your sister-in-law may have problems. In fact, I'm starting to be pretty sure she does. But *I* am not one of them."

CHAPTER FOUR

ELLEN WAS SO mad at everybody she wondered if she might explode. For the past half hour, she'd been sitting under the biggest tree in the orchard behind their new place, with her back against the trunk. She was uncomfortable, but she'd rather be miserable here than cozy back at the duplex.

To let off steam, she was tearing off blades of grass and throwing them as far as she could—which wasn't far, because it was windy and the grass kept boomeranging back in her face.

She didn't want to be in this stupid town—if you could even call it a town when it had only one street with stores, and nothing at all to do. She wanted to be back in Chicago, with her friends.

Or at least the girls who used to be her friends.

She frowned as hard as she could, because she had a stinging in her eyes and a hot feeling in her throat that made her afraid she might cry. She picked up her cell phone for the tenth time in the past minute and checked for incoming texts. Nothing.

She had sent a group text to all her friends at least fifteen minutes ago. She wasn't supposed to use the data package—her dad didn't want her on the internet. The phone was only for emergencies. But she didn't care. She needed to talk to somebody from home.

So she'd taken a picture of herself with the built-in camera, making sure you could see the mountains in the background, and she'd sent it to everyone. She was smiling like she was having the time of her life, and the text said, <3 CO! Epic sky, adorbs cottage. Miss u!

It had taken her a while to think of the perfect words. She couldn't say *duplex,* of course. *Cottage* admitted that it was small, but it sounded quaint and fun instead of pathetic and trashy.

The picture of her was good, too. She'd held the camera high, which made her face look skinnier. Plus, she was wearing the gold earrings her mom had left her, which were very sophisticated. And *real,* which was important. Stephanie said only losers wore jewelry that wasn't real.

But no one had texted back. Not even Becky, who had always been on the fringes of their group because Stephanie didn't like her. Stephanie said Becky was greasy from eating too much fast food. Probably, though, Becky would be allowed on the inside now.

Now that Ellen was gone, and a place had opened up.

The wind rose, tickling her hair into her face, and her eyes stung even worse. She swallowed three times, trying to loosen that tight feeling in her throat, and then clicked on her Facebook app. Maybe she should just post the picture there, so everyone could see.

But Facebook made her feel worse. Her news feed was full of pictures Stephanie and the gang had just taken at the mall, where they'd gone to see a movie. "Less than a minute ago" they'd been horsing around at the Organic Highway counter at the food court. Laughing, throwing stuff at each other, making funny faces.

And, look at that shot! Becky stood so close to Gregory Parr the whole world could see she had a crush on him.

Well, Gregory Parr *was* the cutest guy in school. Ellen had a graph in her diary tracking how long it would take her to lose fifteen pounds, and what she'd do then to make Greg notice her.

Except for Stephanie, who had been held back in first grade and was older than the rest of them, no one in their group had a boyfriend. Not outright. But everyone knew who liked who, and everybody knew you didn't go after the boys your friends had chosen.

But here was Becky, clearly trying to call dibs on Gregory. Ellen's fury rose. If greasy Becky Fife thought she could just move in and take over every single part of Ellen's life...her guy, her friends...

Ellen could imagine her dad's reaction. "Could they really have been friends if they have forgotten about you in a week?"

Could Dad really be that clueless?

Of course they were going to forget her. They hung out together every day, and when you were gone, you were gone. You could hardly expect them to sit around for nine months waiting for you to come back.

Her tears had begun to fall. She reached up and ripped off her left earring angrily. They were only hooked over the edge of her ear, anyhow, because her ears weren't pierced.

Thanks for that, too, Dad.

She yanked the second one, and the filigreed hoop went flying out of her hand into the tall grass around her.

"Oh, my God. No!" She got on all fours and tried to comb the grass, praying to see the winking gold. "No!"

A sudden rustling in the tree overhead startled her. She felt a spasm of fear and froze in place. No bird could possibly be that big. Not even an eagle. Well, maybe an eagle. What did she know about eagles?

She sniffed, trying to keep her nose from running. She hated hick places like this. It could be *anything* up there. A snake, or a cougar, or...

"What's the matter? What are you looking for?"

And abruptly, there he was. A boy, draped over the lowest big branch like the Cheshire cat, his skinny blue jeans and sneakers dangling, his grin and upturned eyes laughing at her.

Suddenly, she was madder than ever. He must have been in the tree the whole time. He'd probably been watching her when she took the picture of herself. *Pictures.* She'd taken fifteen different shots, trying for one that looked perfect.

She blushed furiously, thinking how she'd smirked at herself in the camera, trying to look happy and cute.

"Who are you?" She lifted onto her knees, fists on her hips. "That's pretty rude, to spy on people."

"Hey, now." The boy swung himself down like a monkey and plopped onto the grass a couple of feet away. "I wasn't spying. I was sleeping, and when I woke up, you were there, acting weird. I didn't say anything because I was waiting for you to go away. It's my tree, after all."

"It can't be your tree. This is a school playground. Playgrounds belong to the city, not to people." But then her curiosity got the better of her. "How can you have been sleeping in a tree? Isn't that dangerous?"

The boy dusted off his hands. "Not if you know how." His grin broadened, his sunburned face busting out in white teeth, practically from ear to ear. "I know how."

For a minute, when he smiled, he looked kind of cute. He was a few inches taller than she was, and wiry, like boys were when they had too much energy and never stood still. His hair was blond and thick, and his eyes were a sparkly blue—just about the same color as the sky, now that it was almost evening.

Ellen still thought Greg was cuter, because this guy looked like he might be a hick, with his dirty blue jeans and cowboy boots and flannel shirt with the cuffs rolled back. But he was pretty cute, anyhow. Stephanie would definitely think so. Stephanie had a thing for cowboys.

"So." The boy took a Tootsie Roll out of his pocket, unwrapped it, and stuffed it into his mouth. As he started to chew, he paused. He let his hand hover over his pocket, looked at her and raised his eyebrows. "Want one?"

She did. Though she hadn't noticed it before, she was starving. But she thought about the diet chart in her diary. And she thought about how she'd look like a cow, chewing away at the sticky candy. He certainly did, although he obviously didn't care what she thought. "No, thanks."

"'K." He chewed a little more. "So what are you looking for?"

The sudden recollection of her awful mistake shot through her like a hot poker. How could she have been thinking about cute guys, or even her diet, when she'd lost her mother's earring?

"My earring. It fell off."

"You yanked it off, you mean." But the kid didn't sound judgmental, just factual. He chewed thoughtfully, his gaze scanning the overgrown grass. "What does it look like?"

She held out her hand, opening the palm to show him the match. He walked closer, put his hands on his knees, bent down and studied it without touching, the way he might look at a specimen in science class.

"Is that really yours? It looks kind of grown-up for you." He tilted his head. "How old are you?"

"I'm eleven," she said, lifting her chin to look older, and, she hoped, skinnier. "I'm plenty old enough to wear earrings. Why? How old are you?"

He chewed on his lower lip briefly. "I'm ten," he said.

"What grade?"

"Fourth."

Oh, man. He was a whole grade below her. She felt stupid for having thought he was cute. No wonder he carried Tootsie Roll candy around in his pocket and didn't care if he looked ugly chewing a wad of caramel in front of a girl.

"Well, I'm going into fifth," she said. "And these earrings are definitely mine. My mother gave them to me. It can't have gone far, but the grass is so high...."

She got back on her knees and started ruffling her palm over the grass, inch by inch. "It's important."

She glanced at him over her shoulder. "It's real," she said. Then, in case a cowboy kid wouldn't know what that meant, she added, "like, I mean...real gold."

He nodded, dropped to his knees and started combing the grass, too. He was working an area much closer to where she'd been sitting, and she suddenly realized that was smarter. The earring wouldn't have flown this far.

She subtly worked her way back toward him, but her hopes were fading. This was like the old cliché—finding a needle in a haystack. The thatch of golden-brown dead grass below the new growth was almost exactly the same color as the earring.

And it would be dark soon.

"So will your mom be super mad? Will you get in trouble if we don't find it?"

She glanced over at the boy. It was nice, him saying *we* like that, as if they were partners in the hunt. He didn't have to help. He could have walked away and gone home.

"Not trouble from my mom." She bent her head again. "My mom died. Almost a year ago."

"Aw. Dang." The boy paused and looked at her. "I'm sorry about that."

She didn't respond. If her eyes got blurry with tears, she wouldn't have any chance at all of spotting the circle of gold in the grass.

"Got it!" The boy suddenly jumped to his feet, his fist in the air triumphantly.

Relief washed through her. She stood, too, holding out her hand.

He deposited the earring in her palm with a flourish. "There you go!"

It felt cold, from lying on the ground. She closed her fingers, as if to chafe warmth back into it. She looked up at him, so grateful she forgot to play cool.

"Thank you. Thank you so much...."

"Alec." The boy grinned. "Alec Garwood, rancher, wrangler and part-time treasure hunter."

She grinned back. She couldn't help it. She was so happy that she hadn't lost the only thing her mother had given her directly, with her own hands. And his smile was that kind of smile. The kind you could catch, like a cold.

"I'm Ellen Thorpe. We moved in today. We're renting the yellow cottage over there."

"No kidding!" Alec glanced at the cottage. "That's a cool place. So you've just moved here? Where from?"

"We haven't exactly *moved*. We're taking a year off while my dad works on a resort he's building." She didn't feel the need to mention the shoplifting, the bad grades, the arguments with her dad. "It's more like a long vacation. But I still *live* in Chicago."

He frowned, as if he might quarrel with that way of seeing things, but then he shrugged. "Whatever. Anyhow, those are pierced earrings. No wonder you lost them. Why don't you get your ears pierced, so they won't fall off?"

She straightened. "Maybe I don't want to get my ears pierced."

He looked skeptical about that, too. "All girls want their ears pierced," he said reasonably. "Oh. I see. You're scared to?"

"Of course not. It's just that my dad won't let me."

Alec looked confused. "So?"

She stared at him. "What do you mean, *so?*"

"I mean…so what? How can he stop you?" Alec grinned. "My theory is I'd rather ask forgiveness than permission."

She folded her arms over her chest. "You didn't make that line up. That's famous."

"I didn't say I made it up. I said that's what I do. Grown-ups don't ever want you to do anything fun. They're afraid you'll get hurt." He sighed. "But you gotta do what you gotta do, you know? If you get in trouble for it, well, whatever. They can't eat you, right?"

"Um." She wasn't sure what the correct answer was to that. Even Stephanie wasn't this honest about being bad. Stephanie generally pretended she'd misunderstood the rules, or someone else made her do it. For a fraction of a second, Ellen could see that Alec's honest civil disobedience had a certain nobility to it. "I guess not."

He pulled out another candy. "Well, anyhow, maybe you're really just scared. That's okay. Everybody's scared of something. But if you wanted me to, I could pierce them for you sometime."

Again, she was speechless. Again, even Stephanie…

It suddenly struck Ellen as kind of ironic that her dad had brought her here to get her away from Stephanie's "bad influence," and the first person she met was this troublemaker who casually assumed all rules were made to be broken.

"I—" She squeezed the earrings. This was ridiculous. She wasn't used to being tongue-tied. She always had a comeback. That was why Stephanie had invited her into the group. Stephanie admired people who were chill and sarcastic. "I—"

But then, luckily, she spotted her dad walking toward them across the playground.

"That's my father," she said. "I gotta go."

She moved quickly, hoping she'd meet her dad halfway. She didn't want him to see Alec. He would be impossible about it. He'd probably say a hundred times, "Isn't it great that you've made a friend already?"

He wouldn't see that Alec's being in fourth grade made it impossible for them to be friends.

But after a few yards, she realized it sort of stunk to ditch Alec that way, after he'd been so nice about helping.

She turned. "Thanks ag—"

Alec had already disappeared. She glanced up into the tree, but not a single branch was swaying.

He was just plain gone. She wondered how he did it. He might be only ten, but he was…interesting. Kind of cool. Though not in any way her Chicago friends would understand.

She repeated his name in her head, so she'd remember it. *Alec Garwood.* Cowboy, wrangler, treasure hunter… and, apparently, ninja.

BY TEN O'CLOCK, Penny had done everything she could— at least until the furniture arrived in the morning. It had taken her a couple of hours to shoo away the family, and then she'd emptied the car, hung up her clothes, washed the dishes and investigated every closet, cabinet and cupboard the tiny space had to offer.

After that, as darkness settled over Silverdell like indigo watercolor applied with a thick brush, she grew restless.

It had been seventeen years since she'd moved to a new house—and all of a sudden, though she was exhausted, she couldn't imagine settling down.

The blow-up mattress was ready on the floor, but even with all the extra pillows and blankets Bree and Ro had scattered around, it looked completely uninviting. She'd have to be a lot more tired before she crawled in there.

She stepped onto the back deck, where she could hear the subtle burble of the creek. Though only a few inches deep, it moved quickly. Through the aspen branches, starlight winked like broken crystal on its ripples.

Gradually, she felt herself relaxing into the familiar scents and sounds of a crisp Colorado night. It was comforting to realize that this tiny tributary, which probably would dry up entirely once winter came, was an offshoot of Bell River. The silver thread of the river bound her to her sisters, but with enough room between for Penny to breathe.

"Long day, wasn't it?"

She whirled at the sound of Max Thorpe's voice coming from his deck, which was separated from hers only by an artificial railing. Back when the house had been one residence, this must have been one deck.

He stood at the far corner, leaning against the wooden balustrade, as if he'd been watching the creek, too. The night was fairly clear, with a bright moon, and only about fifteen feet of cedarwood planks lay between them, so she could tell he was smiling.

"Very long." She walked over to the center rail so that she didn't have to talk loudly. The backyard led only to the creek, and then to a small grove that bordered the elementary school playground, but she did have neighbors on either side, and she didn't know whether they considered 10:00 p.m. late or not.

She glanced around his deck and saw that he was alone. "I hope everything in the house is…"

She didn't want to say *satisfactory*. That sounded so stilted. But she didn't know landlady vocabulary yet. "Is set up the way you like it. Jenny—she's the real estate agent—promised she'd have it ready, but I know you arrived a little early, so…"

"Everything's terrific," he said. "Considering we gave her almost no warning, it's fantastic."

She hoped he didn't think she was complaining that he'd come ahead of schedule. She could use extra rent, even a week's worth, to help defray costs. Ruth's town house had brought a decent price, but most of that was set aside to contribute to the Bell River expansion. The rest was in savings, for the day when she could open her studio.

She was determined to support herself. If she could figure out exactly how that would be done.…

"Jenny has been Silverdell's real estate agent since the Gold Rush," she said, smiling. "In fact, I bought this place sight unseen. On just Jenny's word and half a dozen 'virtual-tour' photos she'd uploaded on to her site."

She was babbling. What did he care how she'd decided to buy the duplex? But she wanted very much to be on relaxed terms with her tenant—even if she had made *relaxed* almost impossible with that impulsive kiss this morning.

She should have known word would get back to Bell River. She felt terrible about how peculiar everyone had acted toward him. Rowena had given Max the evil eye so hard that, if he'd been a less confident man, he would have turned to stone.

"Well, she did a great job. We've got everything we could possibly need. In fact, we could probably loan you anything you don't have yet." He glanced toward her side, where the curtainless windows exposed the empty rooms. "I'm surprised you're staying here tonight."

"I remember thinking it would be fun," she said ruefully. "Like camping out. Instead, it's kind of…strange."

Actually, it was more than strange. It felt painfully rootless—like being a vagrant who belonged nowhere.

"I got the feeling your sisters would have liked you to stay with them. I'm sure they'd still be glad to see you, if you changed your mind."

He didn't make any reference to how suspicious they'd been of him, which she appreciated.

"They're terribly protective," she said, wondering how to approach the subject, herself.

She hadn't forgotten she owed him an explanation for that kiss. But how much should she reveal? People often felt self-conscious after they found out Penny's father was a convicted murderer. Or even nervous, as if she could inherit the madness. When she clarified that her father's violence had probably been the result of a brain tumor, they rarely seemed reassured.

And why should they be? Even Johnny Wright's daughters had always carried that doubt inside. What if it wasn't all caused by the brain tumor? What if he was insane? What did that make them?

"Our family…well, things were rocky at home, to say the least. I was the youngest, and Rowena and Bree got in the habit of taking care of me. It's going to be a while before they can create new patterns."

He nodded. "I suppose it's not easy for you, either."

She lifted her chin. Did she seem lonely? Afraid? She wasn't. Not one bit. She fought the urge to tell him how she'd single-handedly fought off an intruder with a can of wasp spray.

"I'm fine," she said. "I know everyone still thinks of me as an eleven-year-old, but—"

"I don't." He smiled slightly. "Believe me, I think of you as very much a grown woman. I just meant…it's a tightrope walk, surely. Breaking free without appearing ungrateful. Turning down all that TLC without hurt feelings."

Her shoulders relaxed. Once again she was struck with

the fact that he was such a *nice* man. She felt again his easy, tolerant vibe—the same laid-back personality that had so appealed to her in the ice-cream store.

He was listening—not judging.

And it was time for him to listen to that explanation she'd been promising.

"I'm awfully sorry about this morning. I put you in a difficult situation. I got the gossip machine buzzing about you, on your very first day...."

She bit her lip. "I hope you know that if I'd had any idea you were my new tenant...or if I'd thought we would be connected in any way, I certainly wouldn't have done it."

He tilted his head. The moonlight touched the amber of his eyes and glistened against the white teeth as he smiled again. "You specifically wanted to kiss a stranger?"

He sounded curious, not shocked. She'd been turning over various half-truths, wondering how she could explain her eccentric behavior without revealing too much. But to her surprise it seemed easy to tell the truth.

"Actually, yes." She sighed. "It was on my list."

His smile broadened. "Really."

"Yes. I have this...list. Not a bucket list, exactly. But a..." She couldn't bring herself to say "Risk-it List," which suddenly sounded too cute.

"Just a list of some things I've always wanted to do but never got the chance. Or never had the courage."

He nodded, but he didn't respond. He simply watched her, waiting, with the murmuring creek in the background. An owl hooted into the silence, and then must have launched into flight, because suddenly the branches above them shimmered and whispered.

He was a good listener. Funny, she'd never realized how much Aunt Ruth had chattered. Their daily ritual had consisted of Ruth talking, reminiscing, teaching, reading—and

Penny as the quiet handmaiden, the receptive vessel into which Ruth's wisdom was poured.

"I've lived a very sheltered life," she said, going on as if it was perfectly natural to be telling him these things. Either he was that type, the type who developed easy intimacy with everyone he met, or their kiss had accelerated the acquaintance, skipping over the early, stilted steps.

"Our family went through a tragedy when I was very young, and the result was that my sisters and I were sent to different homes around the country. I became a caretaker to my elderly aunt in San Francisco. She was a bit of a recluse. So I've essentially spent the past seventeen years like a hermit. In a cocoon. A very loving and comfortable cocoon but—"

He tilted his head. "But a kind of a prison nonetheless?"

She almost protested. Not a prison, she almost said. A sanctuary. A harbor.

But for the first time she realized there might not be much difference.

"Ruth never intended that. But yes, a prison, nonetheless."

"And now you're not eager to exchange one...cocoon for another. That's why you won't stay with your sisters."

She nodded. "I've promised myself I'll do this on my own. I know it'll be hard. I haven't lived in Silverdell since I was eleven—the year my mother died. Even being back here, where so many of my memories are unhappy ones, is difficult. But you can't run away from the past forever, can you? You can ignore it. But that's not the same thing as making it go away."

His smile had faded, leaving his handsome face quite serious. He looked, for the first time, like the label Jenny had given him: a widower. A man who had lost his wife, maybe had his heart broken and his future shattered.

"No." He shook his head. "It isn't the same thing at all."

Perhaps she shouldn't have let the conversation turn so melancholy. She tried to smile a little, to move past the strange emotion that had seemed to pass over him like a shadow.

"So anyhow…I've made a solemn vow to myself. For one year—or for as long as it takes to check off everything on my list—I'm doing this alone. No family, no sisters, no men. No crutches."

He didn't respond. He still seemed lost in his thoughts.

"Anyhow," she said again, "that's why I bought the duplex. And it's why I kissed you this morning. I had just finished making my list as you came in. When you were so good to your daughter, I…"

The flush returned. She felt it inching up her neck. "I just thought, why not cross that one off right now?"

His pensive mood suddenly lifted, and he looked at her with that easy smile. Then he chuckled. "Why not, indeed?"

He shifted, leaning one trim hip against the railing. As he moved, the moonlight slid across his face, tracing the bow of his mouth and the strong angles of his jaw. She caught her breath. He was magnificent, and she remembered with startling clarity exactly how those lips had felt against her own.

A warmth bloomed deep inside, and she had to look away or she would be as easy to read as a book.

A dirty book.

"I know you're probably wondering what kind of crazy landlady you've gotten stuck with," she said quickly. "But I want to assure you it'll never happen again."

"Well, that's a relief." One corner of his mouth tugged up. "Why? Because you've finished everything on your list?"

"No." She shook her head, laughing. "I've hardly checked

anything off yet. It's just that it's not exactly the professional way to act with your tenant. And besides, the rest of the list is…"

"Less exciting? Less…interactive?"

She scanned his face, grateful for his lighthearted tone. How did he seem to know exactly what to say so that she wouldn't feel like an idiot? Laughing was the perfect response. Her behavior had been ridiculous. She knew it, and he knew it, and this way it became a silly joke they shared—not a source of embarrassment that would stand between them, making even a quick hello in the driveway awkward.

"Relatively boring," she said. But then she remembered number twelve. *Make love in a sailboat.*

No way was she going to share that. It would probably scare him so badly he'd move out in the morning, leaving her with no one to pay the rent.

"Well, if there's any way I can help…" His eyes were teasing her. "I know some great places to stay near Mount Everest, if that's on your list."

"Absolutely not!" She tried to imagine herself tackling such an adventure. She, who was struggling to handle one night in a comfortable living room in her own hometown. "This is the baby steps list. I'm starting very small. Unless you know how to juggle, or where to get a really good tattoo of a bluebird."

"Just so happens I do," he said. He lifted a hand sadly. "Unfortunately, it's near Mount Everest."

They both laughed softly, and Penny thought maybe, in spite of the difficult start, things would work out. She also thought maybe she could sleep.

"Dad?" A stripe of lamplight fell across the deck as Max's daughter opened the door to the kitchen. For both units, the kitchen was at the back. It had probably been one big kitchen, once upon a time.

"Hey, Ellen." Max turned toward his daughter with a smile. "Aren't you supposed to be asleep?"

"I can't sleep." The girl still sounded angry. Her posture was stiff, her face deliberately averted from her father. Her tone implied that her insomnia was his fault.

She gripped the doorknob so hard it swayed, making the stripe of light contract and expand, then contract again. "What are you *doing* out here, anyhow?"

"I'm talking to Ms. Wright. You haven't properly met, have you? You were out playing when she came home."

"I know her," the girl said sullenly, scraping her bare foot against the threshold as if she had gum on her sole. "Dad. It's really late."

And then, with just enough noise to show her irritation, but not enough to invite Max's wrath, she retreated inside and shut the door. The deck fell back into silvery moonlight.

Max groaned softly under his breath.

"I'm sorry," he said. "Ellen lost her mother last year. She hasn't…she hasn't found her way out of that yet."

"I understand." And Penny did. She understood so well she could almost feel the knife that was still lodged in Ellen Thorpe's broken heart. "How old is she?"

"Eleven." He rubbed his eyes. "Eleven going on eighteen."

"I was eleven when my mother died," Penny said. "But because I had two older, protective sisters, I was more like eleven going on six."

He lowered his hand, smiling. "I wish. Ellen's an only child, and I haven't been around enough these past few years to be much help to her now. All her friends are back in Chicago. She basically thinks I'm the devil, dragging her down to Living Hell, Colorado."

Poor Ellen. She should meet Rowena. Ro had been that same kind of kid—eternally angry, always defiant, always asking for trouble. Ro would know what to say to her, so that Ellen would know she wasn't alone.

But Penny didn't want to suggest a meeting between Ellen and Rowena—or anything else, for that matter. She'd already overstepped the boundaries of professional interaction between landlady and tenant. By about a mile.

It was time to go in, time to face that blow-up mattress.

"The first night's the hardest," Penny said, talking to herself as much as to him. "It'll get better from here."

CHAPTER FIVE

PENNY WASN'T ORDINARILY the suspicious type, but she had a bad feeling as she arrived at Bell River for the emergency lunch Rowena called a couple of days later.

Something smelled fishy—and it wasn't just the outdoor cookout underway for the guests. Why today? What was the rush? Her sisters knew she was crazy busy. Her furniture had arrived yesterday, and it would probably be another two days, at least, before she was fully settled.

But Ro had insisted. Couldn't wait. That's when Penny knew she had an agenda. As she let herself in the back door, smiling at strangers she passed on the porch, she crossed her fingers and hoped she wasn't in for another argument about why she wouldn't move back to the ranch.

She had to ask three of the college-kid servers where to find Rowena or Bree before someone was sure. "In the back, in the new wing. They're working through lunch, I think," the final young man said as he hauled a huge tray of lemonade pitchers out to the cookout.

The new wing. That had been added since Penny was last here, though of course she'd been sent the plans for approval. The wing was where Rowena, Dallas and Alec lived, and it had been closed off from the rest of the house for privacy.

She imagined the blueprint, mapping it in her head to be sure she could get there without going into the front foyer.

Oh, of course she could. If she just went back outside, then around the side…

She didn't try to talk herself out of taking the long way. Someday, maybe, her Risk-it List would include "walking into Bell River through the front door."

But not today.

When she reached the private quarters, the small dining table was already set for lunch. It glowed festively, all blues and yellows, with a little autumn orange tossed in. It looked more like a party than a business meeting, and her suspicion index rose another notch.

When she saw Ro and Bree, whispering together as they studied a large triptych display—something Alec might have used to enter the science fair—she knew she'd been set up. They were quite clearly plotting something. Pictures and index cards and charts had been taped to the board, and one of the columns was conspicuously labeled *Penny*.

"Okay, you two." Penny paused in the doorway, her arms crossed over her chest. Her sisters looked so much like naughty children, with their heads bent, whispering and giggling, that she didn't have the heart to be angry, but she tried to sound as if she were. "What is going on?"

Ro and Bree looked over their shoulders, twin guilty smiles on their faces. And then, with a grand sweep, they separated, revealing the board.

"Tah-dum!" Bree's voice sounded about fifteen, and almost breathless. "Behold…I have a wedding date!"

"What?" Penny rushed in, so that she could see the board up close. Sure enough, the columns included items like "pictures," "flowers," "food" and "favors." "You've set the date? When?"

"Saturday, September seventh. Almost exactly one month from today." Bree widened her eyes, as if the idea slightly frightened her. "I figured, now that you're here, and we can all be together, maybe I should just break down and let it happen."

Ro laughed, plopping onto one of the chairs. "And thank heaven she did! He's been going crazy, and frankly, he's been driving me crazy, too. If she hadn't set a date pretty soon, we planned to chloroform her, stuff her in the trunk and let her wake up in Vegas."

Bree looked sheepish—a vulnerable expression Penny had almost never seen on her ultracool sister's face. Bree had always kept her feelings on ice—she'd earned the nickname "Ice Queen" as far back as junior high.

"But this is a good thing, right?" Penny smiled. "I mean, you love him, so…"

Ro groaned. "Don't get her started. To listen to her, the man is a god. Apparently, every superlative in the dictionary is listed under Grayson Harper, and—"

"Oh, whatever. You should talk." Bree's fair skin showed every blush, and she was burning pink now. "Anyhow, that's not the point. I just felt…I don't know…as if I should spend more time getting to know him first. It's only been a few months."

She glanced at her sisters. "No one knows better than we do how dangerous a bad marriage can be. After all, Mom must have loved Dad at first, too, and see how that—"

"No, she didn't." Penny shook her head firmly. She wouldn't let Bree lump her upcoming marriage in with the disaster that had belonged to Moira and Johnny Wright. "Not like you and Gray. You know why Mom married Johnny. It wasn't because she'd fallen madly in love."

A small silence blanketed the room. After a quiet second, Penny and Bree sat, too, and the three sisters stared at each other numbly. Penny knew they were all thinking the same thing.

A few months ago, Rowena had discovered that her DNA

and Johnny Wright's had nothing in common. Their mother, Moira Wright, must have been pregnant when she married Johnny. Pregnant with another man's child. And that child had been Rowena.

Even though they'd always understood that their mother wasn't in love with their father, and that she wasn't faithful to him, either, this extra bombshell had been profoundly shocking. It forever altered their own biological relationship to one another. Rowena wasn't technically a full sister.

Thank goodness, it hadn't taken them long to realize that DNA didn't matter. They had grown up together, and they loved each other, needed each other and trusted each other, as only sisters can do. Rowena had been the hardest to convince. All her innate insecurities had kicked in bigtime, to the point that she wasn't even sure she had a right to claim any of Johnny's inheritance—the very ranch they all called home.

But eventually Ro, too, had understood that it didn't matter to either Bree or Penny who her biological father was. In fact, they were happy for her, because this meant she didn't have to continue living under the curse of sharing a murderer's genes.

Whose genes she *did* share, though, seemed destined to remain a mystery. When Ro was reluctant to pursue the information further, Bree had hired a private detective to find out who Moira's secret lover could possibly have been.

Bree had meant well, hoping only to provide her sister with the sense of belonging she'd never known. But Ro had taken her interference badly—at least at first. With difficulty, they'd mended that fence. Still, Ro hadn't ever opened the packet containing her birth father's identity.

At least as far as Penny knew.

"Did you ever—" Penny wasn't sure how to ask. She

wasn't sure she *should* ask. "I guess if you'd looked at the report, you would have mentioned it…"

"I haven't looked," Rowena said quietly.

Penny took her hand across the table. "You will, Ro. When you're ready."

Once, Rowena would have snatched hers away rather than admit she needed comfort, but the new Rowena gripped back with warmth and gratitude. "I know I will," she said. "It's just that the idea of knowing, for sure, is… absolutely terrifying."

"In case he's…"

"In case he's no better than Dad." Ro shrugged. "Or no more interested in knowing his daughter. No more interested in *me*."

Penny nodded. Though it was hard to imagine a gene pool worse than that of a murderer, she knew that, after a lifetime of rejection from Johnny, Rowena was afraid to risk more disappointment and pain.

Watching her sister closely like this, Penny realized that Ro looked terribly tired. Dark circles had formed under her intensely green eyes, and she was even thinner than usual, her personal giveaway that something was wrong.

Penny knew the marriage to Dallas was still strong, still joyous, so it wasn't that.

"Has there been any word from Bonnie and Mitch? Do you think they'll come back for the wedding?"

The disappearance of Dallas's brother, Mitch, who had run off with Rowena's friend and employee Bonnie O'Mara, on the day of Rowena's wedding, was another mystery no one could solve.

Everyone knew Bonnie was running from something, but no one knew what.

Perhaps that was weighing on Rowena's heart. Dallas must be suffering, wondering if his brother was all right, wondering when he'd see him again. And Rowena had grown deeply fond of Bonnie in the short time she'd known her.

"They send postcards now and then, just to let us know they're okay. But they never say where they are. And no talk of settling down. Certainly no talk of coming home." Rowena smiled. "But the cards are full of Mitch's ridiculous jokes and puns, so apparently life on the road is suiting him."

Okay, good. Worry about the nomadic couple wasn't the problem, either.

Getting the dude ranch up and running must be too much for her. This first year was critical—and there were so many decisions to be made. Though the fall season was clearly off to a successful start, they were simultaneously deep into planning for the winter season, which began on January 2.

In addition to getting the new cottages finished, they were hiring staff, arranging for ski instructors and sleigh rides and snowmobiles…and sorting out all the insurance and budget issues that came along with winter activities.

Penny felt a pang of guilt. Did she really have the right to insist on striking out alone at a time like this? Her Risk-it List of dancing and tattoos seemed frivolous compared to the possibility that Rowena was making herself ill with all the work. Shouldn't Penny just saddle up and ride her responsibilities, as their father used to say? She was a full partner—was it right of her not to shoulder a full share of the burden?

"Ro, you look awfully tired. Are you feeling all right? Is running the ranch getting to be too much?"

Rowena squeezed her hand and smiled. "I'm fine. Now that Bree has set a date, and Gray can relax, I'll be great." She put her lower lip between her teeth thoughtfully, her eyes regaining their mischievous sparkle. "Although…if I played the martyr card, would it get you to agree to move back home?"

"Ro." Bree smacked her sister's arm. "You promised. Leave her alone."

Rowena laughed, unabashed. "It was worth a try."

She stood, indicating that she was through discussing her health. "How about if I show you around the new wing?"

Typical of Rowena, putting on a strong face the minute she was questioned. She'd never liked to admit weakness, and though she'd mellowed in many ways, she still didn't enjoy pity.

Penny decided to let it go, though she made a mental note to ask Bree about it privately. "You bet," she said cheerfully, standing. "I can't wait to see what you've done!"

By the time the tour was over, and they returned, chattering happily, to the dining room, a feast of sandwiches and salads had been beautifully displayed on the sideboard. Penny was suddenly ravenous, her mouth watering and her stomach rumbling.

Each of them filled a plate, then sat down to dig in.

After a minute or two devoted to ecstatic appreciation, Rowena spoke. Her voice was full of mischief.

"So…aren't you ever going to tell us about Mr. Dreamy?"

Penny stirred her salad and didn't make eye contact. She was glad to hear Ro sound very much her old, incorrigible self. But she hadn't wanted to open this discussion today.

"Nothing to say, really. It's almost as if no one's over there. He's gone a lot, working. His daughter goes to Millicent Starling's day camp, I think. Remember how awful Starling's was?"

All three of them had been forced to attend Starling's Day Camp at least one summer, so she hoped this topic might divert the conversation away from Max. She looked up and smiled as naturally as possible.

"No one cares about Millicent," Ro said flatly. "Back to the hunky widower."

"He's just a tenant." Penny sighed. "And a pretty good one. He paid three months in advance."

Ro laughed. "Notice how she says nothing about…ice cream."

Penny rolled her eyes. She should have known she wouldn't get away without a debriefing on this. "And you wonder why I am not keen to move back in. I do one impulsive thing in my entire life, and I'm never going to live it down."

"You don't have to live it down," Bree said, shooting their sister a dirty look. "You can kiss every man who walks into the ice-cream store, if you want to. Ro is just being Ro."

It was nice, listening to Bree tease Ro this way—with no real anger or bitterness. For so many years, the two of them had been estranged, and Penny had struggled in vain to help them reconcile. Even if Penny had to be the butt of the joke today, it was worth it to see them act like real sisters again.

"I don't really have the urge to kiss every single man. I don't even have the urge to kiss that one, except that one time."

Even as she said it, though, she knew it wasn't true. She'd had the urge to kiss him again the other night, on the back deck. That urge could become a habit.

"Why?" Rowena ignored Bree's body language, which clearly said "enough, already!" "What was different about that one time?"

"He was with his daughter, who was being a real brat. I expected him to…you know. Say something cruel. Go nuts. I kept imagining what Dad would have been like if I…if one of us…"

She lifted her shoulder. She didn't need to explain further. She could tell they were imagining, too. "Anyhow, Max was surprisingly gentle. And very patient. So...I just felt the urge to thank him for restoring my faith in men."

Darn it. She should have said "in fathers." Restoring her faith in *fathers*. But correcting herself would have been more conspicuous than letting it stand.

Bree looked a little misty-eyed. Ro did, too—although as usual she clearly didn't want it to show. She wiggled her eyebrows dramatically. "Of course, it didn't hurt that he's wildly attractive, right?"

She ducked sideways, anticipating Bree's teasing swat. "Okay, well, as long as I'm in trouble," Ro said, returning to center when Bree withdrew her hand. "I might as well confess that I checked him out."

"Checked him out?" Penny wasn't sure what that meant. Checked out his good looks?

"Yeah. You know. Cyber digging. It's amazing what you can find out, if you're really trying."

"Aw, Ro." Bree put her head in her hands. "You're impossible."

"Well, initially I asked Dallas to do it. He's got all those law enforcement programs that would make it so easy. But he refused. Some ethics nonsense or something."

Ro's eyes were laughing, though she pretended to be serious. "So anyhow, apparently Thorpe is exactly who he says he is. Successful architect. Travels a lot, site planning, construction oversight, stuff like that. Wife died last year of an aneurism. Daughter a little mixed up but not Bad Seed material or anything. Just cranky."

"Ro, what were you thinking—"

But Rowena pretended she hadn't heard Penny's interruption and helped herself to another plate of salad. "He's clean. Bree and I decided he can stay."

"Not Bree and I," Bree corrected emphatically. "You leave me out of this."

Penny was still looking for her voice.

"You…you actually… You snooped into…" She scowled, wishing she didn't turn into an inarticulate child every time Rowena flustered her. "Tell me you're kidding."

"Sorry, Pea." Ro grinned. "It doesn't matter how old you get. I'm always going to be the big sister."

"And she's always going to be an interfering know-it-all," Bree added pleasantly. She winked at Penny. "I've finally made peace with it. You'd probably better just do the same."

She reached down beside her chair and hauled up a stack of pastel binders, each labeled something like Caterers or Bridesmaids Dresses.

"Okay, ladies. If Rowena is finished being insufferable for the moment, we've got a wedding to plan."

ELLEN HATED THE day camp her dad had decided to stash her in while he was at work. It was almost all outdoors, which meant it was too hot, and too…Colorado.

Kids out here thought the weirdest things were fun. They shot arrows, climbed rocks, paddled canoes, rode bikes… No wonder they were so skinny. One of the girls had laughed at her for sweating during the rock climbing. Well, ex*cuse* her if the shopping and movies and YouTube stuff she did for fun in Chicago didn't build up Amazon biceps.

Where she lived, nature wasn't always trying to kill you, so you didn't have to play "survival games."

Today hadn't been the worst, because someone from a place called Bell River Dude Ranch had joined them to teach an art lesson. Alec Garwood had come along with the woman. That was nice, if only because Ellen actually sort of knew him.

His parents owned that dude ranch, she discovered, which was kind of cool, except he said it was mostly horses and more of this outdoorsy stuff—canoes and bikes and rocks and campouts. Still, the other kids looked up to him, you could tell. When he came over and sat next to her during the art class, they all began treating her better.

It didn't seem to matter that he was only ten, and some of the other kids were all the way up to twelve. He was like one of those natural born leaders or something.

He was rotten at art, though, and he laughed about it, adding colors and blobs to his painting until it looked like a picture of wet mud. She was pretty good, and she'd expected him to be nasty about it. Boys sometimes were if they felt stupid. But he wasn't nasty. He kept saying how good she was, and several other kids heard him, which was nice.

She painted a watercolor of some loblolly pines, which she liked the name of, even though she'd just learned it today. Her other choice had been to go to the stables and paint a horse, but horses made her nervous. She didn't want anyone to notice that—especially Alec. She had a feeling he would be like a horse guru or something, considering he owned a ranch.

Anyhow, the pines had turned out really pretty. Even the teacher said so. Ellen found herself checking her watch, hoping it was almost time for her dad to come get her. He approved of her doing art—it was the one thing she liked that he didn't call "inappropriate." Besides, he'd promised to take her out to dinner.

"So did you decide if you want me to pierce your ears?" Alec had tilted his chair back on its rear legs, and he was ruffling his paintbrush through his fingers, spraying paint on his paper. The teacher had stopped reprimanding him half an hour ago, when it became clear his painting was hopeless.

Ellen ran her hands across her drawing, smoothing it out. "No," she said flatly. "Why would I let you do that? You don't know anything about piercing peoples' ears."

"What's to know?" He got his brush sopping wet, swished it around in the green paint, and let loose a spray of dots that looked like Martian blood. They hit the paper, then slid down in blobs, picking up the mud color as they dragged along. "You use ice to numb your ear, I know that. Then take the needle and...bam!"

He jabbed with the paintbrush, mimicking the needle through her ear. She winced, in spite of herself.

"See?" He smiled. "I knew you were scared."

"I'm not scared. I'm just not an idiot. You didn't say anything about sterilizing the needle. You'd probably cut my ear off."

He laughed, then put down his brush, noticing that the teacher was winding up and preparing to leave.

"Suit yourself," he said happily. "She's my ride, so I gotta go."

Something went flat inside Ellen's chest, like a bike tire with a hole in it. She didn't want to be left alone here with these other kids, who weren't nice to her. She looked at her watch. Twenty minutes until her father came. She wondered if there was any way to get Alec to hang around till then.

But as she was searching her mind for an excuse that didn't sound pathetic, Mrs. Starling showed up at her elbow. She hated Mrs. Starling most of all, because she was sun-tanned to the color of leather, and she had muscles so big they looked as if they were play dough mounds added to regular arms and thighs.

"Ellen, your father called," she said with a smile that

was probably supposed to be friendly. But her teeth were so white and square inside that leathery face that it just looked weird. "He's been delayed at work, and you're supposed to go home in the camp van."

Ellen's mouth fell open. "He's not coming to get me?"

The woman gave her a narrow look, as if Ellen might be kind of slow. People thought that sometimes, because she was chubby. She always wanted to take out the picture she kept of her mom, who had been chubby when she was eleven, too, and turned out to be really beautiful and smart.

"Yes." The woman spoke more slowly. "I said, he's been delayed at work."

"Well, what will I do when I get home? Will he be home then?

Ellen knew she was sounding just as brainless as Mrs. Starling suspected, but she was so upset she couldn't think straight. Although, really, why should she even be surprised? Back before her mom died, her dad was always stuck at work.

But he'd promised her. That's why they moved here in the first place, he said. So that he wouldn't have to travel so much, and he could "put her first."

Ha. And she'd been dumb enough to fall for it.

"I'm sure someone will be there by the time you get home," Mrs. Starling said, but you could tell she wasn't one bit sure. She didn't care. If no one was home, it wouldn't be her problem.

The woman walked away to talk to the driver, who had already begun to gather his group over by the front door. Ellen had always felt a little bit superior, because she didn't have to get herded up like one of the sheep. She was one of the lucky kids whose parents could get off work early, or didn't work at all, and always showed up on time.

Well, not anymore. *Thanks, Dad.*

Just then Alec came sauntering by, talking to a couple of the other kids, his hands in his pockets and his mouth full of chocolate. They were heading for the door, following the art teacher. Going back to Bell River Dude Ranch, no doubt.

It sounded so cool. During art class he'd talked nonstop, telling her all about it. Apparently he had a father, a step-mother, some kind of almost-aunt person, and an almost uncle, too. And a ranch manager who played the guitar and sang songs all the time, like in an old-fashioned cow-boy movie. And a cook who baked awesome cookies just for him.

Not to mention about fifty other people who worked for them, making everything nice.

"Hey," she said impulsively. "Alec."

He turned, smiling. That probably was why everybody liked him. He was just plain nice. He didn't smile in a needy way, praying you'd like him. He seemed to smile just be-cause he liked *himself.*

"Hey," he said. He didn't even make it a question. He just stood there, even though his friends kept walking. He didn't look annoyed that she'd stopped him.

"So…I was thinking." She swallowed. "Why don't you come over to the cottage? I think I'm in the mood to pierce my ears."

As Max listened to Acton Adams—retired big-deal golf pro and owner of Silverdell Hills—drone on, he had to sum-mon the "out of body" control he'd learned in Mexico just to keep from throttling the jerk. Adams, who had clearly bought into his own PR, had been holding forth for the past two hours about absolutely nothing.

Max had already been forced to ask Ellen to ride the van home from camp, which she'd probably hated like fire.

If Adams didn't shut up in the next twenty minutes, Max wouldn't get home before the van dropped her off, either.

That was the real problem. But Max also had an issue with feeling trapped, even in a luxurious conference room like this. He tapped his pencil on the green blotter. Under the mahogany table, his thighs burned with the need to stretch, to move, to prove to his brain that he was free....

So he put himself elsewhere. Compared to Mexico, this jerk was a piece of cake. Max evened out his breathing, then put himself on a horse, on his grandfather's farm, with the cabbage, peppers and potatoes greening under the spring sun.

But another ten minutes passed, and Adams was still pontificating, still asking Max the same questions over and over.

Olivia Gaynor, the VP who'd hired Max, had begged him to give Adams the attention he wanted. Adams was hot-tempered, she said. If he decided he didn't like Max, then her job, and a couple of others, were on the line—not just his.

Max didn't give a damn about finishing this resort. He'd completed the architectural plans, which was the part he loved. But he had a background in construction, so over-seeing the construction phase was one of the extra ser-vices he'd tossed in when he left corporate work after the Mexico incident. As he struck out on his own, he'd needed to set himself apart from the other million or so available architects.

He didn't need that anymore. But Olivia liked her job. *Needed* her job. And he liked Olivia. He liked the others, too. So strangling The Big Deal wasn't an option. Sadly, making nice was required.

But so was ensuring Ellen had supervision. Before he came to Colorado, he'd been clear about his schedule with

Olivia and everyone else on the team. They all knew he had to be out of here by four o'clock, every day, no matter what. So, foolishly, he'd assumed he wouldn't need baby-sitter services.

As Adams signaled for more water in his crystal pitcher, Max sighed. *Crap.* He'd have to get a sitter somehow. He thought through his options. Then, coming up with a plan, he offered to get the water. Olivia widened her eyes, but The Big Deal took it as his due.

Max didn't care. All he wanted was to get out of the room. He stepped into the hall, handed the pitcher to a passing office runner and took out his phone.

Penny had given him her cell number, in case he had an emergency with the rental. He hoped she wouldn't mind being asked for a personal favor instead. He wouldn't have asked—in fact, he'd deliberately steered clear of her for the past few days. But Ellen came first, and, other than the people in this conference room, Penny was the only person in Silverdell he knew well enough to trust.

The thought flitted through his mind that he didn't really know Penny very well, either. He'd been in Silverdell maybe eighty hours, and everyone he knew here was the same: an acquaintance of about eighty hours.

But he dismissed the overly literal logic of that. Some things weren't counted in hours. He trusted Penny Wright, and it didn't matter whether he could explain it. Trust was born on some other level entirely.

Luckily, she answered on the second ring.

"Max?" Her ordinarily warm voice was guarded. He wondered if she dreaded seeing his name on her caller ID. Maybe she didn't have a lot of spare cash, and she was afraid the pipes had exploded, or the roof had caved in. "Is everything all right?"

"Everything's fine. Did I catch you at a bad time?"

"No…" Still, she sounded careful. "I'm at the ranch with my sisters."

"Oh." Darn. He'd have to think of a Plan B, and fast. Maybe she could recommend a sitter. "I'd been hoping that… But if you're busy, then—"

"I'm not busy. I mean, I'm not too busy to help, if you need something. We're just chatting."

He heard female laughter in the background. She put her hand over the phone a minute, as if dealing with someone in the room.

When she spoke again, her voice was more normal. Maybe she'd stepped out to get privacy, as he had. "Really, I'd be glad to help, if there's anything I can do."

She sounded sincere. Something relaxed inside Max for the first time since the idiot had begun blathering two hours ago.

"Thanks," he said. "I'm stuck at the office, but Ellen will get home on the camp van in the next half hour or so. Is there any chance you could meet her at the cottage, and keep an eye on her till I get home? It shouldn't be more than another half hour after that."

He looked through the window toward the conference room, where The Big Deal had put his feet up on the table and was leaning back, absently plucking at his belt as if he wished he could loosen it and get comfortable.

Needed more room for all the hot air, presumably.

"At least I hope it'll only be half an hour," Max amended honestly. "And I guess I should warn you…I promised Ellen I wouldn't ever work late like this again. So she's probably going to be mad."

PENNY GOT HOME in fifteen minutes, thinking she'd have time to change clothes, maybe make a cup of tea. She knocked on Max's side of the duplex first, just in case, but no one answered. So she left her door open, listening for the van, and slipped off her pretty flowered skirt, kicked off her heels and tugged on a pair of jeans.

The yellow gypsy shirt, with its smocked neckline and cuffs, would have to stay as it was. No time to take it off. She had an angry little girl arriving any minute.

But another twenty minutes came and went. Penny started to be nervous. She paced out onto the road, looking for the Starling van. She knew it well—she would have recognized it anywhere, even if she hadn't seen it tooling around town, looking just the same as it had seventeen years ago.

Same bright orange paint. Same busted springs and bumpy lurching over railroad tracks. Some childhood traumas you never forgot.

The road was empty. This wasn't a busy street, backing up on the elementary school as it did—at least not until school started again next month. Frowning, she went back inside. Maybe she should call Millicent and see how many stops had been on the driver's route. She might also call Dallas and see if there had been any accidents downtown, the only spot likely to create a traffic jam.

She'd just picked up the telephone when she heard Ellen's footsteps outside the door. Thank goodness.

But then she realized she hadn't heard the van. That was strange. It was so quiet out...just wind in the trees and birdsong. She couldn't have missed the rumble and sputter of a van like that, could she?

She turned, smiling. "Hey, there," she started, and then came to an abrupt stop.

"Miss Wright. Come quick."

Penny's heart raced. Ellen's voice was thin with distress. What had happened? Had there been an accident after all? What about the other children?

She moved quickly toward the door, trying to assess Ellen's condition. The child's face was splotchy, as if she might have been crying, but she stood normally, and Penny couldn't see any blood.

But…what was going on with her ear?

Ellen was backlit by the afternoon sun, so it was hard to be sure, but…

Penny came closer. The little girl didn't move. Penny bent and put her hands softly on Ellen's shoulders, so that she could look more carefully.

Dear heaven. Ellen's glossy brown hair was piled up on her head with plastic toothy clips, but just on one side. And there it was. Penny hadn't been imagining things. On the bared side of the girl's head, a silver sewing needle protruded from her earlobe, which was gently seeping blood.

"Oops," Penny said calmly. Ellen's eyes were wide and panicked. She didn't need an anxious adult screaming questions at her. "What's going on here?"

She tried to touch the needle, thinking she might be able to slip it out quickly, but Ellen flinched and drew back.

"You have to come quick," the girl said again. "Hurry. I don't know what to do. It's Alec."

"Alec?" Penny stood. The needle was very fine, and it had done its damage already. If necessary, taking it out could wait until Ellen was calmer. Right now, Penny needed to find out what was going on with Alec.

Ellen led her wordlessly down her front steps, then up the steps that led to the rental side. She pushed open the door, but she didn't enter. She stood as if frozen, pointing toward the floor.

"There. I think he fainted."

Penny didn't take time to process what she saw in words. If she had, she might have fainted, too. The sight of Alec, mischievous, lively Alec, lying in a heap on the living room floor, was enough to take her breath away.

Instead of thinking, she acted. She knelt beside him, confirmed that he was breathing…thank God, thank God… and slipped her fingers into his mouth. His tongue was where it belonged.

So far so good. His skin wasn't hot to the touch. There was no blood. No limbs twisted at strange angles, no bones jutting out.

She rocked back on her heels and took a deep breath. Maybe he really had merely fainted.

But why?

She was pulling her phone out of her pocket to call 911 when Alec suddenly opened his blue eyes. When he registered Penny bending over him, it seemed to take him half a second to sort things out. Then his eyes went impossibly wide, his mouth formed a perfect circle, as if he were blowing smoke rings, and he clambered to his feet.

"Oh, heck. *Heck!* What the heck happened?"

Ellen, who had tentatively tiptoed through the doorway and now stood just a few feet away, her shadow almost touching Alec's body, made a contemptuous noise. "You fainted, that's what happened, you poser! I *knew* you didn't know anything about piercing ears!"

Alec narrowed his eyes to angry slits. "How did I know you were going to start gushing blood like a stuck pig?"

Penny stood, putting her hands between the feuding children like a referee at a boxing match. Which this might become in a minute or two, if she didn't stop them. Ellen and Alec were both clearly scared to death, and embarrassed—and both were the type who couldn't tolerate those emotions without lashing out.

"Hang on," Penny said, still keeping her tone calm. "I need to know what's going on. And I need to hear it from one at a time." She glanced from one heaving, fiery little body to the other. "Ellen, it's your house and your ear. Why don't you tell me?"

Alec grunted, but he didn't interrupt. Ellen didn't look at Penny while she talked. She kept her furious gaze on Alec, as if daring him to contradict her.

"My dad didn't come get me, so I had to come home on the van. Which he said I would never have to do. Then he wasn't even here. So Alec came over, and he said he wanted to pierce my ears. He said he knew how."

Her delivery sped up at this point, as if to discourage questions. Obviously this was the tricky part, and Penny suspected that the girl didn't have permission to entertain friends when her father wasn't home. *Or* to pierce her ears. Penny didn't mention any of that, though, because right now she just needed the facts.

"But I knew he was lying. He didn't even numb my ear right, because it really hurt." Ellen looked indignant, as if Alec had deliberately tricked her. "And then, the minute he put the needle in, he passed out."

Alec reared up to half again his height. "I did *not*."

"Oh, yeah? What were you doing down there, then? Counting the threads in the carpet?"

"Well, it was gross." Alec hadn't stopped scowling since he stood, but his face was like a thundercloud now. "You're a bleeder, that's what you are, like one of Gray's sick horses. Besides, it's a lie that I *wanted* to do it. You *asked* me to do it. But if I'd known what you are, I wouldn't *ever* have done it."

"Done what?"

A shadow fell into the room as a new, larger figure appeared in the doorway, his back to the setting sun.

For a split second, the tableau of three froze. Penny stood in the middle, arms stretched, one palm gently turned toward each of the red-faced children. Alec's finger was mid-air, jabbing toward Ellen.

Ellen, of course, still had a winking, silver needle hanging out of her ear.

And, of course, her daddy had chosen that moment to come home.

CHAPTER SIX

FIFTEEN MINUTES LATER—after making a call to Rowena—
Penny, Max, Ellen and Alec crowded into the small kitchen,
preparing for surgery. Penny was working hard to remain
outwardly calm, for Ellen's sake, though she was angry
with Alec and just a little flustered by this intimate prox-
imity to an angry Max.

He was powerful and radiated energy even when he
was at his mildest. Now, worried for his daughter and furious with her simultaneously, he was almost overpowering.

"You sure you don't want me to do this?" Max's dark
gaze met Penny's as she plucked an ice cube from his
freezer, having promised to numb Ellen's ear before she
touched the needle.

"Dad, no!" Ellen's voice thrummed. She was perched
on the countertop, her hands squeezing the edge until her
knuckles turned white. "I want Penny to do it!"

Max backed away, and Penny shot him an apologetic
glance. Ellen must have felt a woman would be more understanding. Judging from the frown on Max's face, she
might have been correct.

One of the silver cooking pots was still sitting on a
burner, with an inch of water cooling in it—evidence that
the kids told the truth when they said they'd tried to sterilize
the needle by boiling it. A small jar of alcohol and a blood-
stained cotton ball on the counter told the rest of the tale.

From the corner of her eyes, Penny noted that Alec

wasn't watching the procedure, little chicken. He leaned against the doorjamb and picked at the brand-new wallpaper. Penny touched his shin once with the side of her shoe, to tell him to stop it, and he did. But he still slouched sideways, staring at the wallpaper stripes as if they were the only interesting things in the room.

Penny took her time, making sure Ellen's ear was so cold the little girl couldn't feel a thing. The girl was so terrified Penny wondered how on earth Alec had ever talked her into this in the first place.

"You know, I'm still trying to decide which flowers to plant behind the deck," she said lightly, plucking a topic out of the blue, hoping to distract Ellen while they waited for the ice to take effect. "I want bird feeders, of course. And I'd love to attract butterflies, so I'm thinking pentas and maybe lantana."

No reaction. Ellen wasn't a budding gardener, then. Okay. Something more interesting…

"And I have a gazing ball collection, so I need to arrange that, too. I've been making gazing balls for years. I brought them all with me from San Francisco."

Ellen looked up, finally curious. "What's a gazing ball?"

"They're glass balls people put in their gardens, all sizes and colors. They reflect the light and flowers and things around them. They're really pretty. I make mine out of bowling balls."

As she'd hoped, that got Ellen's attention for real. "*Bowling* balls?"

Penny took that moment to do the deed, sliding the needle free as deftly and quickly as she could.

"Yep," she responded, dabbing a piece of cotton to catch the drop or two of blood that followed. Alec was right— Ellen did bleed easily. "They're superheavy, which is good because they won't blow around in a storm. I put little pieces of colored glass all over them, making pretty mosaics. I'll show you sometime."

She held the needle up in front of Ellen's face. "Here you go."

The girl's eyes widened. "You got it out already?"

Penny nodded, smiling. She hoped Ellen might smile back.

But then, as if her courage had finally stretched too thin and popped abruptly, like a balloon, the girl started to cry. She fell forward onto Penny's shoulder, hugging hard and making gulping, sobbing sounds. Penny's eyes met Max's over Ellen's weeping head.

He looked as if the sight of her tears pained him—but awkward, as if he weren't sure any effort he made to console her would be welcome. Within seconds, Penny's shirt was soggy, and Penny had no choice but to hug her back.

"Oh, brother," Alec said, but Penny bumped his shin again to shut him up.

The doorbell rang, and they all knew it was Rowena. Alec groaned, but he made no move toward the door, since it wasn't his house. Max touched Ellen's back once, softly, and then went into the living room.

Still holding Ellen, Penny listened as Max greeted Rowena. For several minutes after that, Ro's voice was the only one she heard. Her sister was clearly apologizing all over the place, something she was probably getting pretty good at, considering how often Alec was in trouble.

Suddenly Rowena's voice grew louder, and very stern. "Alec!"

Alec blanched. He glanced at Penny, as if she might be willing to hide him.

"Go on," Penny said quietly. "It'll be all right. Nobody actually died."

"Aw, *man*."

One good thing about the crazy kid—he did know how to take his medicine with grace. He inhaled deeply, squared his skinny shoulders, gave Penny a look as grave as a soldier, then marched out to face Rowena.

"Is he going to be in big trouble?" Ellen spoke the question into Penny's shirt.

"Not really," Penny said honestly. "My sister tries to be strict with him, and sometimes she makes a lot of noise, but he pretty much has her wrapped around his finger. Her and everybody else. He's pretty persuasive, as you probably noticed."

She had hoped that might make Ellen laugh, but apparently she was striking out today. Ellen just sniffed.

"Hey, there." Penny touched Ellen's hair. "Want to meet my sister? I think you two might like each other."

Ellen lifted her head, but shook it. "I can't. She'll know I've been crying." Her brows knit together. "She'll think I'm a baby."

"Well, let's see." Penny smoothed Ellen's hair, then brushed away the remaining dampness from her cheeks. When she had adjusted her collar and checked the ear one more time for blood, she smiled.

"Nope." She pronounced the verdict with conviction. "No one could guess a thing. You look fine."

She stood back so Ellen could hop down from the counter, and tossed the cotton balls into the under-counter trash can.

"Besides," Penny added casually, as if it had just occurred to her. "It probably would look more grown-up to come out and be polite. It would show Alec you're doing fine. And it would prove you're not afraid. Which, of course, you aren't."

Ellen frowned. "Of course I'm not," she said, pulling down on her shirt, which was a little snug over her blue jeans. "It was just weird to have a needle hanging out of my ear, that's all."

Penny hid a smile. This was almost too easy. Growing up with Rowena had been like a master class in handling people like Ellen. Once Penny had couched it in terms of pride, Ellen had no choice. She had to stand up and put on her game face. She was desperate to erase the impression of those tears.

She squared her shoulders and lifted her chin, in an unconscious imitation of Alec's earlier moves. *That wasn't really me, hugging you in front of everybody,* the posture said. *That wasn't really me, crying like a baby.*

Penny's heart tugged toward the brave little girl. It wasn't easy being so proud. She'd seen it so clearly with Rowena. If you didn't allow yourself to ask for the love you needed, you often didn't get it.

She had the strangest sense of protective frustration, wishing she could teach Ellen a better way to handle her emotions. She didn't want her to have to wait until she was a grown woman, as Rowena had, to mellow and let people in.

And Ellen was lucky—she didn't really *need* to wait. Unlike Rowena, she had a loving, patient father, just standing by, hoping to get a chance to shower affection on her.

But Ellen wouldn't listen, even if Penny had felt she had the right to tell her any of that. She didn't know Penny well enough yet. She didn't trust her. In fact, trusting people seemed to be one of Ellen's most basic issues.

Well, Penny understood that, too. It was something she struggled with, herself. Only in Penny's case, the person she'd never learned to trust was herself.

So she just held out her hand, as if it would be perfectly normal for Ellen to take it. After a brief hesitation, the girl did. Then, together, they moved through the swinging door and entered the living room.

Rowena stood near the front door, grasping Alec by both shoulders, fixing him directly in front of her. She was clearly not going to let go until he'd made an apology that suited her.

He seemed to be winding down from a long speech. "And so that's it, Mr. Thorpe. I really mean it. I'm really, really sorry."

Alec twisted his head up at Rowena, as if checking to see if he'd satisfied all requirements. Her face seemed expressionless, but its very blankness must have told him something, because he sighed and turned around again to face Max.

"And...let's see...oh, yeah, I'm *also* sorry that I came into your house without your permission, because I know that probably feels creepy to you, doesn't it?"

Max's mouth twitched. Penny had to force herself to stop looking at it, because the motion of repressed laughter was so attractive.

So oddly sexy, given the situation.

"I honestly didn't think of coming off like a creeper," Alec explained. "I was just thinking it would be fun, and that Ellen would be happy to have pierced ears so that she could wear her earrings. And...oh, and I'm also sorry I fainted on your carpet, and I guess I could pay to get it cleaned or something, but to tell you the truth I don't even remember any of that, so if I slobbered or puked on it or anything—"

"That'll do." Rowena made a choking sound. "I think Mr. Thorpe gets the idea."

Rowena suddenly seemed to notice Penny and Ellen. She wiggled Alec's shoulders. "There's Ellen," she said meaningfully.

He screwed up his mouth, but he obviously knew the drill. He walked over to Ellen, and he gave her a serious look. She stared back, equally solemn, still holding Penny's hand. She didn't relent an inch. Though her fingers tightened around Penny's, her gaze at Alec was poker-straight.

"I'm sorry I got you in trouble," he said in his best manly voice. "I'm sorry I sucked at ear piercing. I thought it was a lot easier than that. And I had no idea I'd be so dumb about blood."

He grinned up at Penny—it wasn't in Alec to be somber for long. "I used to think maybe I'd be a doctor, but now I know that won't work. So that's actually a good thing, right?"

"That's a *very* good thing," Ellen answered, though the question hadn't been directed at her. When Alec glanced her way, she smiled—just a fraction of an inch, but he obviously knew he'd eventually be forgiven.

"Want to come meet my second mom?" He gestured toward Rowena. "I call her Rowena, but she's really my second mom. My first mom moved to Paris and had these two twin babies that are like, wow, *disgusting.* You wouldn't believe how awful. So Dad married Rowena, and everyone thought I would be mad, but I wasn't, because she's actually pretty awesome."

Ellen glanced over at Rowena, covering her shyness with a frown. She squeezed Penny's hand, as if trying to send her an SOS.

Penny watched Ro figure Ellen out in a heartbeat. At that age, Ro, too, would have hated the idea of a formal introduction to a stranger, especially a stranger who might be very mad at her.

So Ro just smiled and gave Ellen a friendly "that's okay" wave.

"Ellen probably doesn't want to have much to do with anyone connected to you, Alec," Rowena said. "Anyhow, right now I have to take you to get your head examined.

Literally. Maybe later, if she decides to forgive you, Ellen can come over to the ranch for lunch or something. You can show her Trouble."

"Trouble's my dog," Alec put in, as if afraid Max and Ellen would misunderstand. "It's just a silly name. She never bites or anything."

"Anyhow, we'll get out of your way," Rowena said, glancing toward Max. "Remember, though—this probably really was all Alec's doing. The boy could talk a rabbit into a steel-jawed trap."

"So I'm gathering," Max said blandly. He walked over and held out his hand to Alec. "Thank you for the apology. Your mom brought you up right." He smiled at Rowena. "Both of them."

Rowena smiled back at him. Then she cast a quick, sparkling glance at Penny, as if to say *wow*.

"Ro, I'll head out with you," Penny said quickly, before her sister could start saying embarrassing things. Rowena's matchmaking wasn't terribly subtle, she'd discovered at lunch the other day.

Besides, Max and Ellen would need privacy now, to sort things out. "I'll walk you to the car, and then I've got a ton of unpacking left to do."

She felt a small twitch from Ellen, as if her instinct was to beg Penny to stay. But when she looked down, Ellen's face had gone stoic, any weakness covered with a layer of bravado. She let go of Penny's hand.

Penny's heart tightened again, recognizing the acceptance that she was all alone in this. So heartbreaking—and so unnecessary. If only the little girl could see how staunch an ally her dad would be, if only she'd let him...

"Maybe I'll see you in the next few days?" Penny smiled. "Maybe you could help me decide where to put the gazing balls?"

"Maybe." Ellen swallowed hard. "If I'm not grounded."

Penny glanced at Max—and beneath the impassive mask she saw the truth. He was so darn relieved both kids were unharmed. Any punishment he doled out would be purely a token.

Which, unfortunately, just made her want to kiss him all over again. She flushed, then glanced at Ro, wondering if her sister had noticed.

The twinkle in Rowena's green eyes was answer enough.

She'd noticed, all right. In fact, the tips of her cheeks looked a little pink, too, as if she might be willing to kiss him herself.

"You won't ground her, will you, Mr. Thorpe?" Alec sounded worried. "It's like Rowena said. It was my fault, even if she is a bleeder—"

Laughing, Rowena clapped one hand over her stepson's mouth.

"Come on, Pea," she said. With her free hand, she grabbed Penny's fingers and tugged her toward the door. "I think Alec better quit while he's ahead."

ELLEN DIDN'T FALL asleep until nearly midnight. Max wondered whether that might be too late to knock on Penny's door, but her lights were still blazing, so he took a chance.

He went to the back, leaving his kitchen door ajar so he could hear Ellen if she woke up. She slept hard, and ordinarily nothing disturbed her, not even his bad dreams, during which he sometimes cried out so loudly he woke himself. But he didn't want to take any chances.

Penny answered almost immediately, and it was clear she'd still been up and wide-awake. She wore the same loose, lacy shirt and formfitting blue jeans that had driven him crazy earlier today. She might have the face of a china doll, too sweet and perfect to be real under that fall of honey-brown hair. But her body was 100 percent real-flesh woman.

And, given that he'd sworn that for the next nine months he'd be 100 percent pure father—with nothing set aside for personal things, like sex and dating—that was a lot more woman than he needed right now.

But he had to thank her for today. She'd been unbelievably competent and compassionate.

In fact, she'd been the kind of mother Ellen should have had. How different might things have been, he thought, if he'd waited for a woman like this one?

"Hi," he said. "Sorry to bother you so late. I just wanted to thank you for all your help today. You were terrific."

"It was nothing." She smiled. "And I didn't even realize it was late. I was still up. Still unpacking. It's such a mess, moving in, isn't it?"

He nodded with feeling. But, judging from what he could see over her shoulder, her place didn't look half as chaotic as his. He still had boxes everywhere, and he hadn't even brought any furniture or large items. She'd had only a few days to start from scratch, and everything he could see looked fully finished.

Simple and spare, lots of blues and browns and clean, creamy white. Elegant and welcoming. Flowers on the kitchen table, and beyond that, lamps and armchairs and a colorful braided rug in the living room.

And, on every wall, framed paintings—beautiful landscapes that looked like original artwork. Wildflowers and mountains that could easily have been Silverdell itself.

She glanced toward his side of the duplex. "How's Ellen?"

"She's all right, thanks to your TLC. I don't know how you got her to come out and face Rowena. She usually gets stubborn and defensive."

She smiled. "Appealed to her sense of pride, mostly. It's a technique I learned with Rowena, when we were kids. When she felt bullied or threatened, she covered up by being haughty, or lashing out preemptively. So we all learned to come at her sideways."

He shook his head, thinking how sad it was that Penny, at ten or eleven, had been defter with a difficult personality than he was at thirty-four.

"I wish you'd been around to help me navigate the rest of the night. The minute you guys were gone, Ellen started in on how the whole disaster was my fault, because I reneged on her mother's promise to let her pierce her ears when she turned eleven."

"Oh, dear." Penny still smiled, but her gaze was sympathetic. "Don't tell me. You tried to be logical. And things went south from there?"

"In a big hurry. I ended up having to ground her after all. She got so unpleasant, and I'm so bad at knowing how to stop it. Once, I would have walked away and let her mother handle it. Then, for a while, I just let her get away with whatever, because she'd lost her mom. Now I'm trying to hold her accountable. It's no fun, but I'm trying to stick to it, even when it hurts."

"I'm so sorry." Penny reached up to shove a strand of shining hair from her face. "I feel as if I'm to blame, actually. If only I'd realized they were in the house already."

"That's absolutely not your fault. You couldn't have known she'd be devious enough to hide and refuse to answer the door. Besides, the driver shouldn't have left her when no one was—"

He broke off, suddenly glimpsing what looked like an angry, purple bruise on the upper rim of Penny's cheekbone.

It wasn't large, but the back porch motion-sensitive lights all had switched on when he came through, so the porch was bright as if it were daylight. It was definitely a bruise. She looked as if someone had socked her.

"Oh..." He touched his index finger to the mark before he even thought about it. "What happened?"

She put her own hand to the spot and made a sheepish sound. "Honestly, it's so ridiculous I almost hate to admit it." She smiled. "I'm twenty-seven years old, and I don't know how to juggle. I was trying to learn."

Juggling? Had he heard her right? "With *what?* Your bowling balls?"

She backed away from the door slightly, so that he could see into the kitchen's breakfast nook. There, just beside the centerpiece of daisies, were three stones she'd probably found on the creek bed. Mostly rounded, mostly smooth, but too big and heavy for juggling—at least twice the size of golf balls.

"With *rocks?*"

"Yeah." She sighed. "I don't have anything sensible, like beanbags, so I thought those might work." She raised her eyebrows. "I was wrong."

"Who would have guessed?" He tried not to laugh, but at the moment he felt every day of the seven years between them. How could anyone be so naive? "Did you put something on it?"

She nodded. "I've been defrosting peas on my face for the past half hour, so I should be okay. Do you want to come in? I don't have anything adult to offer you, but I've got hot milk on the stove." She smiled. "And peas."

Hot milk for a nightcap. He thought back to the first day, when he'd seen her pull into the driveway and assumed she was a stalker, maybe nuts. He almost laughed out loud, thinking how wrong he'd gotten that one.

"I'd love a glass of milk," he said, though he knew the offer had probably been perfunctory, and she fully expected him to decline. "I should stay out here, though, so I can hear Ellen."

"Of course." Maybe it hadn't been perfunctory, after all. She looked pleased, and he wondered whether she'd been lonely—in there with only her determination to stand on her own two feet for company.

She glanced up at the silvery-gray sky. "The weather's perfect for it, as long as we don't get any rain."

She was right. The temperatures, which had reached the high seventies in the afternoon, had dipped, but not enough to be uncomfortable. A low blanket of clouds had kept the warmth from dissipating. It also held the resin scent of the pines near the earth, thick and sweet. Overall, a fair trade for the loss of starlight.

She went to the stove, poured out two glasses and brought them out onto the porch in a matter of seconds. She led him to the new wooden table she'd put next to the railing overlooking the creek.

This could become a habit, he thought—meeting his adorable, milk-guzzling landlady each night under the pines, with the babbling water for background music. Max was accustomed to city life, where even the deepest midnight hummed with traffic, television sets set too loud, and the occasional ambulance crying in the distance. The absence of mechanized noises made you intensely aware of yourself, he realized…and the people around you.

She leaned back in her chair, put her feet up on the seat, and nursed her warm milk in both palms. "You're very polite, not even asking me why I was juggling rocks in the middle of the night."

He took a sip of his milk, which was very sweet, and reminded him forcefully—and pleasantly—of his childhood, back when everything was simple and everyone was a friend.

"I know why," he said. "It's on your list. I'm just glad you weren't in there giving yourself a tattoo. I've seen enough damage from needles for one day."

"Oh, that's right. I already mentioned the tattoo, didn't I? The bluebird of happiness. But I must have neglected to mention I plan to put the tattoo on my right hip. I couldn't possibly reach that by myself."

He laughed. "The bluebird of happiness?"

"Yeah. Sounds crazy, right? It's just…a thing from when I was a kid." She smiled. "And I mentioned the juggling, too, didn't I? That one may be my undoing. It's not the scariest thing on my list, but it may be the hardest—for me, anyhow. I'm the most horrible physical klutz."

He found that hard to believe. If he'd ever seen a body put together right…

"What *is* the scariest thing on the list?"

Her eyes widened. "White-water rafting." She laughed. "It looks like so much fun, but at the same time I'm deathly terrified of the very thought. If I ever get a check mark next to that one, I'll feel like a superhero."

Her sparkling eyes looked so alive. He had a sudden, intense desire to see her master all of it—the juggling, the rafting—every darn thing on her list.

She deserved to feel like a superhero. He'd seen her with her family, with their elderly neighbors, with Alec. It was beautiful, how she offered gentle understanding to everyone around her—even to his unpleasant daughter.

But she had more than handmaiden sweetness inside her. She had fire and grit, and he would love to be there when she finally believed in herself.

"Why juggling, of all things? You planning to join the circus?"

"I'm not sure, really. We used to have a wrangler who

could juggle anything. *Anything*. Horseshoes, spurs, boots, bottles."

"Rocks?"

"No." She laughed softly. "Even he never tried rocks. But I could watch him for hours. He said he'd teach me, and we'd just begun lessons when my dad fired him for goofing off too much. It broke my heart."

Max imagined her guileless, sweet-featured face, taken back fifteen or twenty years. She would have looked like an illustration in an old-fashioned children's book, all wide, oversize Bambi eyes, and bowed, pink-cherub lips.

He pictured how earnestly she would have listened to the old wrangler's instructions, and how openly she would have sobbed as he departed.

Max raised his glass with a smile. "So now you'd like to learn to juggle, in his honor."

She grinned, raising hers, too, and clinking them together in a lighthearted toast. "Exactly. But I'm afraid I'm hopeless. If he could see me today, he'd be ashamed of his pupil."

"Well, we can't have that." He set his milk down and stood, thinking about their options. Many of the trees around the cottage were aspens, but taller pines dotted the landscape, too, so there undoubtedly would be cones. He walked the three steps down from the deck, and sure enough within a minute he'd found two that were perfect. Small, more round than oblong, and closed fairly tightly, as if they knew there would be rain before the night was over.

"Here. Let's try these." He tested the weight of the cones by bouncing them in his palm. Good—they were light enough that, even if she missed a catch, no one would be bruised. And the bristles weren't too sharp. His more-callused palm hardly registered a sting, so surely even her softer one would survive.

She looked embarrassed as he climbed back up to her. "Max, I don't think you understand. I'm not just bad at this. I'm *horrible*."

"Maybe. But it must be on your list for a reason," he said. "Let's see what we can do."

Reluctantly, she stood and placed herself a foot or so in front of him. She looked at his hands. "You only have two pinecones," she said dubiously. "We need three, right?"

"Not until you get the hang of two. And we are going to start with just one. Try tossing this one from your right hand to your left."

She did. But she was overly cautious, and the cone moved in an almost straight line.

"Try tossing it higher, so that it traces a rainbow between your hands. We want an arch whose topmost point is just about at eye level."

She tried again. Much better. He put her through it about a dozen times, until her arms loosened up and she stopped being so self-conscious. Stiff arms were the kiss of death to juggling.

Then he had her reverse, and toss from her left hand to her right. She had more trouble with that one, as she was right-side dominant, but eventually, that movement, too, was fluid.

"Excellent," he said, and she gave him a wry smile, well aware that he was cheerleading much as he might have with Ellen.

"Excellent if I were five years old," she grumbled.

But he just laughed and held out the second cone. "See if you can toss the one in your right hand in that same kind of arc toward your left hand. But this time, when it reaches its highest point, throw the one in your left hand up in an arc toward your right hand. Make sense?"

It clearly didn't. She frowned at him as if he were talking in another language. She looked at her hands, made a couple of pretend tosses, like a golfer hitting a practice swing, frowned again and then began to laugh.

"I hear your words," she said, "and in my head I even see exactly what you want. But when I try to make my hands do that, everything gets scrambled."

He could tell she wasn't kidding. "Why not try?" Maybe he could spot the problem.

She grimaced. She threw one cone tightly and, simultaneously, as if mildly panicked, tossed the other one—way too soon. Inevitably, both cones landed at her feet, and her hands closed awkwardly over thin air. She groaned, clearly mortified far beyond the true importance of the thing. She bent to pick up the cones, inspecting them for damage as if she couldn't bear to meet his eyes.

"See? I'm like this with everything physical." She straightened finally, and shrugged. "I can't dance, or jump rope, or play tennis. My fine motor skills are no problem. I can smock and crochet and paint and cross-stitch like a fiend. But hand me a ball, and I'm as clumsy as a fish on a bicycle."

He heard something new in her tone. "That's not even you talking, really, is it? That's somebody else. Somebody who always said you were terrible at sports."

Just as Lydia had always told Ellen she would be fat, if she didn't watch what she ate. It had driven Max mad. Who told a ten-year-old little girl it was time to worry about her weight? Who told a girl of any age such a thing? Worry about her health, yeah, you might say that someday—only after everything else, like making healthy food exciting and making exercise fun, had failed. But warn her about getting "fat"? Never. No one. At any age.

He watched Penny's face, to see if the comment struck home. Would she know instinctively whose voice she'd been channeling? Her sisters, perhaps? Rowena looked the athletic type—had she been scornful of the diffident little sister who excelled at more stereotypically domestic skills?

Or maybe her dad? Had he been a bit of a chauvinist? After it became clear he'd have nothing but daughters, a man like that might grow resentful.

But her face registered no recognition. Whoever it had been, she'd forgotten. She thought the voice in her head was simply the voice of Truth. So of course her brain scrambled the signals about which hand to move when.

"Nobody had to tell me," she insisted, laughing. "I knew. *Everybody* knew."

"Okay," he said. He came around and stood behind her. He put one palm under each of her elbows. "Let's try it this way. When I nudge your elbow, toss the ball."

Instantly, her shoulders tightened and rose toward her ears.

"Hey. No stress." He jiggled her arms to loosen them up. "They're pinecones, not Fabergé eggs. We can smash them all night, and no one will call the cops."

Her shoulders moved in a silent chuckle. Good. That brought them down to a more natural angle. He shook her elbows again, like a shimmy, and the muscles in her forearms relaxed.

"Better," he said. He let a moment of stillness move through her. "Okay?"

She inhaled deeply, then nodded. He pressed up softly on her right arm, and she tossed the pinecone. At the height of the arc, he pressed her left elbow, and she tossed that cone, too. Each of them fell, with pinpoint precision, into her waiting palms.

She laughed, delighted. "It worked!"

"Again," he said, before self-consciousness could return. He nudged, she tossed. Nudge, toss. Nudge, toss. The pinecones passed fluidly between her hands. She tilted back, slightly, as if it helped to have more contact with his torso, his arms, his shoulders. Their warmth blended, with no night air between them. It was as if they were one body, their rhythms exactly matched, tossing the pinecones as one juggler.

And then, out of nowhere, the motions took on a sensuality so blatant it made his heart pound hard against his rib cage. Suddenly, her elbows seemed like the most intimate spot on her body, a trigger point that caused a physical reaction, an exchange of energy so powerful it seemed almost indecent to be doing it out here, in the open, where the moon, and the trees, and the neighbors, could see.

He knew the instant it hit her, too. A tremor passed electrically down her arm and sizzled between the delicate bones of her shoulder blades and into his chest. Her breath stumbled, suddenly awkward, and her arms grew stiff and uncoordinated.

Within seconds, both pinecones lay on the ground between her feet.

And yet he didn't let go of her. He couldn't. They were fused, somehow, their bodies joined so profoundly that no conscious decision could tear them apart.

She stood like that several long seconds, staring out toward the creek, breathing slow, deep breaths, as if she'd been running instead of simply tossing a pinecone between her own two hands.

And then, slowly, she brought her hands up and folded them across her chest. Because his were joined, they followed, and suddenly he was holding her. Holding her up against his hot, pounding heart.

She made a soft sound, and slowly, by degrees, let herself relax all the way into him. Her head cradled itself in the nook of his shoulder, and her feet adjusted, so that the length of her body fit snugly against his, all the way down to the thigh.

The pliant warmth of her curves, and the musky scent of violets that rose from her lace-covered skin were more than he could stand. His body was instantly hard. She would know, of course. The intimacy of this melding left no room for artifice. He could no more hide his arousal than she could hide the pounding of her heart under their hands, or the inhales that grew shallower, faster with every second, until they were more pants than breaths.

He told himself to stop. His brain kept saying the word, but it was like being asleep, screaming at yourself to wake up, yet unable to make any sounds come out.

Stop. Stop. Stop.

Instead he lowered his lips to her neck. He tasted the violet sweetness of her skin, and he skimmed his lips along the arch of her throat until he reached her ear. He kissed the pulse that raced there. He drank the heat.

Finally, she turned her head. Her eyes were closed, but her lips were full, flushed and parted.

Stop. Stop. Stop.

Instead, he kissed her. She made that same soft sound, and he groaned. Their mouths were wet, and very hot. Violets, honey, heat, something sweetly pink, and something very dark mingled in a potent cocktail of desire.

He strained down, and she strained up, and the connection still wasn't enough, so she twisted in his arms and faced him, somehow never letting their lips lose the connection that was, inexplicably, as important as air.

The wind in the trees ticked the seconds away, and the creek took their secret underground, where it disappeared briefly, emerging farther on, swelled and white with cloudy moonlight.

When it began to rain, he didn't at first recognize what

it was. It seemed right that he should be wet, and that a cold heat should sting his skin. But then he knew. He lifted his head and opened his eyes.

The chilly air was shocking against his swollen mouth. He glanced down at Penny, whose face seemed just as unprepared for the onslaught of reality.

Guilt moved through him like an interior rain. "I'm sorry." He shook his head. "I should never have let that happen."

She blinked. It was like watching something solidify right before his eyes. She had been as fluid, as sweetly, heavily thick with passion as some kind of elixir that held rainbows and prisms and diamonds in the depths of one drop. But as she gathered herself, she frosted over and hardened, like water turning to ice.

"It's all right," she said, finally. She stepped away, under the overhanging roof. Ostensibly it was to avoid the rain, but he knew it was because she couldn't think clearly, standing that close to him.

He couldn't think straight, either.

"It was my fault, really," she said. "I started it, with that kiss the other day. Maybe we just had to get it out of our system. But you're right. We can't let our working relationship get even more complicated."

"It's not just that," he said. He joined her under the edge of the roof, while the raindrops pattered briskly against the deck like little silver explosions. "It's not just about the tenant-landlord situation."

Didn't she know he'd be happy to surrender all hope of a "professional" relationship in order to taste a kiss like that? Hell, he'd move out and sleep in his SUV, if that would free them to do this—and more.

He would. But he couldn't do that to his daughter.

"It's also Ellen," he said. "When I brought her here, I

promised her I wouldn't let anything distract me while we were in Silverdell. This year is supposed to be about the two of us—and finding a way to mend our relationship."

"I understand." Penny seemed eager to remove any pressure for him to explain. "That makes perfect sense."

Did it? It had seemed sensible a month ago, when he'd concocted the plan. Now he wondered whether it was just one more way of indulging Ellen unnaturally. Someday he'd have to have a life....

Whatever that meant.

But nine months wasn't too long to wait to "have a life," was it? After years of being a half-ass father, surely he could give Ellen his entire attention for nine months.

This might be their last chance to salvage their relationship. In two years she'd be a teenager, honor bound to hate him. In four years, she'd think she was in love with some gangly kid who would occupy her every waking moment. In seven, she'd leave for college, and would probably never again sleep under his roof except as a visitor.

And that was a best-case scenario. Worst case: she kept stealing, kept following morally bankrupt divas like Stephanie and ended up in jail, or on the streets.

"I haven't been a very good dad," he said. "I've traveled a lot. I—I have to make it up to her, while I still can."

"It's okay," Penny said. She took another couple of steps back, putting even more room to breathe between them. She reached the edge of the roof, and raindrops sparkled against the edges of her hair, creating a halo.

"I lost my mother when I was about her age, so I know how wrenching that can be."

Wrenching. Yes. That was a good word. It was as if Ellen and Lydia hadn't fully made the separation into two people yet, and death had torn the mother part away, leaving the little girl part ragged and incomplete.

He wondered whether that loss was responsible for the fragility Penny projected. She was a mystery, in some ways. All her actions spoke of a surprising intelligence, tact and resilience, but even so the vibe she gave off was vulnerable. Wounded.

Would Ellen be like that, too? Even if she learned to cope, and found a way to succeed, on some level was the death of a beloved mother an insurmountable obstacle? Max himself had never known his parents, who died in a hotel fire abroad when he was only an infant. But he'd always thought of his grandparents as parents and never brooded over the loss of something he'd never had in the first place.

"What about your father? I'd like to think I can help fill the gap, but…" He thought of the widening gulf between him and Ellen. "Maybe I'm just kidding myself. Maybe there's no replacement for a mother, really."

For a long minute, Penny seemed to consider his question thoughtfully. When she spoke, he was surprised at how somber her voice sounded.

"My situation wasn't anything like Ellen's," she said. "In every way that mattered, I lost my father at the same time I lost my mother."

"How?"

She stood very straight as she answered. "He killed her."

Max couldn't find any words to respond to that chilling statement. When she spoke, he felt as if he stood, briefly, at the edge of a bottomless chasm, staring straight down. The endless black hole of those three words made him feel cold, slightly dizzy. Emotionally, he had to step back, simply to keep from falling in.

How had he described Penny Wright? Wounded? Vulnerable? Those were like a child's vocabulary, incapable of describing the monstrous howling of that chasm. Frankly, he was impressed that she could walk and talk and smile, and be kind to bratty little girls. Much less possess the warmth and passion he'd sensed behind that kiss.

"I'm surprised no one in town has filled you in on the details already." One corner of her mouth tucked in wryly. "They will, no doubt. Half the town feels sorry for us, and the other half thinks we're clinically insane. I'm not sure, actually, which half is more irritating."

"Ellen would say the pity half."

"So would Rowena." Penny's smile widened and grew more natural. "They have a lot in common, your daughter and my sister. They both like to come out swinging, just in case."

He nodded. He didn't know about Rowena, of course. But a more apt description of Ellen's temperament would be hard to find.

"Anyhow, now you know. So you don't have to worry about—" She waved her hand over the drenched and gleaming porch, as if it symbolized their kiss, and all the unspoken chemistry that sizzled between them.

"About *all this,*" she finished. "I know you need to focus on Ellen. And you heard all about my situation the other night. I can't afford to be distracted, either. I have to build an entire life from scratch, and I must stay focused. I need to find out who I am when it's just me before I could possibly think of getting involved with anyone else."

"Yes, I remember." He could hear her now, fierce, determined—a fascinating mixture of excitement and fear. "No family, no sisters, no men, no crutches."

"Exactly." She smiled. It was a truce smile. "So you see? It's all right. We got that out of the way, and, as…as nice as it was, we both know we can't let it happen again. We both need to concentrate on the tasks that brought us here. Right?"

"Right," he said firmly, because that was what she

seemed to expect. Not because he was anywhere nearly as confident as she pretended to be. "Now that we got that out of the way," he repeated, with only a trace of irony.

"I hope we can be friends, though." She glanced once again toward his side of the duplex. The rain had grown heavier, and it fell like a silver curtain between the two sides of the house. It was probably splashing into his kitchen through the door he'd left ajar. "I'd like to be Ellen's friend, too, if she ever needs one. I like her a lot. She reminds me so much of Ro. So, if there were ever any way I could help, I would like to think you'd ask."

"Of course," he lied automatically. "And I hope that you'd do the same—if you ever wanted anything." He fought the urge to touch her arm, or her hair, or her cheek, though he had to ball his fingers into a fist to control them. "Anything at all."

"Of course," she echoed blandly, and he knew she was lying, too. It was the polite thing to offer, and the polite response to make.

But neither of them would ask the other for a casual favor, not if they could possibly help it.

The air between them still surged with an invisible current—as if the very raindrops were electrically charged. They hadn't gotten *anything* out of the way, no matter how hard she tried to convince herself.

It would never be safe to pop over and ask for a cup of sugar, or help hanging a picture, or an hour's worth of babysitting. Because the one thing they were guaranteed to want was the one thing they couldn't have.

CHAPTER SEVEN

TWO WEEKS AND a day later, Ellen realized she was never going to have a moment's privacy again, not as long as she lived.

After the ear incident, Dad found a horrible babysitter, a mean old woman named Mrs. Biggars, who apparently used to babysit for Alec before he moved to the dude ranch.

Alec had made a choking sound the first time he stopped by and saw Mrs. Biggars in the house. "You've got Big Ass guarding you? Oh, man, you're sunk now."

And he was right. Every time Dad had to work late, or go in on a weekend, or even rush out to the grocery store, Mrs. Biggars appeared at the door…poof! Like an evil genie in a bottle.

And boy was she nosy! If Alec came over, even for five minutes, to show Ellen something cool like where one of his horses had kicked him in the shin, or a piece of petrified wood shaped like an iguana, Mrs. Biggars always waddled out onto the deck, sat down on the lawn chair and made conversation impossible.

Even inside, in her room, Ellen wasn't safe. She used to spend hours poring over the box of old pictures she kept under her bed. Mostly photos of her mom as a kid. Looking at her mom's thick waist and pudgy legs gave Ellen hope. But now, when she pulled out her box, suddenly there was Mrs. Biggars in her doorway, pretending she just wanted to talk, but really sticking her nose into everything.

Ellen hadn't even tried to look at the pictures for a week now. No way Ellen was going to let awful Mrs. Biggars touch them.

It was hopeless. She might as well be locked away in the Cook County Jail back home. If she'd guessed in a million years that letting Stephanie talk her into putting that lipstick in her purse would lead to this, she would never have...

Well, that wasn't true. She probably still would have done it. It was really hard to say no to Stephanie.

She heard the glassy pinging sound that usually meant Alec was out back. He always lobbed a small pebble at her window, so that he didn't have to knock and run into Mrs. Biggars. She got on her knees, surprised, because he'd said he was going to be at the dude ranch all day, helping teach the kids to ride horses.

But it wasn't Alec. It was Penny, who had apparently dropped a heavy ball that had shattered, sending off bits of something. One of the bits must have hit Ellen's window.

She watched for a minute. Oh...*cool*. Those must be the gazing balls Penny had mentioned. They were so sparkly— all kinds of colored glass pieces, put together like mosaics, like the ones she used to make out of colored beans, back in first grade. Only much prettier.

"I'm going to sit on the back porch and read," she called out from the kitchen. "Okay?"

Mrs. Biggars was in the front room watching her "story," which meant a dopey soap opera. Ellen had tattled on her the first day, hoping her father, who hated soap operas, would fire the old lady.

He hadn't.

"Okay." Mrs. Biggars wouldn't stand up from that TV show for anything short of a fire or a bomb. "Just don't leave the deck."

"I won't."

Actually, Ellen hoped Penny might invite her over to look at the gazing balls, but technically that wasn't leaving the deck, since it was connected.

And sure enough, as soon as Penny spotted her, she smiled. "I was hoping you were home," Penny said, and she looked as if she meant it.

Ellen wandered over casually. She pointed at one of the big globes, a blue one that sparkled in the sunlight. "Are those your gazing balls?"

"Yep." Penny bent over to pick up a bunch of little diamond-shaped pieces of glass. "What's left of them. The movers broke two, and I just broke another."

"But you have so many! They're awesome." Now that she was out here, Ellen saw that Penny had at least a dozen of the balls, in all sizes and colors. The sun was bright today, and it sparked off the bits of glass like hundreds of tiny magic flames. With these things out here, the deck looked like something out of a fairy tale.

Why didn't everyone do this with their backyards? But Ellen knew why. Most people weren't artistic like Penny.

Sometimes, over the past couple of weeks, Ellen had seen Penny sitting out here with an easel and a palette, just painting—and she'd wandered out to watch. In fact, she could watch for ages without getting bored. She loved to try to figure out how Penny created shadows, or water, or how she could make it seem that some things were up close, and others far away.

Penny never seemed to mind being watched, or answering questions about why she put yellow in the clouds, or green in a face. She seemed to like to talk to Ellen—and Ellen felt that they had become friends, in a way, even though Ellen was just a kid. Maybe it was just convenient, because they lived next door. But sometimes Ellen wondered whether maybe Penny didn't have very many people to talk to about artistic things.

Ellen didn't have *any*. If she tried to talk about painting to Stephanie and the gang, it was like…like their ears couldn't even hear her. Ellen would be right in the middle of a sentence, and Stephanie would hold up her fingernails and say, "Do you think I should take off the Dusty Rose and put on Flamingo Pink instead?"

It was different with Penny. The first day she'd watched Penny paint, Ellen had tentatively said, "I like Monet." She'd really half expected to be ignored.

But Penny had nodded and smiled. "And Renoir," Penny had added casually, as she touched her brush to her canvas and turned some of the aspen leaves brown. "Renoir is dreamy."

At Ellen's house in Chicago, her mom had a picture of Monet's water lilies in the living room, so she hadn't been making it up that she liked him. But she didn't know very many other painters yet, not by name. She didn't want to admit that to Penny, who obviously knew them all. So of course Ellen had looked Renoir up on the computer that very night.

Penny was right. Renoir was dreamy. His pictures looked like they'd been sprinkled with pink sugar and happiness. The next day, they'd talked a long time about Renoir.

Eventually they'd talked about other things, too. Now Ellen felt as if she could probably tell Penny anything. She wondered if she could tell her about how annoying Mrs. Biggars was.

But not right now. Now she wanted to help Penny arrange these great mirror balls, if Penny would let her. She'd been waiting two weeks for Penny to show them to her.

She edged closer to the railing between the two decks. "Can I help?"

Penny had just picked up the biggest gazing ball, a fancy blue-green-purple one that looked like a big circle of magical water. It was obviously really heavy.

"Actually, that would be great!" Penny frowned at the ball. "I forgot the stand inside. Would you mind grabbing it for me? It's in a box next to the kitchen table."

Ellen nodded and eagerly jumped over the railing. She loved to be a part of Penny's projects, and she loved to go in Penny's house. It was beautiful, and all the walls had paintings on them. The house didn't smell like perfume and little bowls of sachet, the way her mom's house always used to. Stephanie's house smelled like that, too, and sometimes it made Ellen sneeze.

Instead, Penny's house smelled cleaner. Like fresh flowers and oil paints and clean sheets. Like a summer wind had just blown through.

Ellen poked her head in first, checking the walls before she went any farther. She always did that. It was odd, but she always got excited when Penny put a new picture up.

But, at least from here, the only new picture she could see was on the refrigerator. It was really just a bunch of colorful doodles on a piece of sketch paper, but Ellen was curious anyhow. She went into the little kitchen nook, which was just like her own at home—maybe that's why she always felt so comfortable in Penny's house.

Anyhow, when she looked closer she saw that it was really just a list that Penny had drawn pictures all over. A blue bird at the top, and some vines and random sketches of horses and canoes and stuff at the bottom.

Why decorate a list so much? It must be pretty special. It wasn't really a grocery list, or any normal kind of list. The Risk-it List, it said at the top, and below that the numbers one through twelve, with things written after them.

Things to do, like get a haircut or take a picture of somebody famous.

So just a to-do list. At first, Ellen fought a feeling of
disappointment, but then she found herself curious to see
what Penny thought was cool and fun to do. She had often
thought about asking her dad to invite Penny to go with
them when they had a picnic, or a hike, but she wasn't sure
Penny would say yes.

Some of the twelve things had already been crossed
off—like "buy place in Silverdell." Others hadn't. But one
of them—"Hot air balloon (fear of heights)"—had a date
scribbled next to it, and five exclamation points. The date
was tomorrow. Saturday, August 23, 9:00 a.m.

Ellen kept going. Number Ten had been crossed off so
hard and black Ellen couldn't tell what it said. But later...
Oooh, was Penny really going to get a tattoo?

Some of the stuff seemed pretty expensive for a woman
who lived in such a tiny house and probably didn't have
much money. Like, at the end, for Number Twelve, Penny
had more crossed-off words, and then just the one word,
"Sailboat," with a heart next to it.

Sailboats cost a whole lot.

"Hey, I'm about to drop this on my toe! Is the stand not
in the kitchen after all?"

Ellen's cheeks flushed. Ashamed to have been prying,
and sorry that she'd left Penny holding that heavy ball, she
scooped up the stand and raced outside with it.

"Thank goodness!" But Penny was still smiling, so she
wasn't mad that Ellen had been dawdling. Ellen hadn't ever
seen her mad, actually—which was more than she could
say for her own mother. Mom had been pretty easy to set
off, especially when she was trying to hide how angry she
was with Dad.

"Can you put it over there, by the table?"

Ellen stood the metal base in the corner, where she knew it would look prettiest. Groaning, Penny loaded the ball onto the stand, rolling it into its cradle. It rocked gently, then settled securely.

They both stood back, admiring the effect.

"Thanks," Penny said. "I think I like it here. How about you?"

"I think it looks amazing."

It really did. It reflected blue sky on one side, and on the other it caught one little curve of the creek. The constant movement of the reflected water made the gazing ball seem alive.

Out of the corner of her eye, Ellen saw Mrs. Biggars open the kitchen door and poke her head out, checking on her. Like the rounds at a jail. Bed check every hour, on the hour.

Darn it. She'd have to go in soon, and she could hardly stand the thought of being trapped in there with Mrs. Biggars. She suddenly, passionately wished Penny could be her babysitter instead.

But Dad was obviously never going to ask Penny to babysit again. And that was Ellen's own fault. She'd been bad, and she'd made Penny look like a bad babysitter.

She started to apologize for making such a mess of things. She stopped herself at the last minute, though, realizing it might sound like she thought babysitting her was some kind of special thing everybody wanted to do.

Maybe, she realized sadly, Penny was *glad* she didn't have to. Maybe Penny thought she was a brat, like her Dad did. If only she had more time, away from Mrs. Biggars, to show Penny that she wasn't always like that.

"Are you going to be out here painting tomorrow?" Ellen knew the answer already, because she'd looked at that list. But she tried to sound totally innocent.

Penny shook her head. "Not tomorrow. I've got quite an adventure planned for tomorrow. I'm going on a hot air balloon ride!"

Ellen made an impressed, envious sound. She hoped she was a good enough actress to pull this off. She would be ashamed if Penny knew she'd snooped at her private list.

"Oh, that sounds awesome. I've never been on a hot air balloon."

Then she waited, holding her breath, wondering if Penny might invite her. But Penny was still fiddling with the smaller gazing balls, rearranging them so that they caught the sunlight better, or made prettier color combinations.

"Where does the hot air balloon take off from?" Ellen was pushing, but she couldn't help herself. She wanted to be a part of Penny's adventure so bad. "Whose hot air balloon is it?"

"It's called Air Adventures. And it's over by Montrose, about half an hour from here, I guess. Bell River has an arrangement with their company so that we can bring our guests over as a day trip."

"So it's not some private thing? Can anybody go?"

"Sure." Penny laughed and ran her hand through her hair. "Anybody brave enough, that is. Frankly, I'm terrified—and I just get more terrified the closer it gets. I hope I don't chicken out at the last minute."

Ellen couldn't quite believe Penny was scared of anything. She seemed so comfortable with herself. She did all kinds of things that Ellen found terrifying. Think how she took that needle out of Ellen's ear, for instance. And she rode horses over at her family's dude ranch a lot. Ellen was scared to death of horses.

Penny could paint right out in the open, too. She didn't seem to worry whether other people thought she was any good, or whether they thought she was weird.

And she always wore such cool clothes. She wore colorful, flowing dresses, or narrow pants with loose green sweaters that fell off one shoulder and sagged in the most comfortable-looking way. She never seemed to feel self-conscious about looking different. It never seemed to occur to her that she should wear what everyone else wore.

Plus, she was the only grown-up woman Ellen had ever met who didn't wear makeup, not even lipstick. And yet somehow she managed to still be the prettiest woman Ellen had ever seen.

Except her mom, of course.

It made Ellen feel odd inside, kind of squirmy and inferior, to imagine what Penny would say if she learned Ellen had tried to steal something as dumb as a lipstick. Penny would never understand doing something really wrong just to impress a mean girl like Stephanie.

She'd never understand being desperate to fit in.

"I can't picture you being scared of anything," Ellen said impulsively. She hadn't meant to say it out loud. But she wished Penny would explain where that magical ability to just be yourself came from. She wished Penny could teach her not to care what other people thought. "You seem very brave."

Penny smiled, but to Ellen's surprise the smile had something sad inside it.

"Well, you know what they say about courage," she said, touching the big blue-and-green gazing ball with one hand, as if she needed to steady herself on it. "It doesn't mean you aren't ever afraid to do something. It means you can be absolutely petrified, but you do it anyhow."

SATURDAY MORNING CAME far too early for Max. He stifled a yawn, hoping Ellen wouldn't see it. He was exhausted, having stayed up half the night trying to incorporate Acton Adams's ridiculous requests into the resort's design.

But he didn't want Ellen to know that. She knew it was his habit to sleep a little later on Saturdays—at least until eight or so—and he wouldn't want her to think he resented giving up that luxury today.

He didn't.

In fact, sleep was the last thing on his mind. His daughter had come to him last night, expressing a desire, out of nowhere, to take a hot air balloon ride. Even more amazingly, she wanted to take it with *him*.

So by God, he was going to make it happen.

If he could just find the darn hot air balloon company's building. And they had to find it in the next ten minutes, or else they'd miss the 9:00 a.m. ride.

For some reason getting on that balloon—and *only* that balloon—had become the most important thing in Ellen's world. Until he got home last night, and she began lobbying him, he'd had no idea she even knew what a hot air balloon was, much less cherished a dream of riding in one.

It was a beautiful morning for it, though. Cool, but not cold. A cloudless blue sky that went on forever. Hardly any wind, which seemed like a good thing, though he really didn't know much about ballooning himself.

And he darn sure didn't know how to get to this Air Adventures Incorporated place. They'd given him directions over the phone, when he made the reservations. Plus, he'd asked at the gas station as he left town, just to be sure.

But in these small towns directions were iffy, at best. People said things like, "It's about half a mile beyond where that old elm was struck by lightning in 'eighty-five," or "Just park between the riverbank and that big rock they can't get rid of."

Every landmark was where something *used* to be, or

where something memorable had happened long ago. If you didn't have a history here, you were out of luck.

"There it is!" Ellen bounced in her seat, pointing through the window. "See?"

Max had spotted the small Air Adventures trailer, too, but he let her have the victory. He turned the wheel, smiling—not just because he was glad to find the place, but also because that uninhibited eagerness used to be a hallmark of his little girl.

Maybe five years ago, Ellen had been nothing but laughter and enthusiasm. His nickname for her had been Bubbles. What had happened to all that delightful effervescence?

Was it his promotion, which necessitated the extra traveling? Was it sending her to that ridiculously snobbish elementary school, full of affected, world-weary first-graders? Was it Lydia, or the loss of Lydia? Was it Mexico?

Perhaps it had been all those things.

But identifying the cause, assigning the blame, was pointless. Somewhere along the way, his family had taken a wrong turn on the happiness road, and they'd been wandering in the darkness ever since. The only important thing was finding their way back.

"Good eye," he said, careful not to let it sound patronizing. "If we'd driven past that trailer, we would have been in Nevada before we realized we were lost."

She was clearly not listening. She leaned against her door, craning her neck and squinting, as if the balloon would be difficult to spot and she didn't want to miss it.

Hardly. As they pulled in, cresting a gentle, rounded rise in the land, they suddenly saw the balloon, lying nearly flat on the ground, stretched out in huge, impressive stripes of bold color—blue and yellow and red and white.

"Is that…" Ellen stopped bouncing. "Is that…"

"That's the balloon. They haven't filled it yet, which is a good thing, because it means we're not too late."

He found a good parking space, though a surprising number of cars already filled the small lot beside the trailer. A few yards away from the balloon and its impossibly small wicker basket, a large knot of people in long sleeves and sweaters milled around, avidly watching the process.

Max had been told that the basket held four, and they'd be going up with one or two others. No way that whole crowd was going with them. Must be people waiting for the next flight, or maybe other members of Air Adventures staff.

Someone turned on a large, noisy fan—the din roaring back toward Max and Ellen, even though they had just emerged from the SUV. He felt a small warmth burrow into his hand, and, looking down, saw that Ellen had braided her fingers into his, as she used to do when she was very small.

His heart twisted. His feisty little girl was afraid.

"It's neat, isn't it?" He pretended not to notice. "I'm glad we got here in time to see how they get the balloon filled up. They'll fill it with air from that fan, and then they'll heat the air to make the balloon lift up."

Ellen kept walking, but her fingers tightened as they drew closer. He wondered how much reassurance he should offer. He could tell her how thoroughly he'd checked the company out this morning, while she got ready. Air Adventures had been offering flights around here for more than a decade. The pilot had logged thousands of trips, with no incidents at all.

Licenses, insurances, safety records—it all checked out. But would those details reassure her, as they had him? Or would they just remind her of the dangers?

"The pilot is named Eagle Ed," he said, settling for the

human interest angle. "They call him that because apparently he feels more at home in the air than on the ground."

Ellen glanced up at him. "Really?"

"Yeah. Cool, huh?"

Her grip relaxed slightly, and so did his heart. He wanted to believe he could give her comfort when she needed it— that she trusted him enough to feel safe by his side, no matter what. He'd never felt fear in his life, not until Mexico, and he didn't want her to feel it, either.

They'd almost reached the crowd now, and Max began examining people individually, trying to pick out Eagle Ed from the customers and crew. He'd seen the pilot's picture on the website—not a huge guy, brown hair, a mustache, big smile with white teeth. In the picture, Eagle Ed looked like someone in a 1920's barbershop quartet.

He began eliminating people, one by one. Too tall...too muscular...too female... Darn it, Eagle Ed had better not have handed the flight off to another pilot, not now that Max had used him to calm Ellen's nerves.

And then his eyes collided with a pair of eyes that stared back at him, round and startled. He was completely unprepared, his mind absorbed with locating a man he recognized, not a woman. And certainly not *this* woman.

It was like making sudden eye contact with a deer you were inches away from hitting with your car.

Recognition slammed into him, and suddenly Ellen's urgency to be in this field, on this particular flight, became as clear as the morning air around them.

He was staring into the wide, shocked eyes of the beautiful Penny Wright.

PARADOXICALLY, THE HIGHER the balloon flew, the calmer Penny felt. She wouldn't have imagined it possible, but by the time they cleared the treetops, she had actually begun to enjoy herself.

She'd expected to endure the ride in total terror, much as she had on the only other hot air balloon ride she'd ever taken.

And yet…this time…

The whole experience seemed completely different. Instead of being scary, it was thrilling and oddly peaceful. Up here, everything seemed quieter, simpler. She could look down and see where cars slid along gray-ribbon roads, where roads met green fields, where fields met silver rivers.

As she took a deep breath of the clear blue air, she caught Max's eye.

He smiled. "Feeling better?"

Penny nodded, but before she answered she glanced at Ellen. The girl had obviously relaxed, too. Sometime in the past few minutes, she'd let go of her father's hand and right now was getting a demonstration of the propane tanks from Eagle Ed.

"Much better," Penny admitted. She should have known that Max would sense the anxiety she'd tried to mask. "I'm actually enjoying it, which I definitely did not expect. The only other balloon ride I've ever taken was such a spectacular failure."

He smiled. "Failure? How big a failure? You lived to tell the tale, at least."

"Oh, not that kind of failure, thank goodness." She shook her head, trying to shake off the horror of the memory. "*I* was the problem, not the balloon."

"How so?"

She thought back. Many of the simple, physical details, like the color of the balloon, the name of the company, the season and where they'd flown, were lost. But she remembered the emotions as if they'd happened yesterday.

Penny's father hadn't ordinarily been tough on her—not as tough as he was on Bree and Ro, anyhow—but when he saw her fear, he'd mocked her mercilessly, repeating everything she said in a high-pitched whine.

When he drew tears, as he must have known he would, he issued strict orders. No one was to touch Penny until she stopped crying. Her mother hadn't dared to defy him. But Rowena, who was only eleven, had stepped up and scooped Penny into her arms.

"She *can't* stop crying, you sick bully. Can't you see that?"

He hadn't even looked at Rowena. Without so much as a sound, he'd thrust his arms under Penny's shoulders, ripping her away. Then he held her up and pretended he was going to drop her over the side.

The truly crazy part was that his intention wasn't even to frighten Penny, really. He wanted to control Rowena. And it had worked. Ironically, Penny's tears ceased instantly, because she was completely frozen with terror. But proud, defiant Rowena had ended up weeping, begging him to stop. She'd promised anything he asked, just to make him put Penny down.

For months afterward, Rowena had sat up in the barn, plotting horrible deaths for Johnny—and apparently she worked out her fury in those fantasies. But Penny had never quite been the same. She couldn't sleep alone, because in her dreams she always found herself dangling from clouds, or tree limbs, or cliff edges, her feet blindly churning, trying to find solid ground.

Just remembering it now made her legs start to shake again slightly. She gripped the side of the box and took another deep breath. "Well, I was terrified, which disgusted my father. I don't remember much else."

He looked quizzical. "Disgust seems pretty intense. How old were you?"

It had been three days after her sixth birthday. She'd forgotten that part till just now. Johnny had been out of town on the day itself. The balloon idea had been concocted as a late birthday present for Penny.

She shrugged. "Maybe about six."

Max frowned. "You weren't allowed to be scared at six?"

"My father didn't like weakness. He always said we couldn't be babies, not if we wanted to be ranchers. We needed to grow up."

"Right." Max's tone was cutting. "Because nothing's as annoying as an immature first-grader."

He smiled, and to her surprise she found herself smiling back. Odd, how soothing it was to hear someone stick up for her, even if it was twenty years too late.

"It was a long time ago," she said. "But thanks."

Really, she should have forgotten the whole experience and moved on by now. But somehow, that moment of feeling that her father had been willing to jettison her like so much worthless ballast, all because she was a coward...

It had left something inside her that felt like a permanent stain.

No—more like a broken place that couldn't mend. Like a rotted beam, a faulty support that might let her down at any moment if she put too much pressure on the wrong spot.

A hollow place inside herself, a weak link she couldn't trust.

She watched the ground below them receding, and realized how much better you could understand geography, and distances, and the relationship of one ranch to the next, one town to the next, if you weren't so close to it all.

Maybe life was like that, too. Maybe someday, when she

got enough perspective on it, the events of her childhood would start to make more sense, too.

"According to him, we were a trio of useless, hothouse flowers, and we needed to toughen up. That was one of his favorite lines." She had forgotten that, too. "Given how things turned out, perhaps he had a point."

"Like hell." Max shook his head. "I'm sorry, Penny. But it sounds like your dad was a very sick man."

Penny looked at him, struck by the coincidence. Two decades and two worlds apart, he and Rowena had instinctively chosen the same word.

Sick. And suddenly, as if she'd finally reached the right height to see the big picture, she knew it was true. Her father hadn't been all-powerful, all-knowing, all-seeing. He had simply been a very sick man.

He hadn't possessed the emotional or mental stability to judge or label *anyone.*

Penny wasn't a "coward," any more than Rowena was a "bitch." Any more than Bree was a "fool." Any more than her mother had been a "dirty slut." All the labels Johnny Wright had hurled at others, all those judgments he'd passed that they'd carried inside for so long, were lies.

They were a product only of the delusional rage that festered inside a very, very sick mind.

And just like that, her memory of those horrifying moments faded. It didn't go away entirely, but its sharp edges blurred. When she touched the place inside where the phobia lived, she could feel only a dull ache, no worse than a stubbed toe, no longer a knife edge of pain.

She turned to Max. "Thank you," she said, her voice vibrating with emotion. "Thank you so much."

He looked surprised, but then he smiled.

"Once again, I don't know exactly what I did. But... that's all? Just the words?"

She knew what he meant, of course.

Just words? No kiss?

"Just the words," she repeated. But she smiled, too, and for a minute the look in his eyes was almost as good as a kiss.

"Dad." Ellen suddenly tugged Max's hand. "I thought it would be...like, windy up here."

"Nope."

"Why not?"

Eagle Ed, who stood in the corner, his hand above his head, holding on to the rope that could send another blast from the burner to the balloon above them if they began to lose altitude, answered her. "Because we're going with the wind, not into it."

"Yeah?" Ellen bit her lower lip, and slowly let her hand drop from Max's so that she could hold on to the edge of the basket. "Look, Dad! Everything down there looks like toys."

Max met Penny's eyes over his daughter's head, and they both smiled. Though their temporary intimacy was over, this was good, too. For a minute, it was like being parents together, sharing a milestone in their daughter's life.

Parents together? Oh, dear heaven. What was she thinking? Horrified at her own foolishness, and hoping to God he couldn't read her thoughts, she looked away, pretending to search for the SUV Ellen was pointing to.

None of this really meant anything, especially not to him. She had been through a catharsis, like some kind of regression therapy in which she'd relived a traumatic childhood moment.

He had simply been having a conversation that got out of hand—and he didn't even understand how. This was an artificial intimacy, up here in this small box together, defying the laws of nature.

And he was just…he just had that kind of smile, the kind that made you feel warm, included, important.

He was socially graceful, she'd hand him that. Though he obviously had been as surprised as Penny to realize they'd be sharing a balloon ride this morning, he had handled it smoothly.

As he handled everything. Even their kiss.

Kisses, she corrected herself. Two kisses.

She'd be willing to bet he didn't lie awake, thinking about those kisses. But she did. In fact, that was why she'd accelerated her plan for the balloon ride. She needed to get her mind off her sexy tenant, and back on to her own mission. How better than to tackle one of the really tough risks?

And now mission and tenant had come together, quite by serendipity. How was that for fate? She hadn't invited anyone to go with her, not even Bree or Ro, determined not to clutch at any form of safety net.

But if fate sent her the best of all safety nets, completely unrequested…

Max, who radiated security. Calm. Competence.

Max, who had helped her bury an old memory forever.

Who was she to criticize fate? To heck with the "plan." She looked at him again and returned the smile, deciding to surrender to destiny and enjoy the good luck. And when she did, something in her stomach went *thump.*

It wasn't just security he added to the experience. It was excitement. Glamor.

Sex.

Being up here with him, in this quiet, enchanted otherworld, gave the ride a sense of romance she couldn't have imagined possible, not after the trauma of her first experience. Yet, there it was. She closed her hand over her stomach, as if she could quiet the suddenly fluttering wings that beat there.

Luckily, Ellen didn't seem to register the subtle shift in mood. The little girl shuffled even closer to the edge of the basket, and everyone else adjusted to give her space. Penny and Max ended up shoulder to shoulder, and she shivered as his warmth made its way into her veins.

"Are you cold?" He touched the collar of his gold suede coat, ready to shrug it off. "Want to borrow my jacket?"

She shook her head. "I'm fine. Just a little excited, I think. It's amazing, isn't it?"

"Beautiful." He wasn't looking at the landscape stretching out below them, though. He was looking at her. She felt her heart speed up, and the familiar flush—which seemed ever-present when she was with this man—starting to creep up her neck.

His gaze dropped momentarily, as if registering the flush, then returned to hers. "I take it this is all about checking another item off your Risk-it List?"

"Yes."

"I thought so." He glanced once wryly toward Ellen, who had begun asking Eagle Ed another endless stream of questions, which luckily he seemed quite happy to answer. "Any chance that list is...well, *made public* anywhere?"

Penny thought a minute, then finally she understood. Of course.

"On my refrigerator," she said, lowering her voice. Ellen was still chattering, but it was a very small basket. "I'm pretty sure I even wrote the date and time next to this one."

He nodded, smiling. "And the mystery is solved."

"I'm sorry," she said, feeling ridiculous for not having figured it out sooner. Lucky coincidence? *Sure.* "Obviously you got dragged out on a ruse, and—"

"I don't mind. I'm just sorry we intruded. I know you were eager to do everything alone." He raised one eyebrow. "No sisters, no family, no men..."

She laughed softly. "It's okay this once. Since I had no idea you were coming, I don't think I can be accused of reaching for a crutch."

And now that she was sharing the experience with him, she couldn't imagine how lonely and uninspired it would have felt if she had been alone. Her stomach pinched, thinking of that. Maybe this was the real danger of using a crutch. Walking alone seemed so much harder when the crutch was finally gone.

Overhead, the burner whooshed, emitting a blast of heat. On Penny's childhood trip, that sound had gone through her like an electric current of fear. She'd been certain they were all going to die a fiery death, falling out of the sky like Icarus.

But today the blast was just another piece of the magic. The balloon continued its upward climb. The cars below diminished to ants, and the bends and curves of the river looked like cursive letters—as if someone had written across the hills with a silver-glitter pen.

But the words were in some mysterious language she didn't know. She couldn't tell what their message was supposed to be.

"Are those all propane tanks? Why do we have so many?" Ellen widened her eyes as a new idea struck her, and tapped Ed's arm. "Hey, are there any girl pilots?"

Max grinned at his daughter, who obviously had lost her last shred of anxiety and planned to turn this into a flying lesson. Putting her own irrational mood swings aside, Penny concentrated on the pleasure of seeing Ellen so uninhibited.

Sometimes the girl looked too self-conscious, as if she worried more about the impression she was making than anything else. She smoothed her hair a lot and pulled at her clothes, which were always a little too tight.

Not today, though. Today Ellen's jeans were loose, her sweatshirt well-worn, her hair a windblown mess, and she didn't even seem to notice it. She was too absorbed in learning the ropes.

Eagle Ed was clearly getting a kick out of all the questions. Ellen would probably be ready to take her pilot's test by the time they touched down.

"Penny, look." Ellen tugged at Penny's sleeve suddenly, trying to direct her attention to something she'd spotted outside. "How would you paint that?"

Penny followed the little girl's pointing finger. "You mean our shadow?"

Ellen nodded, raptly focused on watching the outline of their balloon float on the ground below them. It was oddly beautiful, proof that they really were floating up here, defying gravity.

"It's so amazing," Ellen breathed. "But I don't even know what color you'd use."

"Well, let's see." Penny moved a few inches forward and bent down, so that the two of them were looking at it from the same angle. "It isn't really a color, is it? I mean, it's more like a lack of light on the places it covers."

They talked about it for a few minutes, and once again Penny was struck with how easily the child seemed to grasp ideas. She'd never seen anything Ellen drew, so she had no idea whether she had any talent. But she never saw the little girl as happy, or as unaffected, as she was when she talked about art.

When Ellen again began grilling Ed, Penny turned impulsively to Max. Without even realizing it, he'd helped her so much today. She wanted to offer something—anything—that would make his life easier, too.

"I'm going to be working at Bell River next week, giving some art lessons. If Ellen would like to come, I'm sure there's room."

She'd thought Ellen wasn't listening, but apparently she'd been naive. Ellen undoubtedly kept her ears tuned to her father's conversations every second, whatever else she might appear to be doing.

At Penny's words, Ellen made a squealing sound that she swallowed back almost instantly. She didn't say a word, but she turned imploring eyes toward her father, and her hands were clenched tightly in fists against her midriff.

"It's just a couple of hours each day," Penny added. "We'll be taking some nature hikes, drawing some of the things we see. There will be lots of supervision."

Max seemed to hesitate. Penny wondered what the hitch was.

"Dad." Ellen's voice rippled with longing. "Dad, can I? Please?"

"It's a transportation problem, more than anything," Max said finally. "You'll be at Mrs. Starling's camp the first part of the day, and—"

"I'd be glad to pick her up," Penny interjected. "Or, even better, if she'd like she could spend this week doing the Bell River children's activities. We have programs scheduled all day long, so that the parents staying there can do adult things. Rowena and Bree have really put together some fantastic classes."

He was still frowning. "I'm sure it's great, but—"

"Dad, please. *Please.*" Ellen's intensity was radiating out in waves of desperation. "I hate Mrs. Starling's camp. The kids there are mean, and there's hardly any art stuff at all. Everything is so boring. It's like nursery school."

He looked at his daughter for a long moment, then turned to Penny. "Are you sure it wouldn't be an inconvenience?"

"Not at all. I really think she'd like it, and I'd love having her there. So would Alec."

Max smiled, finally. "Okay. Check with the others first, though, to be sure they have room for an extra kid."

"I will," Penny started to say, but Ellen was squealing so loudly she couldn't hear her own words. The little girl grabbed her father's waist with one hand, and Penny's with the other, and wrapped them both in a joint bear hug.

The force of her embrace tilted Penny toward Max, and, as she corrected her feet to find her balance, she ended up practically face-to-face with him. Their eyes were just inches apart, with only the ecstatic little girl between them, her face buried in her father's rib cage.

"Thank you, thank you, thank you," Ellen said, her voice muffled by Max's jacket.

It was the first time Penny had seen Ellen voluntarily embrace her father since they arrived. She looked up at Max, and saw the surprise—and the deep, wordless relief—in his honey-brown eyes.

"Thank you," he said softly to Penny, his lips moving the words more than speaking them.

"My pleasure," she answered, also in a whisper. And she was shocked to realize how true that was. His joy seemed to ignite a similar sense of satisfaction in her own heart.

Somehow, in just these past few days, this little family's happiness had become very important to her.

CHAPTER EIGHT

THE NEXT MONDAY, the first day Ellen spent at Bell River, Max nearly quit the Silverdell Hills project about a hundred times. Acton Adams unexpectedly showed up at the headquarters again, with his girlfriend in tow, and Max spent the entire endless day finding ways to talk the two rich idiots out of making design changes that would turn the golf resort into a Vegas-style monstrosity.

He got home so tired he just barely could stay awake to hear about his daughter's day. He fought to keep his eyes open while Ellen showed off her watercolors of fall foliage and quizzed him with flash cards identifying the native birds of Colorado.

He hoped she didn't sense his exhaustion, which she'd undoubtedly read as indifference. He did his best, registering even with his foggy mind that day camp at Bell River was a darn sight more educational—and apparently more fun—than Mrs. Starling's camp had ever been. And he must have done well enough, because for the first time in a long time, Ellen hugged him good-night.

That night, he slept like a stone. Though Acton drove him nuts, peaceful sleep was one fringe benefit—Max was so exhausted he didn't wake up even once with the Mexico dream. And he didn't have to lie there afterward, thinking about Penny and wondering whether she ever dreamed of him.

But by Thursday, fringe benefits or not, Max had endured all the Acton he could take. In frustration, he directed Olivia to nix the girlfriend's new brainstorm—lobby columns shaped like golf clubs, and a glass ceiling filled with thousands of golf balls, which she thought would be "classy, like Chihuly or something."

"Talk her out of it. Or hell, *don't* talk her out of it. I honestly don't care. Just make sure they understand that either this new lobby goes, or I do."

And then, with Olivia staring wide-eyed at his back, he left. He couldn't handle another minute of this place. If he hurried, he could get to Bell River before Ellen's camp activities were over for the afternoon.

He wanted to see the dude ranch for himself. Ellen had been practically an angel all week, yes-sir-ing and no-sir-ing Max till he wondered whether the Wrights were putting something funny in the water over there.

He'd driven by Bell River before, of course, first out of curiosity, and then, when he agreed to let Ellen attend the camp, with a more discriminating eye. It was a pretty place, great location just east of town, old enough to look established, but fresh and updated. Obviously well loved and well run.

Now he wanted to get up close and personal.

He knew to drive around back to find the car park. When he got out, though, he hesitated a minute, trying to decide whether to head toward the barn or toward the main house. Ellen had explained that mornings were spent outdoors, hiking, horseback riding and playing sports, but afternoons were mostly in the barn, painting, or listening to guests talk about nature and wildlife and local lore.

"Thorpe?"

Max glanced over to the west, toward a building that looked as if it must be the stables. Dallas Garwood was walking toward him, hand outstretched and smile in place, offering the welcome that had been so conspicuously lacking the last time they met.

But what the heck. Max wasn't the type to hold a grudge.

"Garwood." He accepted the other man's handshake, noticing that the man looked warmer, more down-to-earth here in this setting, with his jeans and flannel shirt and cowboy hat instead of a suit.

Also in his favor, Dallas held a wrench in his other hand. Not merely the sheriff, then. Not just the eye candy husband for an heiress wife. Dallas was a working partner in the family endeavor.

Max liked that. On his grandfather's farm, everyone had pitched in on everything. He couldn't remember ever seeing his grandfather without a hammer or a pair of pliers in his pocket.

"I'm glad to see you, Max." Dallas's handshake had been warm and sincere, almost like an apology. "I've been meaning to stop by and say I'm sorry about what a jerk Alec was."

For a minute Max couldn't remember what Dallas meant. He tilted his head quizzically. "Jerk?"

"Yeah. I hear he made quite the fool of himself at your place. Went after Ellen with a sewing needle, and then keeled over in your living room." Dallas shook his head. "I wouldn't have blamed you if you'd skinned him alive on the spot."

"I have to admit I thought about it." Max smiled, thinking back on that crazy day. "Let's just say Alec has a clever way of disarming his opposition."

"I know. Believe me, I know." Dallas chuckled. "One of these days, though, the little devil is going to meet someone he can't charm, and then God help him. Anyhow, I'm sorry he made such a hash of everything. He's mucked out about a hundred extra stalls as punishment, and he's not done yet."

"Might be time to let him off the hook," Max suggested. "I don't think he was to blame for that escapade. You remember how, in chemistry class, if you took the perfect two ingredients, and put them in the same beaker..."

Dallas laughed, tipping his hat back on his brow. "Oh, yeah. I've met Ellen." He glanced toward the barn. "She's got some serious spunk. Plus, she's the first kid who's ever introduced Alec to the concept of humility. I'm definitely a fan."

Max felt himself mellowing, completely forgiving Dallas for their rocky start. There really was no better basis for a friendship between two fathers than this: *you like my kid, and I like yours.*

"So. Are you here to pick Ellen up?" Dallas stuffed the wrench in his back pocket. "Or are you here to see Penny?"

Max raised his eyebrow, surprised that both options seemed acceptable to Mr. *Silverdell Sheriff* Garwood, who little more than three weeks ago apparently had stood ready to slap him in jail if he so much as looked funny at the youngest Wright sister.

"I'm here for Ellen," he said. "Penny ordinarily brings her home, but I got free early, so I thought I'd pick her up myself."

"I don't think they're back yet." Dallas shaded his eyes and looked off toward the western slope. "Ro and some of the youth counselors took them out on a short ride. Nothing to worry about. The younger kids are on our slowest, laziest ponies, so they don't always make it home on time."

"That's okay. I'll wait in the car."

"No, no. Come on in. Penny and Bree are inside. They're working on the wedding plans, of course. All day every day."

"Wedding plans?"

"Bree and Gray. It's next weekend, so we've officially

reached crazy time. Swatches everywhere, and if I have to eat another piece of sample cake or give my opinion on another bridesmaid dress, I'm moving out till it's over."

Dallas grinned again. "I'm not trying to scare you, Max. Just offering fair warning. This is seriously something borrowed–something blue stuff. If wedding plans give you hives…"

Max tilted his head and raised one brow. "Hives?"

"Well," Dallas shrugged. "I mean, if you don't give a hoot whether a petticoat is made of satin-edged tulle or tulle-edged satin, you can always come back later. I won't even mention you were here."

Max nodded, thoughtfully digesting the offer. Then he smiled.

"As you may have noticed, I'm not that easy to scare. Wedding planning is not a problem. I'm a tulle-edged satin man, actually. And I'm happy to tell anyone who asks."

Dallas narrowed his eyes briefly, searching Max's face, as if the two of them had just exchanged an important piece of information. Then, relaxing, he slapped Max lightly on the back.

"Well, good for you, Thorpe," he said. "Good for you. Come on, then. I'll show you where to find the fun."

PENNY KNELT ON the floor in Ro's living room and put her elbows on the coffee table, so that she could get a better look at the pictures she'd spread out there.

The photos Bree had rejected had been tossed aside, into a stack on the far side of the table. The "like" pile was now fanned out so that Penny could study them more carefully, looking for a common thread. She rose onto her knees and stretched, rear end high in the air, so that she could check out the farthest ones.

She thought she spotted a pattern. Bree had picked out all the pictures that—

"Hi, there. You look busy."

Max? *Oh, hell.* Penny almost tipped the chair over, trying to get back in a normal position. She cursed her clumsiness internally, but tried to smile on the outside. She had probably looked like someone's pet monkey, baboon behind in the air....

"Max! I didn't know you were coming to get Ellen." She smoothed her shirt down. "You didn't have to, you know. I was planning to bring her home, as usual."

"I thought I'd surprise her," he said. Then he stopped, just inside the doorway. "You cut your hair."

"Yeah." Self-consciously, she reached up to touch the long bob that now barely brushed her shoulders. Ruth had always told her she shouldn't cut it. A woman's crowning glory...men like it long...

"Does it look that bad?" She tucked one side behind her ear. "It's so much more comfortable. So much easier to take care of..."

"It looks fantastic."

Amazingly, he sounded absolutely sincere. And the look on his face was not disappointment. It was something more complicated. Something that made her insides warm slightly.

The hairdresser had assured her it was a much-sexier look. More approachable, more adult, than the long, straight fall that she usually scraped back in a ponytail. Hearing Ruth's voice in her head, Penny had been skeptical—but in the end she shut the voice up and forged onward. The haircut was for her own aesthetic pleasure, and her own convenience. It wasn't done to appeal to anyone but herself.

However, now she knew that the hairdresser had been right.

Seeing this admiring look on Max's face…this was a fringe benefit she would gladly accept.

"Thanks," she said, fighting down a blush. "It's no big deal. Just another check on the list. Compared to something like the tattoo, or the white-water rafting, a haircut seemed like a cinch."

"I bet." Max came into the room and took one of the other chairs around the table. He leaned back comfortably. "So you must be burning up that list by now. How many is that?"

She smiled. "This makes five. I've got twelve, so I'm almost halfway through. Not exactly burning it up, but pretty good. Especially considering I'd expected to give it a whole year. If I keep this pace, I may have to make a second list—one that's a little more daring."

"Five." He smiled. "Does that count juggling?"

Suddenly her mouth tingled, and without conscious thought she found herself staring at his.

"No." She pulled her gaze free and pressed her lips together. "No, I don't think I'm ready to cross that one off just yet. I tried it again yesterday. I've even bought the right kind of beanbags, and a video. But I'm hopeless."

Like a fool, she found herself wanting to add something flirtatious, something obvious, like, "I probably need a few more lessons."

But she didn't. She wasn't that foolish, thank goodness. Nothing had changed since their last talk. They'd agreed that night that neither of them could afford the distraction of a fling right now. They were both recovering from huge, life-altering events—and everyone knew you shouldn't rush into anything at a time like that.

He'd made vows to Ellen. She'd made vows to herself.

Not that keeping those vows was going to be easy.

Sometimes, when she lay awake at night, listening to the

silence and feeling so painfully alone, she tried to argue herself out of it.

Why shouldn't they fudge on their promises, she asked herself? Just a little? They didn't have to hurt anyone in the process. They could flirt…kiss…even be lovers—all without letting his daughter find out. People had secret affairs all the time.

And so what if she was trying to build a reputation in town as a woman you could send your children to for art lessons—while everyone around her was waiting to see if she had grown up to be crazy, like her dad, or slutty, like her mom? They could keep it a secret from the whole darn town, too.

It didn't even matter that Max was going to be around for only nine months, so that any relationship could never be anything more serious than a fling. She was an adult— she could control her emotions. She could master these feelings, this strangely powerful attraction that came over her like a tidal wave whenever she got near him.

She could be sure he didn't break her heart.

Except that she already knew she *couldn't* be sure of that. Just sitting here beside him right now, she already could feel the temptation of his gentle kindness, his steady strength.

The sad truth was, it would be so easy to fall for him. To put off trying to stand on her own two feet, which was turning out to be so much lonelier than she'd ever bargained for.

Easy—but cowardly. And she refused to be that kind of coward. To those who said it was her destiny to lean on a man, any man, even a man who would hurt her, she could only say…*watch me.*

"Yeah," she repeated. "I'm definitely hopeless."

"You'll get the hang of it," he said gently, as if he could hear her inner turmoil and wanted to assure her that he wasn't a threat. As if he wanted to promise he wouldn't take advantage of her ambivalence. "You're tougher than you realize, Penny. If you decide to do something, you'll do it."

She smiled appreciatively, though she couldn't quite meet his eyes—they seemed to see so far into her.

"Thank you," she said. She bent her head over the pictures and began shuffling them around meaninglessly. It was time to change the subject.

"Has Ellen mentioned that Bree asked her to be in the wedding?"

Max hesitated, then laughed. "I didn't know till five minutes ago there was going to be a wedding. Apparently the dad is always the last to know. Be in the wedding... how?"

"As a flower girl." Penny wondered why Ellen hadn't mentioned it to Max. Bree had asked her days ago—maybe the second day she was here—and she had reported that she'd been given permission.

Maybe Max would think it was inappropriate, given how new their friendship was. Penny wondered if he understood how quickly Ellen had been integrated into the Wright nucleus. Perhaps it was Ellen's motherless, vulnerable aura, or maybe it was her friendship with Alec, but all three of the Wright sisters had taken to the girl instantly. She wasn't the sweet, immediately adorable kind of kid— but then, they hadn't been that kind, either.

They liked spunk, and grit, and a little fire in the belly. Those things, Ellen had times ten.

"It's not a huge commitment," Penny said, feeling the need to downplay it, for fear he wouldn't allow her to participate. Ellen would be heartbroken if she was denied the chance. She'd already spent hours with Bree, picking out the perfect flower garland for her hair.

"Bree's already bought Ellen's dress. Bree used to be an event planner, so you can't get her to delegate anything. We can even get someone to give Ellen a ride, if you don't feel that you can make it, though of course we're hoping you will. Did you get the invitation Bree sent home with Ellen?"

He shook his head, still smiling ruefully. "I guess that must have slipped her mind, too."

"Oh, dear." Penny sighed. "She's probably afraid you might not approve. She does seem to think Alec has a reputation as the demon child."

"*No!* Really?" His eyes twinkled, though.

"Really. And with good reason, I might add. Anyhow, the wedding isn't a big extravaganza. Maybe fifty people, right here on the property, a week from Saturday. I hope you'll say yes."

He hesitated just a fraction of a second. Then he smiled. "Sure. It'll be our pleasure."

For a moment, neither of them spoke. They hadn't been alone together since the balloon ride, and their friendship seemed to have moved to a more personal level that day. Clearly, neither one was quite sure where they went from here.

She fiddled a little more with the photos.

"What are those?"

Either he, too, was looking for a neutral conversational topic, or he truly had just noticed the pictures for the first time. He leaned forward, his hands resting on his knees. "Not family pictures, surely. These are all different brides and grooms, aren't they?"

"Yes." Gratefully, she held up a couple for him to look at. "In college, I used to freelance a little, shooting weddings. I brought some of the prints over today, so that Bree could see them. I'll be doing her wedding pictures, and I wanted to see what kinds of shots she liked."

He edged forward on his chair, considering them more closely. "And these are the ones she chose?" He picked up one or two. "They're all so different. I'm not sure I see a theme."

Penny touched one thoughtfully. "You're right. I was just trying to see if I could spot a pattern. I think I might have figured it out. She's not responding to the poses or the composition, or anything to do with the photography itself. Not primarily."

He frowned. He picked up a photo of an older couple, mid-fifties, maybe, standing at the edge of a lake. Betty and Wally Mosen. Penny had shot them from the back, their heads tilted together, the sunset shining between them with a heart-shaped glow.

He glanced over at Penny. "Not the photography? So what is she responding to, then?"

"Well, I haven't checked every one, but I think she's picked out the *happy* couples."

He laughed. "Aren't they all happy couples? At least for that one day?"

"Of course not." Once, she might have thought so, too. Even with her family history, she had started out thinking that marriages must slowly sour over the years, not start out that way. But the truth was far sadder than that.

She rifled through the reject pile and fished out one particularly obvious example. A whole contact sheet from the Evans wedding.

"See? Mindy and Joe. I knew while I was taking these pictures they wouldn't make it. And boy was I right that time. They were divorced within the month."

She smiled ruefully, holding it out for him to see. "I never even got paid for the pictures."

He took it from her, seeming curious, though his expression was still skeptical. "And you think their doomed marriage is obvious from a photo?"

"It almost always shows," she said. "In this one, for instance...see how they never look at each other? There are thirty-five images on that sheet. Not once did they make eye contact."

He scanned the sheet, nodding subtly, almost as if he didn't realize he was doing it. "No, they don't, do they?" He glanced up, a new light in his eyes that felt like a dawning respect for her analysis. "And it's as simple as that? Make eye contact, happy marriage. Don't make eye contact, divorce?"

"Of course not." She pulled out some more pictures. "There are tons of red flags. Fake smiles, the ones that don't extend to the eyes. In-laws who look as if they're headed for an execution. Or a couple who stand farther apart than they need to. Even a few inches is telling on a day like this."

She fanned the pictures out on the table, looking for the other cues. Many of the signs she registered only subconsciously, and it was a challenge to put those intuitions into words.

"Let's see." She held up the formal Murray wedding shot. "Too much tooth in that smile—can't you tell it's forced? And here, see how the veins are visible in his neck? Oh, and this is a dead giveaway—when they hug, their torsos come together, but their pelvises are tilted back, avoiding contact from the waist down."

He was looking at her with a strange expression, and she wondered whether she sounded a little neurotic. Did it seem as if she reduced something as ethereal as love to a set of physical mechanics?

She didn't. She was, at heart, a hopeless romantic. Having been born of a loveless marriage, and having seen the tragedy that could come of it, she, more than anyone, had elevated love to a near-mystical status. Other children, the ones with loving parents, had always seemed magical to her, as if they lived inside a snow globe that rained fairy dust and rainbows.

That was probably why she had trained herself to spot these "tells." She hated to think that the Real Thing could ever die, no matter what happened. That would leave everyone—including Rowena, Bree and Penny herself—vulnerable to heartbreak and tragedy.

It was far easier to believe that the marriages that didn't work had never been built on true love in the first place.

But she couldn't explain all that. He probably didn't really care. And even if he did, he'd think she was too naive to live.

So she didn't mention the rest of her list. But it was a long one. Was any nonrelative female in the crowd looking directly at the groom, instead of at the bride? Was either the groom or the bride always shifting weight onto the outside foot, as if poised to run away? Was the bride particularly infantile, with heavy Cinderella vibes to her wedding dress, and a cake like a Barbie doll?

He took the Murray photo from her and stared at it, his expression oddly fixed. "Surely, though, some of these things could just be the result of an awkward shot."

Max was smiling, but something about this subject clearly made him uncomfortable. Maybe he was feeling self-conscious, remembering some detail of his own wedding photos. How thoughtless she'd been to spout her theories, when it might hurt him to hear them.

Ugh. Had she really believed this was a neutral topic? Weddings. Love. Divorce. Disillusionment…

He seemed snagged on the picture he held in his hand. He kept looking at the desperately smiling Joe Murray. "One picture. It's not really enough, surely. The camera can catch a saint looking drunk, if it snaps at the worst possible moment."

"Of course," she agreed, suddenly wanting to reassure him. She tried to remember exactly what he'd said the other night. He'd said he had a lot to make up for…that he hadn't been a good father…that he'd traveled a lot.

Reading between the lines, did that mean he hadn't been a very good husband, either?

"If I see only one of the signs, I ignore it," she said, keeping her tone light. "If I see two, my antennae quiver a bit. Any three…well, if I see three, then I still could be wrong. But I make sure I get my check before I leave."

Finally, his spell seemed to break. He laughed, dropping the photo back on the table. "Does Bree know she's having her wedding pictures taken by a psychic?"

"Bree doesn't have much to worry about," Penny said. "At this wedding, I'm the nervous one. Those two are so in love the heat coming off them will probably melt my camera right out of my hands."

It had been the same at Ro's wedding. It had felt like standing next to a bonfire—a bonfire made of the sweetest smelling incense. A bonfire that never dwindled, but seemed somehow to renew itself even as it flamed.

After a few toasts that day, Penny and Bree had been just loosened up enough to admit how much they envied their feisty older sister. With their history, finding this kind of love required nothing short of a miracle.

And now the same miracle had come to Bree.

Penny was happy, deeply happy, for both her sisters. But a little voice couldn't help asking: what were the odds of a third miracle finding its way to the same family? Wasn't it far more likely that one of them would have to live out the script everyone had expected them all to follow?

The poor damaged Wright girl, the poor orphan whose father killed her mother, and consequently could never trust a man enough to fall in love…

Or, even worse, the poor damaged Wright girl, whose weak mother, afraid to be alone, had repeatedly tied herself to the wrong men. The poor Wright girl who repeated that pattern, who always clung to whatever man came close enough and never learned to stand on her own two feet.

Bree stuck her head through the doorway. "Pea, Ro's got Ellen out front." She widened her eyes. "Max! Hi! I didn't realize you were here. If I'd known, I would have brought in the picture of the dress we got for Ellen. Pretty cool she's going to be a flower girl, huh?"

Penny tightened, but Max just smiled easily. "Very cool."

"Well, anyhow, I guess you're the one who needs to know—Ellen's out front."

"Great. Thanks."

Bree looked once at Penny, then back at Max. Then, with a laugh and a wave, she disappeared.

Max stood. "I guess I should let Ellen know I'm here."

"Of course." Penny stood, too, shaking off her earlier thoughts. She was just borrowing trouble. She wasn't going to repeat her mother's mistakes. She was more than tough enough to stand alone.

And someday…maybe…she'd even be tough enough to let herself fall in love. With the *right* man.

"I'll take you around," she said with a smile. "Ellen will be so excited to see you."

Without thinking, she turned toward the kitchen. He caught her elbow lightly and tilted his head toward the living room. "Wouldn't it be closer to go this way?"

Oh. She'd forgotten. He didn't know.

"If you'd like, you certainly can. But I don't go into that part of the house."

He frowned. "Why not? Is it reserved for guests? Surely, as the owner—"

"It's not that." After her mental pep talk about how tough

she was, she felt particularly foolish saying this. But she wasn't going to lie about it, either. It was simply a fact of her life, and whatever he thought about it didn't change anything.

"I don't go in that part of the house because it's where my mother died. It's a sort of phobia, I suppose. But it's easy enough to take the other way around."

He didn't say anything for several seconds. She lifted her chin, trying to warn him not to pity her, or to try to jolly her out of it. She met his gaze steadily, mutely asserting the right to her own truth.

Finally, he smiled. "Absolutely," he said. "Easy enough to take the other way around."

ELLEN TALKED ALL the way home. She didn't mean to, but she'd been so jazzed to see Dad come out of the house with Penny that it was like drinking a bunch of fizzy water, and she couldn't settle down.

In fact, she almost told him about the flower girl thing. She'd been carrying the invitation around for days now, waiting for the perfect moment. If he said no, she'd die a thousand deaths.

But she still couldn't quite bring herself to talk about it. It was crazy, how important it was to her. He might think she only cared because she'd get to dress up and wear a flower crown and be the center of attention. One time, when he was very angry, he'd told her that she was vain, and that she needed to unlearn some of the lessons her mother had taught her.

She hadn't spoken to him for a week after that.

Instead, today, she told him all about the photography class, which had been awesome. When they got to the duplex and went inside, she could hardly wait to bring out her laptop and put in the flash drive to show him the pictures she'd taken.

"I took this one of Alec, but he's a terrible subject. He always has to make some dumb face so that everyone will know he doesn't care whether he looks good or not." She had put the laptop on her dad's lap, and she sat on the arm of the chair so that she could scroll through the pictures and narrate.

She let the one of Alec linger on the screen an extra few minutes. She didn't want to be the one to say so, but she thought the picture was pretty good, in spite of Alec's dumb expression.

"He shouldn't worry about his looks, though," she said. "He always looks good. He's just one of those people."

Dad smiled. "He's definitely photogenic. But I think you caught a great shot there. And you can almost see the devil peeking out of those mischievous blue eyes."

She flushed with pleasure. That was what she thought, exactly, though she wouldn't have known how to put it.

"And here's Penny," she said, finally moving on. "She's easier to do, because she's not nervous. She just acts natural. And she's photogenic, too."

She glanced at him out of the corner of her eye, to see if he'd noticed that she used the word he just taught her. He probably did, because he was smiling at the picture.

"She is definitely that," he said. "That's a lovely picture. Great job."

She wondered whether Alec was at home right now, showing his pictures to his family. He'd taken a whole lot of Ellen. She wondered if any of them were pretty. Maybe. Since they'd moved to Colorado, and she'd been doing all this out-of-doors stuff, like hiking and horseback riding, and even the archery at Mrs. Starling's camp, she might have lost a few pounds.

She wondered if anyone at Alec's house looked at her picture and said, "She's photogenic."

When her dad had looked at every single picture, she asked if she could go out back and take some more shots before it got too dark. She still had a ton of room on her flash drive, and she had an idea that Penny's gazing balls would look great, if she could capture the light just right.

He didn't seem to mind. He had some work to do anyhow, he said.

Didn't he always?

She stayed out a long time, hoping that maybe Penny would come out, too, and they could talk. She took about a hundred pictures of the gazing balls, but they never looked right. The balls always looked flat and lifeless, not at all the way they did in real life. She was hoping maybe Penny knew the trick for making the life show up in the photograph.

After a while, though, she got tired. She was hungry, too. She wondered whether Dad was going to make red rice and tuna for dinner—or whether maybe he'd order a pizza.

She let herself in through the kitchen, and she was glad that it was quiet and dark, which meant he wasn't planning to make red rice. Ellen was sick of that, and she'd be glad to have pizza for a change.

Maybe, she thought, it was time for her to learn how to cook something. The dude ranch was offering a cooking class during camp next week, and she thought she might take it. She wouldn't tell Dad, though. She'd surprise him, and—

She lost her train of thought as she entered the living room. Her father was sitting at the dining table, but he didn't have his computer open. He didn't have any work on the table in front of him. He didn't have the TV on, either, although he almost always watched the news at this time of day.

Instead, he seemed to be looking at a photo album. She squinted and recognized it instantly. It was the photo album full of wedding pictures, from back when he and her mom got married. He must have gone into Ellen's room to get it, because she always kept it by her bed.

She started to say something snarky about that, about how there was such a thing as privacy.

But something about the way he was sitting...

Something about the way he was staring down at the photos, his hands on the table, on either side of the album but strangely loose, as if he'd forgotten he had hands...

Something in the tight set of his jaw, the small, jumping pulse at the edge of his throat...

It reminded her that these were, in the end, *his* pictures. Not hers. Maybe this wasn't a great time to start whining about privacy.

Quietly, she got close enough to see over his shoulder. She expected him to be studying one of the mushier pictures, like the one in which they were kissing, or the one where they were feeding each other pieces of cake.

But it wasn't. He was staring down at a page of photos she'd never liked very much. In these pictures, her mom and dad weren't even looking at each other. They stood side by side, but they leaned in different directions, which looked weird.

Dad's grandfather was in some of them, and he didn't look happy about the whole thing. In fact, he looked almost mad, showing that he hadn't liked his son's bride very much. Which, Ellen had always heard from her mom, was actually the case. One time, her mom had said, "If your great-grandfather had had his way, you wouldn't ever have been born."

She'd never met her great-grandfather. He'd died before she was old enough to remember him. But she hated him anyhow, because he hadn't wanted her to be born.

So why was Dad stuck on these pictures? She had almost thrown them away many times. She would have, if she hadn't felt kind of guilty, as if she didn't have the right.

But her dad should have done it. It was disloyal, keeping pictures of someone who hated your wife.

He must have heard her breathing behind him. He closed the album quickly, as if he had something to hide.

He turned with a smile so fake it took her breath away. "Hey, there, kiddo," he said. "Hungry?"

And all of a sudden, for no reason she could understand, Ellen was angry with him. Really, really angry.

"No," she said. "And that's mine."

She scooped up the album, took it into her room and closed the door, though she was careful not to slam it.

And then she lay down on her bed and began to cry.

CHAPTER NINE

FRIDAY NIGHT—a week and a day before the wedding. Where had the time gone?

Rowena and Bree were coming over for dinner, the first time she'd hosted anyone at the duplex. Penny had spent all day putting the finishing touches on her house—and by "finishing touches" she meant things like rearranging and rehanging pictures, and repainting the hall in a better shade of cream.

She wanted everything to be perfect. She wanted them to see what a good investment the duplex was, and how happy she was living here.

She definitely didn't want to offer any excuse to re-open the debate about whether she should move back to Bell River.

When the doorbell rang, she took a deep breath and composed her face. *Showtime!*

An hour later, as they sat at the dining room table eating a variety of sample food from the caterer—everything from spinach and brie turnovers to caramelized pears and popcorn shrimp—Penny braced herself for the verdict.

Bree took Penny's hand. "It's gorgeous, Pea. You've created a real home here."

For the first time all day, Penny's shoulders relaxed. "You really like it?"

"Like it?" Rowena laughed. "You'd better watch out. We love it so much, with all its charm and peace and quiet, that we'll probably move in, and then you'll never get to open your studio!"

Bree shook her head and tsked. "Don't scare her, Ro. The last thing she wants is to have to fear the invasion of the sisters." Bree turned her placid face toward Penny. "Ro just means it's fantastic. Compared to Bell River at the height of the fall season, it's like an oasis of peace in a desert of absolute madness."

"Plus, we have Alec." Rowena grinned, as if she knew that was the trump card. "We'll be running here as refugees, not as interfering sisters. You'll have to take us in, because you're a well-known humanitarian."

Penny laughed. They were kidding, of course, but she could see she'd scored a hit. When she'd shown them her master plan for opening her art studio, both of them had been almost insultingly surprised at how professional it was. It was as if they never had fully accepted that she was a real adult.

Now, perhaps, they were starting to see. Now, as they laughed with her, she felt that maybe the expression in their eyes was just a shade different. Even their tones were just a microscopic bit less maternal.

More the tone you might take with…an equal.

She'd always be their little sister, but maybe, for once, she wasn't their *tragic* little sister. This day had been a long time coming. But maybe, just maybe, she'd carved out her own space, where she could be close without being smothered.

That was enough, for now.

She waved toward the table. "Let's eat! We have to get this menu decided once and for all. Marianne may be a friend of Gray's but she's not a saint."

For the next half hour or so, the only talk was about the food. Marianne Donovan, owner of Donovan's Dream, had been very patient and flexible, but even she had production realities to deal with. She had to receive their list of final choices by tomorrow.

This was their final tasting party, and Bree frantically jotted down notes about which dishes were the best balance of aesthetics and just plain good eating.

Eventually, Penny gave up. Groaning, she leaned back in her chair. She suddenly wished desperately that she'd worn something loose and flowing, instead of her jeans and sweater.

"I've officially tested my last bite," she announced. "I'm going to pop."

"Me, too." Ro put her fork down and rested her hand on her stomach. She didn't look quite as tired as she had for a while, though she was still unusually thin. Penny watched her carefully, still just a little worried. She'd be relieved when the wedding was over.

"But we haven't decided on the salad yet!" Bree held out the list, showing the blank space where the salad choice should be.

Ro's eyes darkened abruptly. "Too bad Bonnie isn't going to be here. She made this burgundy mushroom salad that was to die for."

Penny hated the sad sound she heard in Ro's voice. "No word at all?"

Rowena shook her head. "It's been two weeks since the last postcard. I can tell Dallas is getting edgy. He's starting to make noises about trying to track them down."

"Well, maybe he should." Penny glanced at Bree to see what she thought. But Bree looked just as mutely concerned as Penny felt. Obviously, there was no easy answer to this one.

"He promised Mitch he wouldn't. Dallas would rather die than break a promise, but…" She bit her lower lip.

"Mitch is his baby brother. He's worried. I know all about that, and I can't blame him for thinking he should do something."

And then, out of nowhere, her green eyes were sparkling with unshed tears. Bree took one of Ro's and Penny's hands in each of her own. Instinctively, Ro and Penny joined hands, too, completing a magic circle.

She squeezed their hands tightly. "Honestly, we're so lucky to have each other back again, aren't we?"

They all nodded, their hands tightening in response. Penny was tearing up, now, too—and even Rowena's eyes were shining suspiciously.

As she looked at her beautiful, complicated sisters, Penny could barely believe this wasn't just a fantasy. Chilly, ultracomposed Bree and sardonic, hard-hearted Rowena— both brought to tears as easily as the baby sister, Penny. Both clinging across the table to the family they'd once told themselves they didn't need.

Penny had dreamed of moments like this, back in Aunt Ruth's house, all those years ago.

If she was dreaming now, she never wanted to wake up.

Ro cleared her throat self-consciously, but she didn't release her sisters' hands. "Okay...so, as long as we're already doing the group hug thing..."

Penny and Bree both turned to Rowena, curiously. They recognized that teasing tone, and that devilish grin.

"I've got...news."

For a fraction of a second, no one reacted. Bree cast a sidelong, almost surreptitious, glance toward Penny, who was sending a similar sneaky glance toward Bree.

"News?" They said the word at precisely the same moment, and with the same inflection—as if it were a foreign expression they had never heard before. It might as well have been a comedy routine they'd rehearsed for days.

Rowena laughed. "Yes, news. You see…I've been waiting to tell you. I'm— That is, Dallas and I—

"Oh, my God!" Bree leaped to her feet. "I knew it! You're pregnant!"

Penny stood, too. It wasn't possible to contain all this happiness and excitement while sitting down. But she didn't speak. She wanted to be sure, absolutely sure. She wanted to hear Rowena say the words.

But Rowena was laughing, letting Bree hug her and spin her around. She shook her head, pretending to frown.

"You guys sure jumped to conclusions. What if I'd been going to say we were moving to Montana? Or we'd won the lottery? Or we'd decided to get a divorce?"

Bree waved that away like the nonsense it was. "I *knew* it. I knew you were either very sick or very pregnant. And you were way too happy to be very sick."

Penny finally found her voice. "Is it true, Ro? You and Dallas are going to have a baby?"

Rowena nodded, and her eyes once again caught the overhead light and sparkled with tears that made them appear to be made of green crystal.

"We are," she said. "That's one of the reasons he wants so badly for Mitch to come home, to be…"

And then she caught her breath on a ragged inhale. To Penny's shock, the tears spilled over and ran down Rowena's cheeks.

"Oh, look at me. I'm being an idiot. It's just that—" She brushed the tears away roughly. "It's just that I never—"

But she didn't need to say the words. They all knew. She had been alone so long, walled off inside her anger and her grief. The love inside her had never found an outlet. Then came the miracle of Dallas and Alec.

And now a child of her own. A new life, a new child. Penny could hardly contain her happiness.

It was, in a way, a chance for the daughters of Moira Wright to completely rewrite the ending of the story.

"Anyhow," Rowena said briskly, as if embarrassed by her display of emotion. "I'll give you all the details later. Right now, since we're all here together, just the three of us, there's something I want to do. And I want you to be here when I do it."

This time Penny and Bree weren't as sure what to think. Ro seemed more muted suddenly, as if the next step wasn't as simple.

"Of course," Penny said automatically. "Whatever you need, Ro. We're here."

Rowena moved into the living room. Her dramatic coloring stood out among the soft blues and browns and creams like a cardinal nesting with finches. She sat on the sofa and picked up her purse.

Bree and Penny followed slowly and sat on either side of her, like bookends, like library lions. It was as if some subconscious protective instinct had dictated their choice.

As they watched, she pulled a large envelope out of the canvas shoulder bag.

At that moment, comprehension dawned—belatedly perhaps, but with a powerful clarity. Penny realized that Ro was finally ready to find out who her biological father had been. His name was in the P.I. report Bree had commissioned all those months ago. It had remained sealed inside that envelope.

"It's time, I think." She put the folder in her lap, smoothed it once and turned to Bree. "I know you didn't understand why I wouldn't look at this sooner. I guess it's the old cliché…what you don't know can't hurt you."

"I understood," Bree said, putting her hand on Rowena's shoulder. "Honestly, I did. Not at first, maybe, but I did eventually get it."

"Thank you." Rowena seemed strangely humble. "Anyhow, something about knowing I'm going to have a baby has changed the equation. This is not my information anymore—not mine alone, anyhow."

She picked up the envelope. Her hands were trembling, and Penny bit her lower lip, forcing herself to wait patiently.

"This name belongs to the baby, too," Rowena said, staring down at the envelope as if it might start moving of its own accord. As if it were something magical, not of this world.

And in a way, it wasn't. It was a name that would take them to another world—the world inhabited by a man none of them could name, but whose blood even now ran through Rowena's veins.

And her baby's.

Rowena raised her chin, and Penny knew that meant her big, brave sister was very frightened. "This is my child's grandfather. I don't have the right to take that away just because I'm afraid."

Penny held her breath. What would the report reveal? Would the name written there belong to someone they knew? It could be a neighbor who lived two houses down, or a stranger living thousands of miles away. It could be a saint or a sinner, a fool or a genius. It could be a living man—or a dead one.

Most importantly, it could be someone who would welcome the news that he had a daughter…or someone who rejected Rowena all over again, just as Johnny Wright had done.

And that, of course, was really why Rowena was afraid. They all were, for her sake. For her sake, they prayed for a father she could be proud of. A father who would be proud of her.

Penny put her arm around her sister's back and leaned in. "We're here," she said again. "No matter what, we're here."

Bree elbowed Ro and shot her a teasing smile. "And, hey. No matter what, you're trading up. Nothing is worse than what we were born with, right?"

Ro nodded. She took a deep breath, ran her finger inside the envelope's seal and opened it. Quickly, as if she feared she might change her mind, she slid out the paperwork inside, held it up and scanned it.

Bree and Penny looked, too, of course. If she hadn't wanted them to, she wouldn't have held it where they could see.

And there it was. The name that for so long had loomed so large in all their imaginations.

You could almost hear the tension fizzle out of the room, like carbonation escaping an uncapped soda bottle.

Dr. Rowan Atherton Reese, it read. Age: Fifty-six. Occupation: Surgeon. Marital status: Married. Children: Four.

Address: 1923 Eaton Drive, Crested Butte, Colorado.

"But…" Bree sounded dazed. "But…"

The bewilderment was an echo of Penny's own. How could it be? How could it possibly be true? None of it meant anything to any of them. Could the P.I. have made a mistake? They'd never, ever heard of this man.

Then Rowena turned the page, and the next sheet was a photo, printed from the staff page of a Crested Butte hospital. *Dr. Rowan Reese, head of surgery…*

And there it was. All the proof their bewildered minds could ever need. Dr. Rowan Reese was dramatically, elegantly tall and thin. His posture was proud and unyielding. He was long-limbed, weather-beaten, outdoorsy, athletic. Handsome, passionate, driven, fiery.

His salt-and-pepper hair had clearly once been jet-black. His lips were full, sensual, his smile wide over shockingly white, strong teeth. His eyes showed intelligence, wit—but most importantly they were burning coals of green fire.

He was all the things Johnny Wright could never be.

He was Rowena's father.

MAX WAS IN the basement in Mexico, but he was screaming. That was how he always knew he was dreaming. He hadn't ever really screamed in Mexico. They would have killed him, and he had to stay alive. He had to get home to Ellen, no matter what it took.

But in his dreams he screamed. In his dreams, he always thought someone was nearby, someone who might hear him and call the police.

He woke himself up with the noise, even though Lydia told him that the sound he made didn't really qualify as a scream. It was more like a choking, with a high-pitched something deep in his throat.

It was really more like a gagged person *trying* to scream, she'd said with a faint thread of distaste. After a couple of months, she'd slept in the guest room. It was just too disturbing, she said, especially since he wouldn't ever talk to her about it afterward.

It drove her crazy that he wouldn't talk about it. But it would have driven him crazy if he did.

Max slept in sweatpants, but he rarely wore a T-shirt over them, because he always soaked it through on the nights he dreamed about the basement. It was easier just to keep one by the bed and drag it on if he had to go check on Ellen.

Tonight, he didn't bother. He pulled himself out of bed. He poked his head through Ellie's doorway, saw that she was out cold, then wandered onto the back deck shirtless and shoeless. At three in the morning, he wasn't likely to run into anyone but owls and possums, who really didn't give a damn how he was dressed.

After the dreams of the musty, unventilated basement, he welcomed the sting of cold air against his skin. He went to the railing and put the heels of his hands on it, stretching his torso up, as high as it would go. He breathed deeply. In through his nose. Hold. Then out through his mouth. Over and over, until his lungs believed there really was enough air, and his muscles believed it was safe for them to relax.

The wind moved through the trees briskly, as if it had a timetable to meet and somewhere to be. The shifting branches winked silver, then olive-green, then silver again in the moonlight. He bent over, hands still gripping the railing, and stretched his torso.

Out of the corner of his eye, he saw movement on Penny's porch—but when he looked, it was only the gazing balls, reflecting back his own strange stretches and bends. When he inhaled deeply, light fractured in half a dozen balls, all of which were aimed at him from one angle or another.

It should have been eerie, but it wasn't. It was oddly comforting, as if they were conscious things, aware of his distress and sending him a signal that he was not alone.

He smiled, appreciating the irony. A few mirror-covered bowling balls were a heck of a lot more company than Lydia had ever been.

"Max, are you okay?"

For a minute, he wondered if his imagination had truly run away with his sanity, and he had let the gazing balls start talking. But then he glanced back at Penny's kitchen door. She stood there, wrapped in a blanket, her new haircut mussed and spiky.

"I'm fine," he said. "Just getting some fresh air."

She blinked, then reached up with one blanket-covered

fist and rubbed at her eyes. "It's just that—you called out. You sounded…upset."

Hell.

He moved toward the railing that separated their two decks. "I'm sorry," he said. "You heard me all the way over there? I can be a pretty noisy sleeper, but I had no idea I was that bad."

"No, no. Not bad." She frowned. "Sad."

"I'm not sad," he said, trying to keep it simple. "Just noisy."

She looked unconvinced, but sleepy enough that she was more confused than skeptical. "Do you have bad dreams?"

He thought about lying. But then he realized he simply didn't want to lie to her.

"Yes," he said. "Often, I do. Luckily, Ellen sleeps like a rock, so I don't disturb her much. I'm really sorry I disturbed you."

"I don't mind." Her eyes were more focused now. Apparently the night air was clearing her head. "I have bad dreams sometimes, too. About my mother." She said it quite matter-of-factly, as if it were only natural that some tragedies would live on in the subconscious.

She moved a couple of steps toward him. She was barefoot, too. "Would it help to talk about it, do you think?"

For one crazy second, he actually considered it.

He'd never had the urge to share his story with anyone. His company had sent him to a psychiatrist, but he'd hated the whole process, and eventually he'd just resigned from psychiatrist and company all in one fell swoop.

Instead, he struck out on his own as he'd always dreamed of doing. Why wait? If Mexico had taught him anything, it was that everything you knew could end in an instant. If death was around every corner, then freedom, satisfaction and courage had better be right here, right now.

Talking about the past just kept it alive.

But all of a sudden, he thought that he might like to tell Penny about it. Maybe it would make the whole thing seem less poisonous. Maybe it would be like opening windows in a mildewed room.

That innocence he had noticed wasn't just superficial—it was without question a profound part of her essence. But it wasn't the innocence that drew him toward her right now. Sometimes, when he looked into her eyes, he could tell she knew every bit as much about grief and pain as he did. He had that click of recognition, as if she wouldn't think it strange that he had to steel himself to walk into a basement, or that the sound of a car backfiring could drop him to his knees.

A shudder passed through him.

"You're cold." She shrugged the moonlight-blue blanket from her shoulders and held it out. "Here. Take this."

Under the blanket, she wore a T-shirt, gray and shapeless. Across her breasts, letters sparkled in the moonlight, spelling out Keep Calm and Paint Something. For a helpless fraction of a second, he couldn't take his eyes off the soft swelling beneath the cotton.

Then, below the words, the curve of her hip, and then the pale gleam of her naked legs, like the slim stalks that held a flower.

Oh, he was in trouble. Big trouble. He wanted her. Every nerve ending in his body had caught fire. He didn't want to talk to her, confide in her, turn her into his psychiatrist. He wanted to lower her to the deck and make love to her in the moonlight, until neither of them had room for words, or ghosts, or pain.

The wool of the blanket brushed against his shoulder as she nudged it toward him. He lifted his forearm, an instinctive blocking motion, as if he had to protect himself against the force of her beauty, slamming into his awareness without warning.

"I'm fine." He put his arm down, but the rest of him remained clenched. "Penny, listen to me. You can't be so naive that you don't see how risky this is. If we're going to stick to the promises we made the other night, you need to put that back on."

She didn't feign confusion. She was so breathtakingly honest, sometimes... Their gazes met.

"And what if we decided to break the promises?"

For a split second, the possibilities glimmered in front of him. Break the promises. Yes, of course. Wasn't that what the cliché said that promises were actually *made* to be broken?

And who would it hurt, really? Couldn't they just indulge these powerful urges once? Just once, with no one the wiser? They were consenting adults, unmarried. They would be careful. He hadn't taken a lover in almost a year, not since Lydia died.

And he hadn't *made love* for a long, long time before that. Sex, yes. Empty, ugly nights of pity sex, or duty sex, or last-hope sex, with the wife he tried and tried to make himself love.

Didn't he deserve this? Penny was kind, and honest, and pure in a way that had nothing to do with her sexual experience and everything to do with her soul. She could have had a hundred lovers, or none, and it would make no difference to Max. He just wanted to rest himself beside her. Inside her. He wanted to drink from that pure spring of gentle kindness, and be restored.

What was the harm? He heard the phrase in his head, over and over. What was the harm? He wouldn't take more than she was willing to give. He wouldn't leave her sick, or pregnant, or betrayed, or in any way diminished....

He felt like an addict, trying to rationalize one fix, just one. What could one night hurt?

But like an addict, he wouldn't be able to stop with just one. The remaining sliver of honesty inside his hungry body knew that.

And yet…

Then, like a life raft floating by, he remembered the one reason he couldn't ignore. *Wouldn't* ignore.

"Ellen is just inside," he said.

Penny bit her lower lip. "Of course," she answered softly, obviously embarrassed. "I wasn't thinking."

She took the edges of the blanket and folded them across herself, so that she once again looked like a tired little girl.

"Besides…you know you would regret it," he said, unsure whether he was convincing her, or himself. See? He had already hurt her. She felt unwanted. He cursed himself and tried again.

"Penny, you're determined to prove something to yourself, and I respect that. More than you can possibly know. I don't want to get in the way. I don't want to be a mistake you regret whenever you remember me. I would like to think that, when I'm gone—"

"You're right." She broke in, as if she didn't want him to finish the sentence. As if the phrase, "when I'm gone" had somehow slapped her into clarity.

"I'm sorry," she said, her voice artificially chipper. "It's easy to lose track of common sense, when I'm only half-awake…in the middle of the night like this."

She turned back toward her kitchen door, moving in her moonlight cocoon of wool. At the last minute, she paused, looked over her shoulder at him and smiled. "Guess that's why they put all those infomercials for expensive Fountain of Youth exercise machines on at 3:00 a.m, huh?"

"Maybe." He gripped the railing hard. "But just for the record…"

He took a breath and somehow managed a smile of his own. "You probably should know I don't find you all that easy to resist in broad daylight, either."

CHAPTER TEN

THE DAY OF Bree's nuptials couldn't have been more perfect. By the time the sun began heading westward, turning Cupcake Creek amazing shades of violet and copper, Penny leaned against the garland-festooned trunk of a loblolly pine and watched the reception get underway with a sense of happy satisfaction.

The wedding itself had been simple, but heartbreakingly beautiful. Performed on the banks of Cupcake Creek, next to the "glamping" tent where Gray had lived when he first came to work for Bell River—and where he and Bree had fallen in love—the tone had been informal. And yet, somehow, the depth of love these two people felt for each other, and which came through in their personally written vows, had been absolutely magical.

"Glamorous camping" wasn't an exaggeration for this large, elegant tent, which overlooked the sweet creek, and was right now about to become the setting for the happiest feast and dance the world had ever seen, with Barton James and the Rockin' Geezers providing the music.

Penny sipped her champagne, savoring the lull in the excitement. It wouldn't be a long one. She could already hear the band tuning up for "Red River Valley," which would be the newly married couple's first dance.

"Congratulations, Penny. This has been a day your sister won't ever forget."

She turned, recognizing Max's voice, and her heart

leaped up in her chest. Silly to react so intensely, but she couldn't help it.

He'd arrived early to be sure Ellen was here on time, so he'd been around for hours. But Penny had been so busy she hadn't been able to do much more than exchange the most basic questions and answers—like, "Have you seen the preacher?" and, "Would you mind helping Mrs. Marvell find a seat?"

Now she registered once again how elegant he looked in his beautifully cut business suit. Most of the other men were wearing cowboy casual, which she liked just fine. But Max's crisp white dress shirt and blue rep tie were so…elegant.

And yet, beneath the elegance, lay those amazing abs, that muscled, tapering back. Aunt Ruth used to say "it's better to leave something to the imagination," but Penny had assumed she was, as usual, being a spinster prude.

Now Penny understood.

"You're not leaving already, are you?" She tried not to sound too upset. "No one should miss the Rockin' Geezers."

He looked toward the dance floor. Just a couple of hours ago, the bride and groom had stood on that spot, exchanged vows and rings and kisses. But now half a dozen couples already stood there, waiting for the Geezers to get the party started.

"I'm not sure I'd have the heart to drag Ellen away," he said with a smile.

Penny spotted the little girl in the crowd, clutching her garland headdress, and had to admit it would take a fairly hard heart to do that. Ellen was clearly having the time of her life.

Penny herself had taken the official preceremony photographs, but since Penny was one of the bridesmaids, Bree had hired Selena Sanchez from town to take the rest of the pictures

Selena was good, but she couldn't be everywhere. So disposable cameras had been provided at every table, encouraging the guests to take candid shots. Those had been a big hit, especially with Ellen and Alec, who were running around getting everyone to pose for them.

They were so adorable in their fancy clothes that no one could resist the request. Alec's yellow-aster boutonniere had long since come off and, no doubt, been trampled in the grass, but Ellen guarded her lovely blue-and-yellow wildflower crown as if it had been gilded with twenty-four-karat gold.

"She's been practicing the electric slide all week," Max said wryly. "Same song. Over and over. If they play 'Born to Boogie' tonight, I may start twitching."

Penny grinned. "I've been practicing all week, too. I haven't danced since I was her age, though, and I think I've already demonstrated what a klutz I am. I'm hoping I can check 'dancing' off the Risk-it List tonight, but we'll see."

Max chuckled, but he didn't contradict her. She liked that. He had already gone on record as saying she had some kind of inner block that kept her from expressing her physicality—not an actual lack of coordination. She'd recognized the logic of the theory, but she honestly couldn't think whose voice she might be hearing. Her dad was the most likely suspect, but he hadn't paid enough attention to any of them to care whether they were good at sports, or dancing. Or juggling.

Still, she liked that Max didn't intend to push his theory. Though he had every tool he needed to be domineering—brains, good looks, money, confidence, personal charisma—he clearly just wasn't the bullying type.

It was a virtue tailor-made to touch Penny—or any of

Johnny Wright's daughters—deep in the heart. Dangerously deep, in fact.

They stood in silence, watching as Bree and Gray took the floor for their dance. The delicate, poignant strains of Barton's fiddle floated in the air like a perfume, and mingled with the burble of the creek behind them. Other than that, the evening was full of a reverent silence.

Penny's eyes stung. Bree was always beautiful, so cool and pale and elegant. But tonight she was beyond description. She was as serene and composed as ever, but there was nothing icy about her. She glowed, as if she were a sunbeam that Gray had caught and danced across the floor in his arms.

As if she were entirely made of happiness and love.

Penny sent up a prayer of thanks to whatever fates controlled these things. *Thank you,* she said with her aching heart, *for making Bree whole again.*

When the dance was over, Penny took another sip of her champagne to cover her emotions. Everyone was laughing and spilling onto the floor to congratulate the couple and begin the dancing.

She saw Fanny Bronson, the bookstore owner, scan the crowd, obviously hunting for a dancing partner, and willed the woman to look anywhere but at Max. She didn't want him to leave her side. Not yet…

"How about you?" Somehow, Penny kept her voice casual. She realized she was twirling the ribbon streamers of her wildflower headpiece like a flirtatious teenager and forced herself to stop. "I don't guess big-deal architects in Chicago spend much time line dancing."

"I might surprise you," he said. "I'll bet I've been to more barn dances than you have, considering you came of dancing age as a San Francisco hermit. Before I was a Chicago architect, I was a Carolina farm boy."

She looked up at him, too surprised to pretend not to be. "You were?"

"I was. But when I mentioned that to Ellen, she nearly had a breakdown. I've been warned that I'm too old to line dance. Under no circumstances am I to attempt the Tush Push, or she'll fall right down and die."

Penny laughed. "I guess that means the Badonkadonk is off-limits, too?"

"She didn't specifically mention it, but I'm guessing yes. She might survive if I waltzed once or twice, maybe." He didn't seem terribly disappointed. "Are you still heading up command central, or could you maybe keep me company at the old folks' table?"

She felt her heart grow light. "I'm officially off duty, thank goodness. But the old folks' table sounds terrible. What if we take a short walk?"

He hesitated a second, then nodded.

In her long, ecru gown and silly heels, she knew she couldn't go far, but she could at least put a few yards between them and the crowd. She moved away from the creek, because everyone who wasn't dancing had congregated there, watching the sun set on the water. Instead, she led Max in the direction of the pine stand, where the shadows were long and cool and deep hunter-green.

"So," he said as they slowly made their way over the bumpy grass, "are you glad it's over?"

She nodded with feeling. "I'm glad it's *safely* over. None of the possible disasters occurred, so I can finally relax."

"I had no idea a wedding was so dangerous." He raised his eyebrows. "What disasters?"

Penny ticked them off on her fingers. "Let's see. Rain, cold, foraging bears. Lost rings, torn gowns, missing clergy. Bad food, burned food, dropped food. Jane Eyre–like last-minute objections to the union."

"Who on earth could have objected to this union? If ever a marriage seemed made in heaven…"

"Well, Bree's obnoxious ex-boyfriend, Charlie, could have shown up. He's apparently done it before, the sleazeball. That awful Esther Fillmore, the official Silverdell witch and part-time librarian, who thinks the Wright girls are the devil's spawn, could have crashed. She wasn't invited, but that wouldn't necessarily stop her."

"Sounds terrible," he said, obviously amused.

"She is. And…well, I guess the only other possible problem might have been old Grayson, Gray's cranky millionaire grandfather. He's not big on keeping his peace at the best of times. He thinks his money gives him carte blanche to be rude."

They'd reached the edge of the stand of trees, as well as the geographical limits of good manners. They were still in sight, but not quite within earshot. She leaned back against the smooth, papery bark of an aspen that was trying to hold its own among the larger pines. She gazed at the wedding scene, now at a discreet distance, like a pretty film they were watching.

There was Grayson, as if her comments had made him materialize. He was actually on the dance floor, cane and all, with his housekeeper at his side. Penny couldn't help smiling, thinking how transformed the old guy was. Just being near the kind of love Gray and Bree had was good for people, apparently.

"For a while there, old Grayson was adamantly against the relationship," she explained to Max. "He felt sure his playboy grandson would break Bree's heart."

"I wouldn't put any money on that bet." Max glanced down at Penny, his eyes tilted with a smile. "Would you? What does your crystal ball, the camera, say?"

She made a mock-offended huffing sound. "Look, Mr.

Thorpe, I know you think I'm crazy, but pictures really do show—"

"I don't think you're crazy." To her surprise, his eyes sobered, and his voice dropped out of the teasing register. "After we talked the other day, I went home and looked at some of my own wedding pictures. The signs were there. All the ones you mentioned. And then some."

She wasn't sure how to respond to that. He had never told her that his marriage hadn't been happy. He'd said only that his wife had died.

She ran her fingertips over the aspen bark, buying time. "But you and your wife didn't divorce."

"Only because she died—a freak thing, a brain aneurysm. I'd already retained a lawyer, and he was in the process of drawing up a settlement offer. If she'd lived, divorce was inevitable."

Why? That was the question Penny always wanted to ask couples like that. If the relationship had been wrong from the start, so wrong the truth seeped out through the wedding photographs, why had they married in the first place?

"Lydia was pregnant," he said, as if he'd read Penny's thoughts. But when she looked at him, she could tell he was merely following his own inner trail. And logic had led him there, to the heart of the labyrinth. *Why?* Why had he married a woman he didn't love?

"I was shocked to see how obvious it was, in the pictures, that we weren't in love. I was so determined to make it work, I think I had convinced myself that I did love her. I figured I must. What kind of man doesn't love the mother of his child?"

Penny could have answered that. *All kinds.* A million million men around the world faced this same dilemma. People couldn't summon love the way they'd summon a waiter, merely because it was time to pay the bill.

At least, she could have said, he didn't *kill* his unloved, unsatisfactory wife.

But what Max needed right now was someone who would listen to him while he asked himself these questions—not someone who would try to provide facile, simplistic answers.

"We limped along for several years. For Ellen's sake. But then—" his face changed suddenly "—some things happened, and I grew a lot less patient. I guess I just stopped trying. So Lydia found someone who *would* try. A couple of someones, actually. She was a very beautiful woman."

Of course she was. And Ellen would someday look just like her, no doubt. Penny wondered whether that affected Max's feelings toward his daughter. But then she remembered the misery on his face when Ellen had been crying over her impaled ear, and she was certain that it didn't.

She knew what it looked like when a man did not love his daughters. And she also knew what it looked like when a man *did,* if only the way she might recognize a positive by having seen its negative.

"When I discovered she was cheating, I wasn't even angry." He took a deep breath. "I thought she wanted out, and I was more relieved than anything else."

He paused. But Penny didn't speak, so he went on, as she'd hoped he would.

"She didn't want out, though. She'd only taken lovers because she thought that, if I got jealous enough, if I feared losing her, I might wake up and appreciate what I had."

Penny wanted to touch him, to offer just a simple gesture of understanding, but she didn't. She didn't want to risk closing off the flow of words.

He put his hands in his pockets. "I don't think Lydia ever accepted the truth. Right up to the very end, I think she clung to the hope that I'd change my mind."

He stared at the fairy lights and flower garlands in front of them. He was silent a long time. Then he turned to Penny, a half smile on his lips. "I'm not sure why I'm telling you all this."

She raised her shoulders. "Maybe because I didn't know her. It's easier to confess things to strangers."

His brow furrowed slightly. "Strangers?"

"Well, you know what I mean. People who aren't…aren't part of your normal life. You don't have to live with the consequences of what you tell them, because they're temporary—they're just…"

She flushed, remembering what he'd said the other night. He knew he would end up merely a memory for Penny, and his only concern was that he didn't want to be a *bad* memory. "They're just passing through. Or, in this case, you are."

He seemed to be studying her face, squinting, as if the shadows made reading it difficult.

"Maybe," he said finally. "Or maybe it's because you're easy to talk to. Because you listen without judging. Because you have a good moral compass and a kind heart."

She had to look away. The intensity of his gaze on her skin was almost like a physical burn. "I don't think very many people would judge you harshly, Max. It's a sad story, but it is also sadly common."

As she stared toward the dance floor, she caught another glimpse of Ellen. She and Alec were working hard at their beginner's version of the electric slide, but they kept bumping into each other and then collapsing into laughter.

"Does Ellen know? That you and her mom were probably going to split up?"

He shook his head. He had followed her gaze and was watching his daughter, too. "We decided it would be better not to tell her, and then, after Lydia died, there didn't seem to be any point."

Penny still knew it was probably best if she didn't volunteer anything. She didn't know Lydia—and what she knew of Max was too isolated, too separate from his normal life, to be considered a true picture.

But she did know something about children who were frightened and hopelessly confused.

"I think you ought to consider telling her," she said. "Kids always know when something is wrong. They know if something, or someone, in the family is on the verge of collapse. But if no one will tell them exactly what the problem is, then they fear everything. There's no safe harbor. No load-bearing wall can be trusted to protect you from the disaster you know is coming."

She realized that, halfway through that speech, she had switched from *they* to *you*. If she'd gone on another sentence or two, she would have been saying *I* and *me*.

But she didn't really care. At the very least, he already knew the basic facts of her family's history, because she, herself, had told him. At worst, he'd get an earful from awful Esther Fillmore.

Heck, even Millicent Starling could have provided some of the juicier details.

The gossips especially loved the bit about how Penny had attended her mother's funeral in her blue party dress that was still stained with her mother's blood.

"And you have no idea what other people might have said to her already." Penny wished she could make him see how likely this scenario actually was. One of Ellen's friends had probably spotted her mom with another man, or heard gossip that Max always took the long way home.

"One day, at school," she said, "a friend of mine called me an 'accident' baby, because I was so much younger than

Rowena and Bree. So I came home and asked our house-keeper if that was true."

He was watching her carefully. "What did she say?"

"She laughed so hard she almost dropped the cake batter she was stirring. She told me I wasn't an accident baby at all. Instead, I was what she liked to call a 'padlock baby.' I was the padlock on the stable door that made sure the frisky filly didn't get away."

"Good God." He frowned, hard. "I hope your parents fired her."

"They didn't know." She put her hand on his arm gently. "That's my point, Max. You won't know, because she won't tell you. If you want to make sure she understands, you'll have to tell her yourself."

ELLEN WAS HAVING so much fun she felt like crying when Dad said it was time to go home. She loved it here. She loved the creek in the moonlight, the old guys playing cow-boy music, all the people line dancing and laughing and acting like idiots.

She only calmed down when Alec reminded her that she would be coming back for camp next week, and then for the "camp-in," a sleepover for all the Bell River day camp kids that they held in the big barn. Her dad had actually agreed to it—without any fuss at all.

That was probably because Rowena had asked him. He liked Rowena, she could tell. Rowena had explained that there would be story time and art and games and the Gee-zers were coming to do a talent contest.

It was going to be awesome, and with that ahead of her, she was willing to leave without complaining.

She had thought about taking some pictures of the wed-ding and putting them on Facebook so that Stephanie and

Becky and everybody back in Chicago could see how cool it was in Colorado.

But she never got around to it. People had always been coming up, asking her for something, as if she were part of the family, as if they really needed her. They asked her to dance with old Mr. Harper, who shocked her by being awesome, in spite of the cane. They asked her to get some coffee from the tent for the lady who had started crying because the flowers were so beautiful. They asked her to talk Alec into singing "Red River Valley" with the Geezers. Dallas, Gray, old Mr. Harper and at least two of the boys from day camp had all asked her to dance slow dances.

Even Dad danced with her. He was a pretty good dancer, too. And of course, she and Alec got up for every single line dance, but that wasn't like a couples thing, so it didn't mean anything. He was too young to dance with, like that, and besides he kind of felt like a brother.

"Penny is a really good dancer, isn't she?"

She and her dad were driving home. They were about halfway there, and she'd started to get sleepy. She had her eyes shut, and her head was resting against the window. She almost felt as if she were talking to herself.

But her dad clearly heard her.

"Yeah." He sounded surprised, almost as surprised as Ellen had been. She'd never seen Penny dance even once, and yet their landlady was clearly the best dancer in the room.

"I could hardly stop watching her," Ellen admitted. She probably wouldn't have said it, except that she was tired and so strangely happy. "Her bridesmaid's dress was pretty. And she doesn't really look exactly like anybody else, does she?"

Her dad hesitated a minute. "No," he said, finally. "She doesn't."

"But it's more than that." Ellen tried to think it through.

"She's not show-offy when she dances, but it's like…it is like she dances the way she paints."

Though her eyes were still closed, she heard Dad turn toward her. "What do you mean?" he asked.

"I'm not sure." Ellen wondered if this would make sense to anyone who didn't paint. He just drew blueprints, which were different, all hard lines and no color or swooshing. "It's like…like she's really paying attention to what's beautiful about music, and what's beautiful about people dancing."

Her father was quite a minute.

"Yes," he said, then. "That's a good way to put it."

Penny's dancing had been so special, in fact, that Ellen had secretly begun trying to imitate it.

But she didn't want to tell her dad that part.

Penny's dancing had been really feminine, but not in a fake or trashy way. Her mom had been feminine; Ellen had always known that. When Lydia Thorpe walked down the street, men turned around to stare at her, and they didn't even try to hide it. But there was something about their stares… They always made Ellen uncomfortable, as if they were thinking things they shouldn't be thinking about somebody's mom. Behind their eyes, their thoughts looked hot and dirty.

Men looked at Penny, too. But they didn't look hot or dirty when they did it. They looked the way puppies looked when they watched their owners drive up, and they sat at attention, tails thumping on the ground in excitement. Or else they looked kind of happy-stunned, like maybe they'd just seen a fairy, or a ghost, or something else they'd only read about in books.

Only a few of the men who watched Penny didn't look happy. They just looked quietly sad, as if she made them homesick. As if she made them think about something that was gone forever, but they were still glad for the chance to think about it.

She felt herself drifting toward sleep. She couldn't remember quite how she'd gotten on to this subject...

Oh, yeah. The Facebook pictures. The ones still locked in her camera. With one thing and another, she'd never gotten around to posting any pictures.

And suddenly she realized that was probably a very good thing.

Stephanie wouldn't think a bunch of old cowboys line dancing outside under a string of lights and a garland of wildflowers looked like fun at all.

"Oh, well," Ellen said, yawning as she opened her eyes heavily, and briefly glimpsed the moonlight pouring by in creamy white streams. "That just shows how stupid Stephanie is."

"What?" Her dad glanced over toward her side of the car.

She smiled and shut her eyes again. "Nothing."

CHAPTER ELEVEN

THE THURSDAY AFTER the wedding, Barton James pulled up in front of a tattoo parlor. He scowled at the storefront, then transferred his scowl to Penny. Though it was only three in the afternoon, on a beautiful fall day in a safe little city like Silverdell, he obviously didn't approve.

"You sure you don't want me to wait for you?"

"I'll be fine," Penny said. "I could walk home, if I had to. It isn't two miles back to the duplex."

The tattoo studio was on the far side of Elk Avenue, but in a town the size of Silverdell nothing was very far from anything else. She was telling the literal truth. If her car wasn't out of the mechanic's by the time she needed to leave, she really could walk home.

It wasn't as if getting a tattoo left you laid up, like getting your appendix removed.

She patted his shoulder and opened her car door.

"Well, *I* think I should wait," he grumbled. "You know what kind of people hang out in places like that."

Penny laughed. "People like me?"

"No." He lowered his tangled white eyebrows over his sharp blue eyes. "You don't *hang out* in places like that. You may go in there, this one time, but that's not the same thing. No sir. Whatever bumblebee has itself stuck under your saddle, I have no idea. But I'd be willing to bet you haven't talked to Rowena about this. Or Bree, for that matter."

There wasn't much he could have said that would have

been as irritating as that particular comment. She got out, shut the door behind her, then leaned in through his open window, giving him a scowl that was every bit the match of the one he'd given her.

"I don't need my sisters' permission to get a tattoo. I'm twenty-seven. I can get drunk, join the Blue Angels and have 'Johnny Depp' tattooed on my rear end if I want to, and neither Ro nor Bree has anything to say in the matter."

He grinned, though he tried to bite it back by chewing on the inside of his cheek. "Nobody said anything about getting permission, Spitfire. You go to your family to talk things over because nobody's head is right every single time. Now and then, you've got mud in your eyes, and you need somebody else to help you see what's what."

Yeah, Barton James was the best. She knew he had called her *Spitfire* the way people called a shy girl *Chatty* or a giant man *Tiny,* but she liked the sound of it anyhow. Maybe that's what she'd ask the guy to give her—a tattoo that said *Spitfire.*

"I know what's what." She touched her purse with a smile. "I've got a numbered list of what's what."

"Whatever that means." Though he rolled his eyes, he moved the gearshift to Drive. "But I've said my piece. My momma always told me, say what you've gotta say, but then let it be. Cornering ain't the same as convincing."

"Smart lady, your mom." Penny extended her arm a little farther and wiggled her fingers, indicating that she wanted a goodbye hug.

He took her hand. "Oh, well. At least get a good one. No Johnny Depp. I'm begging you, Spitfire. No Johnny Depp."

She shook her head, gave him one last squeeze, then pulled her hand back. "Bye, Barton."

As he drove away, she turned toward the tattoo studio. It definitely wasn't trying to blend in. Its signage was all yellow letters on red background, big letters in some font she subliminally associated with the circus. Needles 'N' Pins, it said, and under that, in the same font, only slightly smaller, Art Tattoos and Body Piercing.

You couldn't see into the shop. Every inch of the plate-glass windows was covered with examples of the artist's work. Mermaids, guns, barbells, hearts, American flags, dragons, Celtic knots, fairies, about fifty different scripts of the word *Mom*. She moved to the window to the right of the door.

She wondered how they managed to make the tattoo look exactly like these samples. Did it matter whether the artist was…well, an artist? Did tattoos ever go horribly wrong? She was pretty sure she'd heard of misspelled words. And then, of course, there was the dreaded "I thought I'd love you forever, but it's only been six months, and already I hate you" problem.

Her stomach fluttered, and she realized that she probably should have done some more research. She hadn't, because every time she did an internet search on the word *tattoo* the pictures scared her to death. People lying on their stomachs while being drawn on with needles by men who appeared to be wearing elbow gloves made of starbursts and skulls with rainbows and roses growing out of the eyeholes.

But she probably should at least have looked into which of the employees here was the best. And when he would be on duty.

She walked on beyond the studio, trying to get her stomach to settle down before she went in. This stupid fear— this was why she *had* to go through with it. If she was ever going to master her fears, she had to start somewhere.

Easier to start here, than, for instance, on the white-water rafting trip, where every minute would feel like imminent death by drowning.

Or in the front foyer of her childhood home. Or at her father's graveside.

She had almost reached the ice-cream shop when she squared her shoulders and turned around.

She retraced her steps. Bookstore, diner, drug store, ski shop. Tattoo studio. But she kept going, down the other end, the less chi-chi end. Payday loan, dollar store, thrift store, do-it-yourself pest control. U-turn, and back again.

Maybe she should just quickly stop in at the bookstore and see if there were any books about tattoos. There might be a checklist, things to watch out for.

She probably would run into someone she knew. At least Fanny Bronson, who had taken over for her father some years ago. Penny liked the woman, who was Rowena's age, just a few years older than Penny herself. Fanny was a little odd, but smart. She had to be, in this new world of digital book-buying, to continue to defy the odds and make a profit.

But she also had discretion. She probably had guessed a thousand Dellian secrets, based on who ordered a copy of *Bankruptcy Law* and who spent hours in the self-help section, then purchased *Winning Back Your Wife*. But she'd never been known as a gossip.

So she wasn't likely to broadcast that Penny Wright had been leafing through a book about tattoos. Not that it mattered, Penny told herself sternly as she pushed open the door and marched in. She was getting a tattoo, for pity's sake, not robbing a bank.

As it turned out, Fanny wasn't even there. But Max was.

He stood in the children's section with a large stack of books under his arm. Penny tilted her head to catch a glimpse of the titles. Art books. How-tos as well as big, colorful coffee table volumes on Monet, Renoir, Sargent, Picasso. The expensive kind with gorgeous color plates.

The sight made her feel warm inside. What a super dad he was! She remembered asking her own father for a sketchbook once. He had swiveled his desk chair, reached across his ledgers and handed her a stack of printer paper.

She wondered if Ellen had any idea how lucky she was. Probably not. And maybe that was as it should be. Maybe a little girl should be able to take her father's love for granted.

"Hi, Max," she said, quietly enough that she didn't draw a lot of attention from the other customers. Bronson's Books had been a fixture on Elk Avenue for three generations, and people tended to hang out there whenever they had time to kill. Waiting for car repairs, as Penny was. When their table at Donovan's wasn't quite ready. While a spouse played around at Miller's Hardware.

Today, there were at least half a dozen customers in the store. Max was the only one in the children's section, though.

"Hi, there," he said, looking pleased to see her. They had both studiously avoided the back deck, especially at night, so in spite of the fact that they technically lived under the same roof they hardly ever met. "Everyone at the ranch recovered from the wedding?"

"Absolutely. Actually, we're a bit bored without all the excitement."

"How are the newlyweds?"

She grinned. "Disgustingly blissful. It really shows you why people take honeymoons. It's not for the married couple. It's to spare everyone else the embarrassment of watching them drool all over each other."

In the week since the wedding, the drooling showed no signs of abating. Bree and Gray's honeymoon had to be put off because he had a prize mare within a few days of foaling, but they didn't seem to mind a bit. In fact, Penny wasn't sure they'd even noticed.

They'd more or less been holed up in the cute little three-room apartment he'd built at the new Gray Stables facility, emerging every now and then, with swollen lips and glazed eyes, to check on the horses, or to go out for Chinese.

Gray's horse-breeding business was on Bell River land, technically. They'd given him a ninety-nine year lease for a hundred acres out on the western slope. Rowena and Penny had agreed to rent it for a song, because when he fell in love with Bree, he knew that meant he'd have to relocate here, instead of taking her to his ranch in California.

She'd only just found her way home, to Silverdell, to Rowena, and to making peace with her past. Gray saw that he couldn't ask her to pull up roots, even for him. So he'd done the pulling, and started over with her.

Which was one of the reasons their love qualified as a mini-miracle. How many men would be willing to do all that?

They'd build a bigger house someday, Bree said, but right now they were happy to live in each other's pockets, hardly able to move around the little apartment, which would someday belong to the stable manager, without bumping into each other. But bumping into each other was their favorite thing, and apparently it was making quite a honeymoon. Penny and Rowena teased Bree mercilessly, but she knew how they really felt.

"I'm getting some art stuff for Ellen." Max patted the stack of books under his arm. "And she asked me to pick up some books for Bell River's story time day. Apparently there's some kind of tradition?"

Penny laughed. "I'm not sure the ranch has been open long enough for anything to qualify as a tradition, exactly, but yes. Several of the families who stayed there this last year decided to buy books for story time. The kids love the program, so when they go home they leave behind copies of their favorite books, with notes inside, explaining why the book is so wonderful."

"Ellen has *fifteen* favorite books, apparently, from *A Little Princess* to…oh, that reminds me. Do you have a problem with vampire cheerleaders?"

"Nope." Penny grinned. "The kids love *Vampire High*. Bring it on." She touched the spine of the Sargent book. "Mind if I play with these while you shop? They look so gorgeous my mouth is watering."

He started to hold them out to her, but decided instead to set them down on the stairs that led to the Cozy Corner. Penny dropped down beside the luscious stack of books and opened the top one eagerly. Beautiful, intelligent-eyed women stared at her, their satin and lace and velvets glowing, so real it was hard to believe she couldn't reach in and touch them.

After a few minutes, Max sat down on the other side of the stack, a smaller pile of novels in his lap. He watched as she ran her fingers reverently across the plates, one after another.

She looked up, smiling sheepishly. "Sorry. He's a favorite of mine, and this is such a beautiful volume."

"I'm not complaining. I'm enjoying. Ellen has that same look when she's painting. Or even talking about art. I'm never going to be able to thank you, or the people out at Bell River, adequately for helping her find that passion."

She shrugged lightly. "She would have come to it on her own, eventually. The harder thing would have been to prevent her from finding it."

"Maybe. But finding it right now was a real gift." He leaned back against the pillar behind them, which was covered in Tigger-colored fur. "So what brought you to town? Surely you didn't know I'd be here, holding the perfect book of Sargent prints."

"No. I was just…" She glanced around the bookstore. The cashier had earbuds in, and, judging by his drumming hands, was listening to hard rock. None of the other customers was close enough to be listening.

"I'm downtown because it's tattoo time." She tried to sound enthusiastic, but it came out almost a question. It's tattoo time? Like a kid asking if it's really time to get the tetanus booster, or take the dreaded math exam.

"Yeah? This makes number seven, right? Moving through that list like a buzz saw." He smiled. "And yet… somehow I'm not getting that *thrilled* vibe."

"No." She had to laugh. He could read her too well. "I'm nervous, naturally."

"Do you want some company? Not that I'm getting a tattoo, you understand. I just mean…for moral support."

She would love that, actually. It would change the experience entirely, to have him by her side.

But it would also negate the value.

"It would be heavenly to have you there," she said honestly. "But then *you'd* be conquering my fear, not me. I'm actually far more frightened of the rafting than I am of the tattoo. So if I can't do this…"

He put one knee up and draped his hand over it, getting comfortable. "Wasn't dancing on the list? You didn't seem afraid of that the other night. In fact, your Casanova Cowboy is so good I'm calling foul on the whole 'I'm uncoordinated' excuse."

"I'm pretty sure that was just the champagne," she said, wondering whether her moves had maybe been a little too uninhibited. Several people had remarked that she seemed to have a flair for dancing, especially for someone who supposedly had been a virtual recluse since she was eleven.

At least she knew it wasn't totally awkward or unattractive, because she'd seen Max watching her. And his eyes…

"So champagne is the key to shutting up the little voice that says you can't do physical things?" He looked intrigued, his eyes alert and interested.

"Maybe. It seems counterintuitive, but apparently I'm not as clumsy when I'm tipsy."

"Okay, then, how about maybe adding a little champagne to the juggling practice sessions?"

"I already did," she said ruefully. "When I got home that night, I gave myself a juggling lesson."

"And?"

"And I was still terrible. Liquor doesn't seem to be the answer. I'm not sure there is an answer."

His smile spread slowly. "Oops. Well…is the Risk-it List open for revision, if it becomes necessary?"

She bit her lip. It was a question she'd been asking herself for the past half an hour, as her anxiety about getting a tattoo grew to ridiculous proportions.

"I don't know. I hate the thought that I might give up too soon, instead of pushing through. Once you start saying you *can't,* where does it end?"

"Maybe it ends in self-awareness." He clearly wasn't teasing anymore. "Some limitations are self-imposed, obviously. But there are going to be at least a few things you really *can't* do." He lifted one eyebrow. "I can't be Sargent, for instance. Or Baryshnikov."

She smiled.

"And, similarly," he continued, "there are some things you are afraid to do—not because you're a coward, but because they really are mistakes. Sometimes fear is your subconscious trying to warn you away from trouble."

"But how can you learn the difference between the two?"

"I don't know. It takes a long time, I think." When he spoke this time, his mouth was a flat line. For whatever reason, he was deadly serious about this.

"A couple of years ago, when I was on a business trip in Mexico, I had a gut feeling that something wasn't right. I was nervous about a certain place, a certain person. But I told myself it was ridiculous. I hated the idea that I might be giving in to some irrational fear."

"And were you?"

"No. My subconscious was right. I shouldn't have gone. If I'd listened to my gut…"

He trailed off. "Well, it doesn't matter, really. I should let you get back to your day."

He stood, brushing Tigger fur from his jacket with one hand, holding the books with the other. "I'm just saying that maybe, if you're not comfortable with a plan, it's not because there's something wrong with you. Sometimes there's something wrong with the plan."

IRONIC, MAX THOUGHT, that the occasion of Bree and Gray's wedding had provided him so much more happiness than his own ever had. But the evening at Cupcake Creek had been joyous, and the week since had been pretty good, too.

At the reception, Penny's companionship and conversation had been deeply satisfying, in an easy way that amazingly wasn't all tangled up every single second with thoughts of making love to her.

Even more important, he'd spent a truly pleasant evening in his daughter's company.

She was back—the real Ellen, the one who had once laughed when he called her Bubbles, and embraced the world with so much happy passion.

At the reception, Ellen had stood on his shoes and laughed in his arms as they danced. She'd bustled around the party, eager to be of use. She'd tended old ladies and old men like a princess, and then she'd bopped and wiggled on the dance floor with Alec like a barefoot urchin.

It was brief, but it was beautiful.

So it was doubly hard to even consider broaching the conversation that he feared might send her scuttling back into her sullen shell. He'd put it off for a week now.

He dreaded the thought that he might lose his daughter all over again. But after seeing Penny at the bookstore, he recognized that he was being a coward.

If Penny could tackle her fears, surely he could do the same.

His chest tightened, just thinking about it. *Damn it, fatherhood was hard.* But Ellen wasn't a baby. She had undoubtedly picked up confusing signals through the years of her parents' troubled marriage. She had probably been trying to process those signals, and arrived at half-truths, or completely unfair self-blame.

So it didn't matter how much Max dreaded the talk, or how hopelessly inadequate he felt to find the right words. She deserved the truth. Even if it hurt. Confusion and self-blame hurt, too. In the end, she was strong enough to deal with it.

And so was he.

Just after lunch, his arms full of the books she'd asked for, he knocked on her door. Technically, he hadn't needed to knock, because, for once, she hadn't shut the door. She'd left it ajar as she sat on the bed, cross-legged, drawing in her sketchbook.

"Come on in," she said absently, as though that were routine. As though she hadn't slammed that same door in his face every night for almost a month now, up until this past week.

"Hey," he said, pausing just over the threshold. He aimed for as normal a tone as possible. If she assumed they were friends, he would do the same. "I brought the books. And… are you busy? I'd like to talk a little, if it's a good time."

She closed her sketchbook, but it wasn't a rude gesture. More protective than anything, as if she weren't sure the drawing was ready to be viewed by any eyes but her own. She kept her purple watercolor pencil in her hand, as if to say she'd need to get back to drawing in a minute.

The same way he went into a meeting with his secretary primed to buzz him if it ran too long and he needed an out. He smiled at the universal instinct to preserve options.

"I'm not busy," she said. Her voice had acquired a thin thread of wariness, but she seemed receptive. "I'm just fiddling around. What's up?"

"I just hoped we could talk," he said. He set the books down on her nightstand, but she didn't turn to look.

Instead, her spine straightened slightly. "Talk about what?"

"Us," he said. He'd already decided there was nothing to be gained by beating around the bush. She was smart. She'd see any serpentine segue coming a mile off.

"I guess…Mom, mostly. The anniversary of the day we lost her is just a few days away. I wondered if there was anything special you'd like to do."

Her brows drew down. It was like watching a thundercloud overtake a blue sky, inch by inch. He wanted to throw out his arms and hold back the rain.

"I would have liked to visit her grave." She shrugged tensely. "But she doesn't *have* one."

They'd been over this before, so he knew how tender a spot it was.

"That was Mom's decision, remember. She had it specifically spelled out in her will. She wanted to be cremated. Even if we don't like it, we couldn't let what we wanted be more important than what she wanted."

Ellen's scowl deepened, but he recognized that for what

it was—an attempt to hold back tears. Not true rage. Not yet, anyhow.

"Yeah. I guess." Ellen rolled the watercolor pencil through her fingers. "Whatever."

Okay. "I also wondered whether there were any questions you would like to ask me. About Mom, or the way things were between us when she died. Or…" But why suggest topics? "About anything, really."

Ellen ruffled the pages of her sketchbook. "No. Not really."

"There's *nothing* you'd like to talk about? Nothing that… confused you or upset you?"

"No."

"What about the time I was gone, then? The months I was in Mexico. Would you like to talk about that?"

"No."

God. She sure wasn't going to make this easy, was she? Or maybe he just was awful at encouraging intimate dialogue. Lydia had certainly thought so.

The truth was, in his heart of hearts he had desperately hoped Ellen wouldn't want to ask much about Mexico. Even Lydia was easier to discuss than that.

Squaring his shoulders and girding his will, he came in and sat on the edge of the bed.

"Nothing? That doesn't really seem possible," he prodded gently. "For instance, I know you must have noticed that Mom and I were fighting a lot."

"*She* was fighting," Ellen said, glancing up briefly, her eyes as cold as marbles. "You weren't really there. You didn't *care* enough to fight."

A streak of heat moved through his chest. For a moment, he heard her mother's voice in those words. "Goddamn it, Max," Lydia had cried, night after night. "Where *are* you? You don't even *care* enough to fight!"

He was taken aback, in spite of how prepared he thought he'd been for any anger. When had she heard these words, in that exact tone? Had Lydia repeated her complaints when they were alone, seeking a sympathetic ear in her daughter?

Or had Ellen overheard the words, listening through the walls in the middle of some sleepless night, as Lydia hurled them at her cold, unreachable husband?

"I cared," he said, keeping his voice and face steady. "But just not the way she wanted me to. It was very frustrating for your mother, having a man like me for a husband. I'm too repressed, not open enough with my emotions— especially after Mexico. We weren't interested in very many of the same things. Again, that was worse after Mexico. Some experiences change your perspective on everything."

But that wasn't fair. He hadn't been happy in his marriage, hadn't been interested in Lydia's clothes and gossip and parties, since long before Mexico.

"Plus, your mom and I married very young. People change as they grow up. Over the years we'd both changed a lot."

"You weren't *very young*." Ellen sounded disdainful, also an echo of her mother. "You were twenty-four. People have families, and go to war and die, and become senators, and everything, by the time they're twenty-four."

More Lydia, like a parrot mimicking the sounds it heard. When he had pleaded with Lydia to accept that they'd married too young, she'd countered with exactly those arguments.

"God, Max," she'd said caustically. "That's such a copout. You were twenty-four. Bill Gates founded Microsoft at *twenty*."

Or Steve Jobs started Apple. Or Orson Welles directed *Citizen Kane*. It was always some example that proved twenty-four wasn't so very young. He sometimes wondered whether she looked up examples on the internet, so she'd have new ones to toss at him. As if this were a debate she could win on merits. For someone who professed herself emotional, as opposed to the frigid automaton she'd married, she certainly had been clueless about whether you could debate someone into loving you.

It had been horrible, having the same pointless arguments over and over. They never made progress, because she wouldn't ever agree there was a problem. Not even when she confessed her affairs. She'd felt so justified, as if his emotional inaccessibility after the Mexico ordeal had left her no choice.

Maybe it hadn't.

"Being grown-up isn't simply a matter of age," he explained to Ellen now, trying to set his resentment aside. Maybe he could succeed with his daughter, where he'd failed with his wife. "I wasn't very mature for twenty-four."

In fact, he'd been a raging, overconfident jerk. Just out of grad school, cocky, holding the world carelessly by a string, poised to rise like a meteor above his farm-boy roots.

Bewitched by Lydia's pretty face, bedroom eyes and incredible body. Unaccustomed, in those years, to denying himself anything.

And so sure, so stupidly certain that he was marked for greatness. He had honestly believed that the little matter of a missing condom wouldn't be a problem.

Fate intended him to be a famous architect. A star. No way one quickie was going to derail plans like those. He knew other methods. He'd been careful. *Ha!*

"So what does that mean?" Ellen jutted her chin out. "You like…outgrew her? When you finally got mature, you didn't want to be married anymore?"

Ellen scowled, but her voice had a suspicious tremor, and

she plucked compulsively at her book. "You didn't want to be a *father* anymore, either?"

"No!" Instinctively, he reached out, as if to hug away the very thought. But she flinched, backing up against the headboard. She picked up her sketchbook and pressed it to her collarbone like a shield.

He let his hands fall.

"No," he repeated calmly, though his heart pounded hard against his rib cage. "I never, ever didn't want to be a father. Having you was the best thing that ever happened to me. And to your mom. We didn't agree on very many things, but we always agreed on that."

She narrowed her eyes. "That's not what *she* said."

Oh, Lydia. For a minute, he felt helpless, defeated by the unretractable words of a dead woman.

Lydia, you short-sighted fool.

Deep in his heart, he'd always feared this. He hadn't been able to imagine what else could account for Ellen's intense antagonism. Sure, he could have been a better father, but he hadn't exactly been a demon, either. Yeah, he was gone a lot. But lots of fathers were. Lots of mothers were, too, for that matter. Families did what they had to do.

But he'd always assured himself that Lydia wouldn't poison his daughter against him. She wouldn't fill Ellen's heart with ugly lies when they were alone—not while he was in Mexico, praying just to stay alive. Praying to get home to his little girl.

He took a deep breath, appalled to realize that it shook. "What did Mom say?"

"She said you wished you could just walk out, but you couldn't, because of me. She said you wished I hadn't ever been born."

Dear God. It was all he could do not to release his anger

in some kind of physical movement, or verbal outburst. If Lydia had been here, he had no idea what he'd say to her.

But she wasn't here. And that was, of course, the whole point.

Lydia had died without warning, without time to set anything right—without time to tell Ellen the truth. Surely, if Lydia had known she would have to leave Ellen motherless, with only Max's love to sustain her, she would have retracted her lies.

"Listen to me, Ellen. It's important that you hear this. I've loved you from the first moment I set eyes on you, and every moment since. Whether I was here or away. Whether you wanted me to or not. I have always, always loved you. And your mother never doubted that for an instant."

"Are you calling her a liar?"

"I'm saying she was wrong to tell you that. She knew it wasn't true."

"That means liar." Ellen's hostile eyes glistened. "Why would she have lied to me?"

"Because she was angry with me. Because in a very irrational way, it made her feel better to say bad things about me, and to make you mad at me, too."

The frown was back. But so was a hint of uncertainty. "That's ridiculous."

"Is it?" He searched for an eleven-year-old's corollary. "Haven't you ever done anything like that? What if…what if Stephanie hurt your feelings? What if she wouldn't let you in her group? You might say bad things about her behind her back, just because you felt so crummy. You might even be glad if you could make other people dislike her."

Ellen pursed her lips, but she wouldn't look at him. "No, I wouldn't."

He let the denial fall on silence. He could tell that,

with some small part of her heart, she knew what he said was true.

When he spoke again, he didn't return to that. He could feel Ellen closing off, and he knew he didn't have much time to make his point.

"Look. Your mom isn't here to explain, or to admit why she said what she said. But I am here, and the only thing I need you to hear is this. I love you."

Ellen bent her head to her chest and shut her eyes.

"I love you," he repeated. "And your mother loved you, too. We had a lot of problems. We weren't really good for each other, and our marriage wasn't very happy. But that wasn't your fault. You were the best thing our marriage ever created. Not one single bit of the trouble was your fault."

Ellen's eyes opened, but they remained focused on the sketchbook, and her chin dug deeper into her collarbone. She mumbled something inarticulate.

"I couldn't hear that," he said mildly. "What did you say?"

"I said I *know*."

In spite of her tone, hope rose in his chest. If she could see that she wasn't to blame, maybe she could let go of the anger. Not today, maybe, but someday. If she could even entertain the idea that her mother might, just might, have been wrong…

He waited, hoping for more. "You know?"

"Yeah." Finally, she raised her gaze to his. Her mouth was set. Her blue eyes, the spitting image of her mother, glittered with hot tears.

"Of course I know it wasn't my fault," she repeated, her voice cold, a disturbing contrast to those scalded eyes. "How could it be? It was *yours*."

CHAPTER TWELVE

THAT SATURDAY NIGHT, the night of the Bell River sleepover, was stormy. The rain was a torrential, tree-thrashing battle to the death in the heavens, ripping the sky open every few seconds with swords of lightning.

It had been raining when Max fell asleep on the sofa of his duplex, which felt oddly empty with Ellen gone.

When he woke up, he was in the basement.

And he was screaming.

Recovery from the dream always followed the same pattern. The first thing he had to do was sit up, because he felt as if his lungs were collapsing. When he was upright, the pressure slowly eased, and he knew he wouldn't suffocate.

Over the next several seconds, sometimes minutes, he identified where he really was. He pinpointed whatever sound had triggered the dream—a car backfiring, a television shoot-out, something heavy dropped in the next room. In this case, thunder.

Gradually, his head cleared, and his heart slowed.

And, eventually, life went on.

But tonight he couldn't get his heart to settle down, no matter what he did. It was like being in a car with no brakes, racing downhill. He stood. He turned on every light in the house. He walked around the duplex. He drank a glass of water. He checked his phone, to be sure Ellen hadn't called, to assure himself that, though she wasn't in the house with him for the first time in a year, and she'd left on bad terms, she really was all right.

But nothing helped. He couldn't slow his heart. He couldn't get the smell of oil out of his nose. He couldn't get enough air...there simply wasn't enough air in the entire world....

He didn't know whether he would have a heart attack or go mad, but he knew he couldn't stand it another minute.

He grabbed a T-shirt, dragged it over his head and down his damp chest and went out the front door. The rain pummeled him, and a bolt of lightning streaked jaggedly across the black sky. But he didn't give a damn. He quickly loped down the steps to the small plot of front yard, crossed over, his bare feet sinking into the sodden grass and his hair dripping into his eyes, and climbed up to Penny's porch.

The rain, driven sideways by a crazed wind, still beat against his back angrily. He knocked on her door, belatedly trying to read his watch. Was it too late to bother anyone?

But he couldn't read the glowing blue numbers. It could have said 7:31, or 2:27, or 4:59. It was as indistinguishable as if the rain had been made of acid and the display had melted away.

It didn't matter anyhow. He needed her. He knocked again. He would have prayed for her to answer, but he didn't pray anymore. Not since Mexico.

It probably was only seconds before he heard her turning the knob and opening the door, but it felt like hours. He put his hands on the doorframe, just so that he wouldn't put them on the door itself, and push his way in like the wounded animal he was right now.

Her face was a pale oval in the wet light. "Max?"

"May I come in?" He'd chosen those words carefully, in the hours...seconds...he'd stood here waiting. He didn't want to sound as crazed as he felt. "Penny.

Please." Water sluiced off his lips when he formed words. "May I come in?"

"Are you all right?" She didn't answer him with a yes or a no. She just flung the door open and gathered him into her arms, apparently not caring that he tracked mud and grass and puddles of rain into her pristine and lovely living room.

The rain raged behind him, slanting in, but she shut the door. Instantly, the noise in his ears diminished. The room smelled of violets and clean sheets. The smell of dusty gas and oil began to clear out of his nostrils.

"Come," she said. Keeping her arm around his back, she led him into her bedroom.

"Take those wet things off." She turned toward the bathroom, which was lit by a pinprick of honey light—a night-light, a candle, a flicker of warmth and hope. Light was good.

He'd flicked on every fixture in his house, and it hadn't helped. But here, one tiny night-light was enough to poke the first hole in the darkness inside him.

He heard the sound of a cabinet door shutting, and suddenly she was back, silhouetted against the dimly lit rectangle. She held a stack of towels.

"Take those off, Max," she said again, softly. But he couldn't. He couldn't. She was too beautiful, and he was too weak. He could feel his body responding to her, in spite of the fact that his heart still raced, and his head still spun. He hardly knew who he was, or where he was. He could hardly even see her in the darkness, but he knew he wanted her.

"It's okay," she said. She came closer and smiled, a small gleam against the watery darkness. "We just have to get you warm and dry."

When he didn't move, she came closer still. His heart went crazy.

She tugged at his shirt, pulling it halfway up his chest.

When he felt its dull prodding at the underside of his arms, he lifted them, like a child, and let her tug the soaked cotton over his head.

She handed him one of the towels. He put it to his face, then ran it hard over his hair. At the same time, she took another, shook it open and scrubbed his chest, his shoulders, his neck. Whenever she moved across his heart, he registered her touch as if it were made of fire.

He grabbed her hand and stilled it there, right over the thudding. He pressed it hard against his skin, pushing the soft terry like a tourniquet, as if maybe it could close off the flood of blood that coursed through his veins, forcing his heart to keep this frantic pace.

"You need to get those pants off." She held out the last towel. "Do you want to go into the bathroom and maybe just put the towel on instead? I don't think I have any clothes that would fit, but—"

"Penny." He kept her hand against his heart. She must be able to feel how it raced, how it couldn't possibly go on like this forever. "You know what I want."

"No, I don't. I can't tell. You seem…" She tilted her face toward his, her eyes searching. "Something is very wrong, Max. I can see that you're hurting, but I don't know what you need. Do you need a lover? Or do you just need a friend?"

"I…" He closed his eyes and let rain drop from his hair, over his brows, through his lashes and onto his cheeks. "I want both. For once in my life, I…"

He looked down at her. "Is that too much to ask—just one night with a woman who is both a lover *and* a friend?"

She held her breath for a moment. Then she let the final towel drop and lifted her hand to his cheek. She skimmed her fingertips across his cheekbone, fading back toward his ear. She cupped his cold, hard jaw in the soft warmth of her palm.

"No," she said. "It's not too much to ask."

She took the towel he'd used to dry his face, and let it fall on top of the other one. Then she took her hand away from his heart and put her fingers under the waistband of his pants, pulling the rain-soaked fabric away from his hip bone gently.

She did the same with the other hand, sliding warm fingertips in and slowly stretching the waist until she could slip the sweatpants down, letting the cotton find its way over the contours of his body without discomfort.

It made no sense to feel particularly exposed—she knew how helplessly turned on he was, had known from the start, because the drenched cotton had outlined every inch of him as clearly as if he'd already been naked.

And yet, as she knelt before him, shoving the discarded clothing to the side and using the soft terry towels to dry his feet, his shins, his thighs, his...

He almost came right then, though she touched him so briefly, and only through the towel. But he was so tight, so swollen and inflamed, that it was as if every nerve ending had been distended to twice its size and twice its sensitivity. Any contact with his flesh was dangerous—even the warmth of her breath as she bent toward him, ministering to him, was nearly enough to explode his fragile control.

Or maybe it had shattered already. A strange shivering seemed to have started inside him, like a tiny fire made of ice. It rippled out in waves that rode his bloodstream from nerve ending to nerve ending. His legs began to tremble.

What was wrong with him? He had never wanted anyone as much as he wanted this woman, and he wasn't going to be able to control himself. He wasn't going to be able to make it right for her....

He shut his eyes and held his breath. He reached out and found the edge of the wall, tightening his legs to try to make the desperate pulsing stop.

"It's all right," she said. "Just let go, Max. Just let go."

She spoke the words only millimeters away from the thrusting length of him, and her breath was like honey fire. He cried out once, and she cupped her hands around him and slid him into her mouth...just in time...just in time....

He jerked, and the entire world seemed to disappear inside that warm, moist place. Sizzling fingers of electricity exploded out through his limbs, and thick currents of release pulsed through him and into her.

It went on. And on. Seemingly endless cresting waves of mindless pleasure—as if he had waited too long for this, and he would never be able to get enough. But finally the waves eased to ripples, the roar in his ears died down and the world reformed around him.

When he could think again, the first thing he recognized was the silk of her hair under his hands, braided through his fingers as if he'd held on to her desperately, through it all.

And the second thing he recognized was the peaceful, steady beating of his no-longer-aching heart.

PENNY WATCHED THE lightning play over Max's face as he slept. Though it was three in the morning, she didn't feel the need to rest. Every now and then, she would shut her eyes, thinking she might drift off, but then she'd open them again, just for the joy of being able to stare at him without any barriers.

In the relaxation of sleep, the sweetness of his features was uppermost. All the drive, the competence, the confidence, even the intelligence and wit, were erased by slumber, and all that was left was pure structural beauty—and

an unusual degree of kindness, an amazing lack of ruth-
lessness or aggression, especially in a man's man like Max.

He'd been asleep for about an hour. He'd fought it, clearly
uncomfortable with the way he'd given in to his need for
release. But he was like the survivor of some natural disaster, like a plane crash or a train wreck. He had been
functioning on sheer adrenaline and willpower, and it had
drained him completely.

She'd let him lower her to the bed, and she'd savored
every gentle, sensual kiss... Wow, but that man could kiss!

But she'd counted on nature to do its work. And it had.
Once her soft pillow cradled his head and his exhausted
muscles had the chance to relax, all she had to do was
use her embraces to massage his shoulder, the back of his
neck...

He kept fighting, heavy-eyed, for several minutes. But
finally he lost the battle and succumbed to the sleep he so
desperately needed.

Her body hummed pleasantly. For her, it was the best
of both worlds. She got the joy of intimately learning the
secrets of his face—and, when he finally woke, she knew
he would give her all the physical pleasure she could ever
desire.

Odd, she thought as if from a great distance, that she
didn't use this time to try to talk herself out of any further
intimacy. But somehow this interlude didn't seem to vio-
late anything that really mattered.

It definitely wasn't a surrender to loneliness or fear on
her part. She hadn't gone to him, looking for a crutch.
He had come to her. This time, she was providing the
strength—for whatever reason, his dreams tortured him,
and he had come to Penny for relief.

And, with Ellen gone until midday tomorrow, at the
"camp-in" at Bell River, this night posed no threat to his

vow, either. He would give 100 percent to Ellen, whenever she needed him. But right now, she didn't.

Tonight he didn't have to be a father first.

Penny didn't kid herself. Whatever they found together tonight, it would not survive the coming of daylight. He'd actually said the words, straight out. Just one night. For just one night, he wanted to take some comfort from a woman who was both a lover and a friend.

She appreciated the honesty more than he could ever know. She didn't want to be lied to. She didn't want to be any man's fool.

The lightning crashed outside, and thunder rolled. But in here, Max slept on.

She got out her sketch pad, which she kept by the bed always, and flicked on the low-wattage bedside lamp. It wasn't bright enough to disturb him, but it allowed her to see well enough to draw.

Over the next few minutes, she made several attempts to catch whatever subtle magic made him both angel and man, both tender and tough. She missed every time and kept flipping to a new page, annoyed, but eager to try again.

It must be in the lips. No—it was in the gentle hollow where the cheekbone met the eye.

No. It was the chin—the perfect proportion, that square jaw ending in the surprise of the rounded, dimpled chin. Strength without ego, power without brutality.

No. Maybe it was the brows…

She sighed, leaning back against the headboard and shutting her eyes. Either it really was magic, or it was elusive beyond her ability with a sketching pencil.

"Hey, there."

She turned, and Max's eyes were open. He still looked sleepy, like a little boy. But she knew the power of the naked body under that sheet, so softly molded to his torso. The warm, low buzzing she'd had inside her ever since he arrived intensified slightly, and she put her hand on her belly, as if she could feel it through her skin.

Lightning flashed, but farther away now, so that it was just an opalescent shimmer against his skin, not the white strobe it had been a few minutes ago.

"Hi." She smiled. "How are you feeling?"

"Fabulous." He arched his neck, stretching the muscles awake. He twisted to look above the bed, toward the window. "It's still raining. How long did I sleep?"

"Not long. About an hour, I guess."

He widened his eyes. "Not long? That's an entire hour wasted. I had plans for that hour...."

He lifted on his elbow, but as he closed the distance between them, his chest encountered the sketch pad she'd let fall on the bed between them. It made a crinkling sound. He paused and angled back so that he could retrieve it.

"Oh, I should move that..." She felt suddenly too self-conscious to allow him to look at it. "It's just—"

But he'd already looked. He saw, of course, that the first sketch was a picture of him, drawn from just above, and to the side...a picture of a very handsome, naked man, sleeping with only a thin sheet to cover his trim, muscular body.

He turned the page. Then again. And again. Over and over, the same man, the same sheet-draped body. Sometimes the face dominated, as she'd tried to capture his essence. But sometimes the body was her focus...that beautiful, powerful body....

For a minute she couldn't find any words. It looked obsessive. It looked like the fixation of a woman in love.

"You have a...a difficult face to draw. It's very interesting, artistically speaking. I mean, if you're interested in form and shadow...that angle where your cheek and your jaw..."

She gave up. "You're very beautiful," she said. "I couldn't help trying to see if I could capture it in a sketch."

He leaned over her, his naked chest brushing against her shoulder, and the rain-washed scent of him teasing at her nose, and set the pad down on her nightstand. When he rolled back to his side of the bed, he caught her by the shoulders and rolled her over with him.

She wasn't quite on top of him, but close enough. She could feel the contours of his legs, the jut of his lean hip bones, the already-rigid length of his arousal. The buzzing inside her became a swarm, and things in her midsection seemed to be shifting blindly, contracting and relaxing, swirling, agitated, as if searching for another arrangement of parts.

Their faces were only inches apart. "*I'm* beautiful?" His eyes were tilted up, filled with both seduction and laughter. "Have you looked in a mirror lately, Penny Wright?"

She laughed breathlessly. She wasn't beautiful, but he made her feel that way. All this swirling inside made her feel more alive, more vibrant, as if she must be rosy and glowing.

"No," she said. "Not really."

His arms tightened, pulling her closer, until her breasts touched his naked chest. "You don't know what you're missing." He lifted his head and kissed her neck, moving across her skin with a slow, trailing heat.

If she was going to stop this—she was going to have to stop it now. Later—even a few seconds from now—would be far, far, too late.

She put her hand up, and slid her fingers between the skin of her neck and his lips. "Max," she said softly. "I think we should talk first."

He drew his head back. A frown had appeared between

his brows. "You're not saying…you're not saying you don't want this."

Her heart hammered its own response, but she shook her head, knowing he'd need a clear, unambiguous green light. He wasn't the kind of man who would claim a prize he hadn't won.

"You know I want this," she said. "I just hoped we could talk first. I hoped you would tell me what happened tonight. It was another bad dream?"

He nodded. "Yes."

"But why? What are these dreams that can hurt you like that?" She put her head on his chest, and listened for his heartbeat. Before, it had been racing like an electronic toy spiraling out of control. She'd actually been afraid for him and had wondered whether even the orgasm he so clearly needed could possibly be safe.

To her great relief, his heart drummed with a calm but powerful rhythm. "You don't have to tell me, if you'd rather not."

For a minute, she thought he would choose not to, just as he had in the past. But then, under her ear, she felt him inhale deeply. He laid his palm against her hair and stroked it softly, as if she were a kitten.

"Two years ago, I worked for an architectural firm out of Chicago. Alexander and Floyd. They're one of the biggest. My main job was site consulting. I traveled all over the world, checking out locations. One of those trips took me to Mexico. It should have been simple. I'd been on a dozen trips to Mexico already. But this time, I got an invitation to dinner. Someone I didn't know, but who said they knew one of the VPs at Alexander and Floyd. I had a strange feeling about the meeting, but I went anyway. And, as I told you the other day, I should have listened to my gut. There was no dinner, no man who knew the VP. I was taken hostage."

She felt her body jerk slightly, startled. She'd known it was something bad. But *kidnapped*...

"How terrible," she said. But she didn't lift her head. She didn't want to interrupt his flow of words.

He stroked her hair soothingly—though she had the feeling it calmed him as much as it did her. Rhythmic, gentle, controlled.

"It was all about money, of course. I was nothing to them, personally. I wasn't rich enough, but Alexander and Floyd was. So, essentially, I was just the kidnappers' product. They owned me now, and they intended to sell me back to my company."

She tightened her arms around his waist. Still his heart beat normally. But she wasn't sure hers still did. "What happened? Did they agree to pay?"

"Not at first. I didn't know what was going on, of course, not at the time. But when I got back to Chicago, Alexander explained that they'd been required to negotiate. The asking price was so high...no one ever pays the initial offer... the stockholders would mutiny...."

"Oh, my God." She closed her eyes, thinking of the jackals who could make those kinds of cold-blooded calculations while a man was being held hostage. Stockholders? "How long were you there?"

"About two months."

She finally had to look at him. Two months... Two months away from his family, not knowing whether he'd ever see his child again. She lifted her head and met his gaze. It was dark, but not haunted and lost, not like when he arrived tonight.

"How bad was it?"

"It could have been worse," he said. "But it could have been better."

She shook her head. "Don't. Don't pass me off with meaningless half statements like that. What happened?"

She wanted to know.... But more than that, she wanted him to talk about it. He had all these dodges ready on the tip of his tongue. All these canned phrases that he had undoubtedly used for two years now, to avoid letting anyone know the truth. He probably told himself that stoicism was strength. That a refusal to brood and wallow and whine was courage.

But the dreams said otherwise. The dreams showed that stoicism was just denial dressed up in a fancy name. The dreams proved that a refusal to brood was a refusal to process. A refusal to face pain consciously would inevitably drive that pain to find its outlet in the subconscious.

In the dreams.

"Where did they keep you?"

"In a basement. It was dirty and cold, and it reeked of gas and oil and power tools. But the hardest part was that it was dark. It was always, always dark. Day or night, it was all the same. It's more difficult than you think it will be, doing without any way to visually orient yourself. You lose your sense of reality, somehow. You hear things. See things."

She shivered, but she let him go on.

"You could get to the point you almost hoped for one of them to come, because they brought a flashlight. It was almost worth it, just to remember where the walls were, and where the ceiling was. It can give you a strange sort of vertigo, having no way to be sure you still know which way is up, which way is down."

"But couldn't you feel your way to the walls? Couldn't you at least touch the floor?"

"No." His eyes clouded slightly. She had to fight the urge to put her hand on his heart again, like a stethoscope, just to be sure. "No. There were chains that were attached to the ceiling. In the middle of the room. I'm sure you've seen it in movies. I had. I just didn't understand that things like that weren't just film props. That they existed in the real world, too. And that real people—normal, everyday people—could find themselves hanging from them, in rooms like that."

She was going to cry. She fought it hard, knowing how absurd and pointless and just plain *not helpful* her tears would be. But she couldn't stop them. They hung at the bottom of her eyes, stinging, for several seconds. And then they spilled over, down her cheeks and onto his bare, taut belly.

There was more. Of course there was more. The men would have been angry, frustrated that their requests for money were being thwarted. There would have been beatings, punishments... Maybe no food, no water, no time out of chains to let the blood return to his hands...

"You don't have to stop telling me the details," she said. "I'm crying because I'm angry, not because I'm frightened. I'm crying because I want to kill them, and I can't."

He smiled, and he put his hand against her cheek. "I knew you were fierce, under all that little-girl exterior."

"I can be," she said. "If anyone hurts the people I care about..."

She stopped, realizing that she'd probably said more than she should.

But he didn't seem alarmed by it. He moved his thumb softly behind her ear, and the sensuality of that small motion was oddly distracting.

"I'll tell you anything you want to know, Penny. But I hope we won't have to waste tonight talking about Mexico. The truth is, I don't care very much about all that right now. For the first time since it happened, that basement seems a million miles away and a million years ago."

She found that hard to believe. How could anyone be strong enough to put such a thing behind them?

"There are just a few hours left of this night." He reached down, put his hands under her arms and raised her up where he could look straight into her eyes. "Let me use them doing something beautiful, instead of reliving something ugly."

She nodded. In this position, she could tell that his desire had never abated. He was as firm and ready as he had been since waking.

She flicked the sheet back, baring his body to the dimly lit room, so that the fading storm could shimmer on every magnificent inch of him. She moved her legs so that she straddled him. He groaned softly and slid down, so that they no longer touched hip to hip, but so that she knelt just below that beautiful chin she'd spent so long trying to understand.

He lifted her nightgown and pulled it over her head. Then he put his palms on her bottom and tilted her forward. He smiled and murmured softly, and she realized they were so close she could feel his breath touch her most tender places.

"Max." She tried to lean over and reach the nightstand. "We can make love safely," she said. "I have condoms."

She started to explain why she had them—because after what happened to her mother she would never, ever risk having unprotected sex. But she didn't bother, partly because she knew he didn't really care, and partly because she was having trouble breathing, which meant that forming words was difficult.

"Good," he said, but he didn't let her reach the drawer. He brought her back to his lips and then pressed in with his palms, so that she rocked forward and met his mouth. She felt his tongue move into her, and she cried out as different parts of her body simultaneously liquefied, stiffened... and caught fire.

"Condoms are nice," he murmured as he used his palms, and his tongue, and his lips, to guide her into a subtle, torturous rocking motion that made her want to scream for more.

"But I'm afraid we won't be needing them for a long, long time."

CHAPTER THIRTEEN

WHEN PENNY WOKE, the sunlight was as bright as a mountain of diamonds. Oh—how late was it? She started to check the bedside clock…then remembered it had toppled off the nightstand hours and hours ago.

And with that, the memories flooded in, hitting her with a heat that was almost physical. Her body flushed and tingled, and she became aware that, under her light covering of sheet, she was completely naked.

She was also alone.

"Max?" She got no response. She lay completely still for a few seconds, listening, trying to discern whether there was any movement in the house—the shower, or the faucet, or even the light sound of a bare, male foot across her hardwood floors.

But the house was silent. The sunlight streamed across the bed in brilliant white bands, spotlighting the empty place, rumpled sheets and cockeyed pillow where Max had been…but was no longer.

The night was over.

She sat up, clutching the sheet to her breastbone with both hands, and shivered slightly, her body remembering. She wondered, numbly, whether it would ever forget.

No. She shook off the melancholy that hovered around the edges of her heart. She wasn't going to be sad already.

She had known what she was doing. She'd understood that they had plucked last night out of real life, the way you might pluck a diamond from the walls of a mine. It was beautiful, and it was a joy—and while it might have been forged by extreme pressures deep in that gritty earth, it could never be fully integrated back into the rock and soil from which it came. It would always be a thing apart.

But for those delicious, life-altering hours, she had held the diamond in her heart, and she planned to hold its afterglow as long as she possibly could.

She swiveled, tossing the sheet aside and putting her feet on the floor. Now that she faced the nightstand, she saw that the clock had been restored to its regular position. It stood on her sketch pad, which was open—to a sketch that she could tell in an instant wasn't her own.

She slid the clock aside and pulled out the sketch pad. She held her breath without knowing why, as she realized the drawing was of Penny, herself.

In the sketch, she lay asleep. The perspective was tricky, but effective. She must have been lying on her left side, but at some point had tilted three-quarters of the way toward her back and had thrown her arm over her head. Her face was turned toward her elbow, so that it was drawn mostly in profile. The sheet covered her, but had slipped a little, exposing one breast—represented in the sketch by little more than a curve, a point of darkness in the center and a shadow beneath.

The picture was breathtaking. No one had ever sketched her before. She hadn't known anyone who liked art enough to bother. But she should have known Max had talent. Ellen's own abilities must have come from somewhere, and an architect would have been trained....

Even so, the sketch moved her, almost to tears. The woman here was far, far more beautiful than Penny could ever hope to be. She was both vulnerable and strong, both tender and erotic. Her deep peace and physical ease told anyone who looked that she had been deeply, repeatedly satisfied by the lover who watched her sleep.

She pressed the sketchbook up against her chest, feeling her heart throb slowly against the paper. It might be only a goodbye. A thank-you, not for the sex, but for the comfort and the kindness.

Only a goodbye. But, as goodbyes went, this one was fairly wonderful.

Suddenly she heard a knocking—as startling as a gunshot. It was someone rapping on the front door.

Her first, leaping instinct said...Max!

But then her gaze snagged on the clock. Eleven-thirty already? And suddenly her heart stopped. It wasn't Max. It was her first student. Arriving for the first art class of Penny's much-anticipated new career.

Yesterday, seventy-year-old Margaret Johnson's watercolor lesson had loomed large—the first step in establishing Penny as a full-time working and teaching artist. Today, that milestone had been eclipsed by a few pencil scribbles on a nine-by-twelve piece of two-hundred-and-twenty-gram white paper.

Perspective. It really all came down to perspective, didn't it? She looked once more at the picture before closing the book and dashing toward her closet to find something suitable to throw on.

Not just in art, but all of life. And falling in love, as she'd been foolish enough—and lucky enough—to do in Max's arms last night, had changed her perspective forever.

ELLEN COULDN'T SEEM to hang on to a mood these days. She could feel happy one minute, and then the least little thing could make her really mad, or sad. Alec told her it was her hormones, but she didn't think he was any kind of expert on moods. And besides, she didn't like the idea of "hormones."

It made her sound as if she wasn't even a real person, but just a collection of chemicals, like a science experiment.

She had been extra happy last night, when she was sleeping over at Bell River. She'd been able to forget all about Dad, and their fight.

At home, everything he said seemed to play, over and over, through her head, until she wanted to scream at it to stop. It had to stop, because every time she heard it she felt herself getting closer to believing him.

But believing him would mean believing her mother had lied to her. And she would never do that.

But here at Bell River, the memories went away. Everything had been just as awesome as they promised—maybe even more awesome. Great food, fun games, lots of art projects and sing-alongs. All the kids were nice to her, even.

It had been perfect timing, because tomorrow was the one-year anniversary of her mom's death, and she definitely needed something to distract her.

Plus, school started Monday, and that was beyond awful. She said so aloud to Alec. It was the easiest part to talk about. She didn't want to mention her mom.

"Why is school awful?" Alec paused and turned around with a curious look on his face. He was about five feet ahead of her on the grass, leading the way to see some baby kittens that had been born out behind Mr. Harper's house. "Are you sure you're not just cranky?"

"I'm not cranky."

Alec just rolled his eyes and started walking again. He knew she was mad because she'd been invited to stay for the afternoon and even dinner, but Dad had said no. He said he had to come get her right now, but then when he got here Bree invited them to come see Mr. Harper's new foal, which had just been born last night. And of course he said yes.

He wasn't really in all that much of a hurry to get home, was he? Not when there was something *he* wanted to see.

And then, when they got out to the Harper place, out on the west side of Bell River, Penny had showed up, too. That should have been nice, but it wasn't, not this time. For some reason, Penny was the center of everyone's attention today.

Ellen had wanted her dad to notice that she was still angry with him, still refusing to speak to him or show him the pictures she'd drawn at the camp-in.

But with Penny here, he didn't even seem to be aware that Ellen was giving him the cold shoulder. He didn't try to draw her out, or make nice so that she'd forgive him. He just kept looking at Penny.

Ellen noticed these things. No matter where Penny went, or who she was talking to, Dad's eyes followed her.

Ellen felt jealous, even though she knew that was stupid. She didn't want Dad and Penny to be good friends. She wasn't sure why.

No, she was sure. It was an embarrassing reason. She had a terrible feeling that they would like each other better than either of them liked her.

Alec yanked a few leaves off a low-hanging branch as he went by and began ripping them apart just for fun. "So, seriously. What's wrong with school starting?"

"I don't know." Ellen pushed away the swaying branches that almost hit her face. "I guess so far I've been able to pretend I'm on vacation or something. But starting school— that makes it real. It's like I really *live* here."

Alec turned again. "So? It's awesome here."

"Not if you're used to Chicago."

"Well, I think I'd *hate* Chicago."

"That's because you're not used to it. The city is really fun. We always go shopping, and to the mall, and…"

Annoyingly, she couldn't really think of what else they

used to do. And she knew that Alec wouldn't think the mall was very exciting.

He screwed up his face. "You like going to the mall more than you liked riding Clapsaddle to Little Bell Falls?"

"No. But—"

"You like shopping better than you like taking pictures of the deer on the western slopes?"

"Well, no."

But why couldn't he see how confusing it was to see herself changing like this? It was as if the Ellen of Chicago was disappearing. And if that Ellen disappeared, what would happen to her mother?

Several times, since her talk with her dad, she'd had the most awful, disloyal thoughts about her mom. That was so messed up—how could you think bad things about a person you loved?

It was almost as confusing as the situation she had with her dad, where she couldn't help loving him, even though she was mad at him almost all the time.

It was as if love and hate, respect and disrespect, had somehow mixed together, like an emotion stew. It was too complicated, and it made her heart hurt. All she could think was that her mom wouldn't like this Ellen, the one who smelled of horses, and got her knees dirty, and didn't always brush her hair or worry about whether her shoes matched her purse.

"And, come on, you know you wouldn't really rather go to the movies than—"

"Shut up!" Her chest felt hot, and she stopped in her tracks, stamping her feet. "What are you trying to say? Are you trying to say I'm changing? Are you trying to say I'm turning into some kind of cowpoke who *belongs* out here in the sticks?"

Alec's mouth fell open. If she'd morphed into a fire-breathing dragon right in front of his eyes, he couldn't have looked more shocked.

"Is that what you're saying, Alec Garwood? Because if it is, you're dumber than I thought. And you don't know me at all!"

But there was a reason Alec was one of the most popular kids in Silverdell. He was like the ultimate of cool. He didn't get rattled, and he didn't get mad. He just raised one blond eyebrow, which made him look a lot like his father, who was obviously a superhandsome man.

"I guess you're right. I must not know you very well. I *was* thinking you might be cool enough to belong here *someday*. I was thinking maybe you had some spunk, under that city-girl sissyness."

Heat was rising from under her shirt. She'd been walking too long, and she'd started to sweat. She was breathing heavily, and she couldn't decide whether she wanted to punch him, or sit right down on this path of pine needles and cry.

"That's what I *was* thinking." Alec shrugged one bony shoulder, then tossed away the leaves he'd been shredding. "But hey, if you'd rather go back to Chicago and try on lipsticks at the mall all day, feel free. I don't see anybody trying to stop you."

GRAY HAD BEEN showing Max and Penny the stables, and they'd finally reached the new mare and her foal. She felt awkward, but she couldn't help smiling at Gray. He looked as proud as if the whole idea of horses had been his invention in the first place.

"We don't always turn out on the first day, but Young Jolyon here is a strapping thing. Great balance, really steady on his feet already."

Gray leaned against the stable door, his arms crossed,

outwardly all calm, casual elegance, but Penny had come to understand him pretty well during these weeks she'd been back, and she knew he was as thrilled as a kid on Christmas. The foal, Young Jolyon, was the crown jewel in his breeding program, and hopes ran high for this particular bloodline.

"The weather's perfect, too, which is amazing after last night's storm and this morning's relentless heat. So we thought we might give them both an hour or so in the private paddock this afternoon."

Gray glanced out of the front doors. "In fact, it's probably a good time now, while we've got some cloud cover again. Their eyes are sensitive, you know. This morning was way too bright—and of course it was too soon."

Gray yawned, the only giveaway that he'd been up all night supervising the foaling, then consulted his watch. "Do you mind if I check with the wranglers, to make sure someone's free to spruce up the stall while we turn out?"

"No, of course not," Max said politely. He glanced toward the adorable foal, who was walking around like a kid just learning how to use stilts, and smiled. "We're enjoying the show."

Penny's heart sped up a little as Gray moved away, already calling to the wranglers, who were in other parts of the large stable, tending to other horses. Gray was so caught up with his new pride and joy that he had barely noticed Penny and Max the whole time, but at least he'd provided a buffer.

When she came to Bell River after Margaret Browning's art lesson, she hadn't expected to see Max. The camp-in had technically been over for hours, and she assumed he would have picked up Ellen and taken her out for the day, if only to put distance between himself and Penny.

But here he was. And Ellen, too. It had been awkward,

trying to remember exactly how people acted who weren't burning up with memories of naked skin against naked skin, damp with sweat and steaming with passion....

What did ordinary folk say? How long did they maintain eye contact? Did they hug casually, or did they not dare?

As soon as Gray was gone, Max turned to Penny.

"I'm going crazy," he said quietly. "I can't stop thinking about last night."

All the simmering memories shot to the surface of her skin, and she knew she was as pink as a candied apple. "Yes," she said. "Me, too."

For a moment, Penny thought Max might be going to kiss her. His eyes darkened. His head dipped slightly.

Then out of the corner of her eye, she caught a new movement. Glancing over, she saw the curious foal toddling toward them. His spindly legs and liquid brown eyes made him look a little like Bambi. Even in all the years here at Bell River as a child, Penny had never seen such long legs on a foal. This one might well be a champion.

He almost ran into his mother as he moved toward the stall door—he didn't have great driving skills with those stilts just yet, but he was remarkably steady for a foal only about fourteen hours old.

Both Penny and Max turned to watch—it was hard to resist, and it provided a way to break the frighteningly powerful current that was arcing between them.

But the current only grew less electric—it didn't disappear. Max stood so close to Penny that their shoulders touched, and an unseen heat pulsed in waves between them.

"They're so helpless when they're newborns," Max said. "It was that way with Ellen. I couldn't have dreamed, then, of ever doing anything to hurt her. I couldn't have dreamed I could ever wish I could be alone...away from her..."

"I can imagine," was all she could say.

"And yet, this morning all I could think was—when will we be alone again? When will we get another chance?" He closed his eyes. "Does that make me a horrible father?"

"No," she said. But that seemed too glib. "I don't know. I don't really know what to think about anything, anymore."

He stared ahead, his face stony, and yet, to her, still the most beautiful male face she'd ever seen.

The inner conflict was tearing him apart, and now, just as last night, her instinct was to try to make it hurt less. "You love her, Max—anyone can see that. Even she can see it, though she may not always want to admit it. Her happiness will always come first for you. It's just that…you're a man, too. And sometimes…sometimes you need a kind of comfort that only another grown-up can give."

He turned his head toward her. "How can you be so… so damn *good?* Why don't you encourage me to ditch her, farm her out somewhere, spend more time doing whatever I want to do?"

Penny hesitated.

Because I love her, too.

That was what she wanted to say, but she couldn't. He would probably think she was lying anyhow. It sounded too fake, more like a subtle version of luring him away from his responsibilities than a truth.

She wasn't even sure she could believe it herself. And yet, something in the word felt right. She cared about Ellen, not just because she was an extension of Max, but because she was talented and brave and tremendously loyal. Because of all that, and because of…nothing. Just something intrinsically wonderful that was her own unique self.

"I suppose it's because I don't believe that's the way to happiness. I saw too much of parents doing whatever they wanted and letting the children take care of themselves while I was growing up. I know what it leads to—and it's not happiness, not for the children, and not for the adults, either."

He shook his head slightly. He looked once toward the stable door, through which Alec and Ellen had romped off five minutes ago, in search of newborn kittens. The doorway was empty. The children were nowhere in sight.

He turned back to Penny. "What is happiness? I'm not even sure I believe in it anymore. Except...last night..."

His eyes fell toward her lips. They tingled under the scrutiny.

"Last night...." He repeated the words as if they were a kind of music.

And then he kissed her.

It was only a fraction of the passion he'd poured into her last night, but she felt her lips start to bloom in bright colors anyhow, like watercolor-pencil marks, which intensify and spread when you touch them with the tip of a fine, wet brush. He took her face into his hands, holding her near, and moved across her as if he were painting a picture across her lips. And the picture was so...

They pulled apart as Gray and Bree and a couple of wranglers came ambling in, chatting. The wranglers carried a metal pitchfork, a shovel, a broom and a couple of implements so sophisticated even Penny didn't recognize them.

"Sorry, guys," Gray said. "They're going to be working on the stall, but if you want to watch, we can go out by the paddock. It's pretty cute when the little guy gets turf beneath him for the first time."

"We were just about to leave," Max said with a smile. He had recovered faster than Penny, who still felt a little starstruck and dazed. She touched her lips, as if they might still be gleaming in pinks and roses and gold.

She glanced at Bree, to see whether her sister had noticed anything amiss, but even Bree was too enchanted with the foal to care what was going on with Penny and Max.

"Maybe we should go see if we can turn up those little rascals," Max said pleasantly, smiling down at Penny.

"Alec and Ellen?" Gray was distracted, patting the mare to assure her that he meant the colt no harm by coming into the stall. But he was still trying to be polite to his guests. "I saw them in the office just a few minutes ago. They were playing with the closed circuit cameras. I told Alec I'd kill him if he broke it. Mrs. Soames here has done her work, but I've got three more late-term mares we're watching twenty-four hours a day, and—"

"I hate you!"

Everyone turned. Ellen stood in the stable doorway, her hands on her hips, and fury on her face. Alec stood beside her, looking miserable, but not trying to stop her from whatever she intended to do.

"I hate you!" She moved toward her father, and when she reached him, she pushed the heels of her hands against his chest. "I knew you didn't care about Mom. I *knew* it! She hasn't even been dead a *year*."

"Ellen," Penny interjected. "Ellen, your dad is just—"

"I hate you, too!" Ellen whipped around to face Penny, though she kept her fists on her father's torso. Her features were blurred with tears, twisted with anger and pain. "You never cared about teaching me to draw, did you? You just *used* me so that you could hang around my dad."

Shocked, Penny discovered she couldn't respond.

Ellen wasn't listening, anyhow. She had turned back to her father, lifting her tearstained face to his.

"Tomorrow is the one-year anniversary of the day Mom died—did you even remember that? Did you even remember that when you were *kissing* somebody else?"

"WELL, IT *IS* a spy camera," Alec said an hour later, as Rowena wound down from her furious lecture.

He kicked the side of the porch steps with his heels, clearly tired of the grilling he'd been getting by the three women who were his surrogate mothers. "So if people end up using it to spy on other people, I guess you shouldn't be all that surprised."

"Ro, Alec is right." Penny, who sat on Bell River's back porch swing, leaned her head on her hand. "It wasn't the kids' fault. They had no idea what they were going to end up seeing."

"We sure *didn't*," Alec agreed fervently. Trouble, his dog, lay staunchly next to him, thumping his tail every time Alec got emphatic. "Nobody would deliberately watch grown-ups kissing and hugging and being completely gross on TV."

Ro, Bree and Penny all exchanged a look, but to their credit no one even smiled.

"Seriously, though, Rowena." Penny continued to plead for leniency with Alec. "I should have remembered the closed circuit system was on. Max didn't even know it was there, but I did. I should have remembered that nothing on a ranch is really private."

"Now you know how *I* feel," Alec grumbled irritably. "I can't do *anything* without getting caught. Stinks, huh?"

Penny sighed. "Yeah. Stinks big-time."

"Okay, go on, then," Rowena said, relenting. "Go help them with dinner. And you'd better hurry, before I change my mind."

He looked cautious, so she motioned pointedly to the back door. "Go. You're off the hook, thanks to Penny. But you and trouble better not even find yourselves in the same county—do you understand?" She patted the dog's head. "Not you. The other kind of trouble."

Alec wrinkled his nose. "For how long? I mean, I'll try, but you know how hard it is for me—"

"Forever." Rowena shook her head. "Or at least until I forget about this one."

Alec grinned. "Okay." He stood, climbed back onto the porch and started toward the door.

As he passed Penny, he paused. "I'm sorry you got in trouble. It's so ironic, isn't it? I used to try to make Dad kiss women all the time, starting with my math teacher. But he never would. Not even Rowena. Ellen doesn't want her dad to hook up with anyone, and she can't keep him away from the ladies."

"Alec." Rowena's voice was stern, but Penny could hear the laughter she was holding back. "Shut up."

He wrinkled his nose. "What? I'm just saying it's ironic. And I looked ironic up, too, so I know what it means."

Rowena shut her eyes. "Goodbye, Alec."

When he finally was gone, the three sisters sat quietly, watching the late-afternoon ranch activities bustling around them. Even a month ago, neither Rowena nor Bree would have had the luxury of a few free minutes this close to dinner. But Gray's investment in the breeding program, and Penny's infusion of cash from the town house sale, had eased the cash crunch.

And as soon as they learned Rowena was pregnant, everyone insisted they hire extra help.

Right now, though, Penny wished her sisters had urgent appointments somewhere else. She sat sideways in the swing, so that she could enjoy the view of the sunset dropping golden paint on the western slopes. She kept one toe on the floor and used it to sway the swing gently, so that its creaking filled the silence.

She knew Rowena and Bree were waiting for her to start

explaining, but she didn't feel like it. Most people who wanted to kiss a guy could just do it. For her, however...

It seemed as if every time she and Max decided to lock lips somebody took out an ad in the paper to announce it.

Okay, maybe not every time. Last night, at least, was still private. She wanted so badly to keep it that way. She didn't want to listen while her sisters performed a conversational autopsy on the event. Especially now that it looked fairly certain that last night was all she'd ever have, she wanted desperately to protect it. If she had to talk about Max right now, she might break down and cry. She had lost him, and that hurt enough.

She had to pick her next moves very carefully, if she didn't want to undo all the progress she'd made in the past few months. She thought maybe she'd just go straight for the white-water rafting. It frightened her, but think what a victory it would be.

It might restore her faith in herself. She needed that more than she needed anything else on earth.

Except Max.

"Okay, so..." Bree, who sat on one of the Adirondack rockers, lost the silence contest. "Who should we be worried about here, Pea? Just Ellen? Or Ellen *and* you?"

"Just Ellen," Penny said, determined to sound calm. It shocked her to realize that, even now, her inner child was tempted by the thought of these loyal shoulders to cry on. "I'm fine."

"What Bree means, I think," Ro put in, "is that—"

"I know what she means." Penny slowed the swing. She felt herself growing angry, though she knew it was only a shield to put over the sadness that made her feel so vulnerable and lost.

"Bree means she wants to know whether Max Thorpe has broken my heart. You *both* want to know whether you should call Dallas to arrest him, or ask Gray to take him out to the woodshed for a whipping."

She shook her head, knowing she sounded harsher than she should. But better harsh and independent than adorable…and helpless.

"Or maybe you just want to do an internet search on his romantic history, to see how many girls he's loved and left. Find out whether he's good enough to allow near your baby sister."

Bree and Ro exchanged a glance.

"Well, the answer is no." Penny put both her feet on the porch, and sat up as straight as she could. "Instead, you should take off your mother-hen glasses and see what's going on under your noses. I've grown up, ladies. I'm not your baby sister anymore."

Bree looked sad. "I know," she said. "*We* know. It's just that we love you, and we don't want anyone to—"

"If you love me," Penny broke in, "then trust me to make my own decisions. If I make colossal mistakes, trust me to handle the consequences. But Max is not a colossal mistake, so relax. I'm fine." She swallowed hard, wishing she were out on the white water right this very minute. Anything was preferable to this.

"I'm fine."

Rowena looked suddenly as if she might cry, and that made Penny feel as if the tears she'd been holding back might break free, too. And of course, if both of them were crying, nothing on earth could stop Bree from joining in.

Oh, no, no, no… Impossible. They had guests coming and going all over the ranch, for heaven's sake. What great fodder for the scandalous Wright family legends, if guests reported seeing all three Wright sisters sobbing on the back porch.

"Ro, don't." Penny gave her eyes the lecture of her

life. No burning, no blurring, *no tears!* "What on earth is wrong? What have I said to make you cry?"

Rowena came over and sat beside her on the old swing, which creaked and bounced slightly. Her green eyes were glassy with unshed tears.

"I'm sorry," she said. "It's probably just the hormones. They say the first three months…"

She grabbed Penny's hands. "But… Oh, Sweet pea. It's also that I know that sound. God help me, I know that sound *so* well."

Penny frowned. "What sound?"

"The sound of a proud woman covering up a broken heart." Still hanging on to Penny, she turned plaintively to Bree.

"Damn it, Bree," she said. "Penny's fallen in love with the man."

WHEN PENNY GOT home that night, Max's SUV wasn't in the driveway. But she could see lights on in his side of the duplex, and the bulky frame of Mrs. Biggars moving around behind the shades.

So probably Ellen was there.

She climbed the steps to the Thorpe side and rapped softly on the front door

Mrs. Biggars answered quickly. The older woman and Penny had become friendly over the past couple of weeks, bonding over their shared interest in gardening and their mutual affection for Ellen.

"She says she doesn't want to see you." Mrs. Biggars was a no-nonsense kind of lady. She obviously knew what had happened this afternoon. "But I told her that's rude, so come on in. She's in her bedroom."

Penny hesitated. "Maybe, if she's really not in the mood

to talk—" She held out the framed picture she'd brought with her. "Maybe you could just give her this for me."

Mrs. Biggars took the picture and turned it over. It was one of Ellen's photographs from the wedding, in which she'd beautifully caught the moonlight on the creek, and the strings of colored lights on the flower garlands, and the silhouettes of people dancing. It was probably about 75 percent beginner's luck, but it was perfectly composed and oozing with emotion.

"Did you take this?" Mrs. Biggars looked impressed.

"No. This is Ellen's shot. I had it framed."

Mrs. Biggars' eyes widened. "In that case you definitely should come on in."

"Thanks." Penny smiled as she entered the house. "If it's okay, I'll go give it to her myself."

Ellen's room was brightly lit, the bed made with a softly colorful spread, duster and pillow shams that all looked as if they might have been patterned after Monet's *Water Lilies*. She had a chair, a television, a desk and a bookcase full of books.

She sat on the chair, over by the side of her bed, her back to the corner, where she could see the entire room. It was the power position, the way a queen on a throne will survey the great hall, her back shielded so that no one could sneak up on her.

But Ellen didn't look powerful. Her hair was limp and lifeless, as if she'd forgotten to brush it. Her mouth, one of her beauties, was turned down in a frown that seemed to have become permanent. Even her eyes, which looked so much like her father's, were sunken and dull.

She was not ready to make peace and be friends. Shoulders tight, drawn up practically to her ears. Hands white-knuckled in her lap. Legs as stiff as nutcrackers.

"I told Mrs. B I didn't want to see anybody."

"I know." Penny didn't sit, because that would have implied too much familiarity, but she did cross the threshold. "I'm sorry about that, because I know it's annoying to have your wishes ignored. But I wanted to give you this picture, and I wanted to tell you I'm sorry I upset you today."

Ellen raised her chin. "You didn't upset me. My dad did."

Penny shrugged. "Maybe. But it seemed as if I had upset you, too. I'm sorry. I didn't mean to."

"No. You didn't think I could see. You thought you could just sneak around with my dad, and I would never know."

In some gallows-humor sort of way, Penny felt like smiling. It wasn't altogether untrue.

"I think your dad and I were both worried about upsetting you. I guess he knows you pretty well. He obviously was afraid you'd react...well, exactly the way you did react."

"Because he knows it's true. He didn't love my mom." Her chin quivered. "And he doesn't love me."

"That's not true."

Penny stated it flatly, knowing her certainty would probably anger Ellen. But it had to be said—and by someone on the outside. Max could tell her he loved her till he'd used up all the air in the universe, and she would assume he was only trying to restore his reputation.

"I don't know what was going on between your mother and your father," she said. "I wasn't there, and I never met your mom. But I do know how your dad feels about you. He loves you."

Ellen stared, stony-eyed. "How do you know?"

"If I'm going to tell you that, I'm going to need to sit down. It's a long story." She touched the tip of the wooden desk chair. "May I?"

The girl frowned. Then she shrugged. "I don't care."

Penny placed the photograph, faceup, on the bedspread,

and then sat. "Did anyone ever tell you any gossip about my father?"

Ellen flushed. "It's not gossip. It's just the truth. Alec told me, because it was Rowena's father, too."

Well, not exactly, but close enough for this story. If Ellen hadn't heard any of this story, Penny wasn't going to be the first to share it. But if she already had heard, then probably the best thing Penny could do was clear up ghoulish fiction from fact.

"Okay. What did Alec tell you?"

"Just that your dad…he had a brain tumor or something, and it made him crazy. He ended up…like…sort of…pushing your mom down the stairs. And she died."

"Yes. All of that is true." Penny marveled that Alec hadn't felt the need to embellish. He was ordinarily a big fan of the theatrical.

"The point is, I know what it's like to have a bad father. A really bad father."

"What's it like?"

"It's scary. You never know what kind of mood he'll be in, or what will make him furious. You're afraid to mention anything you need, or want, or anything that's wrong, because it might be the trigger that sets him off. He might be in a good mood sometime, and he'll bring you a ridiculously expensive stereo, or a pet canary. But then, the next day, he'll be in a bad mood, and he'll smash it against the wall."

Ellen's eyes grew round. "The stereo? Or the canary?"

Penny looked straight at her. "Both of them."

"Oh."

"And there are little things, too. He won't sign your permission slips for school, because he doesn't like your teacher. He'll keep you from doing your homework, because he wants to go somewhere, and he wants to take you. There isn't always enough food in the house, or anyone willing to cook it, even if there is. Sometimes no grown-up comes home all night, and you have to try to sleep when you're scared of every sound you hear."

She left a little silence, for the implications of all that to sink in. Then she stood.

"So anyhow, I'm just saying you might want to think again when you start to say your father doesn't love you. Ask yourself if he's ever screamed at you, or broken your things, or let you go hungry, or left you alone all night."

Ellen's shoulders had begun to slump.

"I know it's easy to take the little things for granted, or to be angry because you wanted life to be different. But that's not fair, and it's not kind. And you know what? The bottom line is, I don't think you really want to hurt your father this way. I think you're a better person than that."

For just a millisecond, she thought Ellen might relent. The girl blinked, as if tears threatened at the back of her eyes.

But then she heard the front door open. And she realized Max was home.

Ellen's eyes hardened. They blazed with unshed tears and inexpressible anger.

"I guess that's what you were waiting for, huh? Well, he's here. So you can stop pretending to care what I think and go see my dad. It's not like I didn't know that was all you wanted anyhow."

CHAPTER FOURTEEN

SOMEHOW, MAX AND Olivia had managed to get Acton Adams, golfer extraordinaire, to approve one plan long enough to push through permitting and run the red tape marathon. Finally, ground-breaking day for Silverdell Hills Golf Club and Resort had arrived.

It arrived on the same day Ellen started school, for which Max was now very grateful. After the weekend he'd had with Ellen, and the emotional observance of the anniversary yesterday, he wasn't in the mood to bring his angry daughter to an event with this much news coverage.

The Hills was big enough to make a splash in a spot as small as Silverdell. Most of the big businesses had sent representatives here today. Even Bell River. Gray Harper came over and shook Max's hand.

"The resort is going to be fantastic," he said pleasantly. "Congratulations."

"Thanks." Max had been particularly uncertain about whether Bell River would be receptive to the arrival of another tourist resort. They might easily have seen The Hills as competition. Instead, they seemed to have taken the "high tide floats all boats" approach.

"Yeah, I'm hoping golfers with too much money and time on their hands will fall in love with the idea of raising horses." Gray smiled. "Or at least riding them."

"I think you can count on it."

Gray hadn't mentioned the dustup at the stables this

past Saturday. One of the qualities he liked best about the Bell River clan was that they weren't gossips by nature. Far from it. Maybe they'd just been the subject of rumor and innuendo too long to have an appetite for it, or maybe they simply preferred weightier topics.

Her preference for real conversation was one of the things he valued most about Penny. With Penny, he never felt the need to tune out. In fact, he barely wanted to blink, for fear one of their limited number of seconds together would get away from him.

"Well, you've got a public waiting, so I'll let you get on with it." Gray deftly found another acquaintance to talk to, freeing Max to deal with Fanny Bronson, who was making a beeline for him.

"It's all so exciting," Fanny said, beaming. "I'm already scouring my distributers, to see what new titles I should stock. Do golfers read anything other than books about Tiger Woods, do you think?"

Max saw the twinkle in her eye, and knew she was joking.

"Better not let Acton Adams hear you say that," he cautioned, glancing toward the spraying fountain, the one completed selling point, where The Big Deal was signing autographs and posing for pictures. From a distance, in the sparkling sunlight, he looked twenty years younger than he was, and every bit as arrogant.

"I won't, of course." The assessing look in Fanny's eyes was so intelligent that Max suddenly understood how she'd been able to keep her bookstore going when all around others were failing. She was a born businesswoman. "In fact, I've found a biography of him, and I'm thinking maybe we could set up a book signing event."

"Sounds great."

"I'll wait until the resort opens, of course." She smiled,

switching fluidly from businesswoman to flirtatious in a heartbeat. "Will you still be in town then?"

He wouldn't—not unless, for the first time in the history of construction anywhere or any time on this planet, the resort finished ahead of schedule. They planned on eleven months. He was in Silverdell for only nine.

Nine months. And one of those was almost gone already. The calendar suddenly seemed tragically short.

"No. I'm afraid I'll have gone back to—"

"Max." Gray appeared suddenly, placing a palm on Max's shoulder. His other hand held his cell up to his ear. "Max, can I steal you for a minute?"

Gray tilted his head, clearly directing his next words into the phone. "Yes, I'm going to tell him. He deserves to know. Bree, trust me. He deserves to know."

Something deep in Max's stomach went hideously cold, in spite of the warm sun. He gave Fanny a rote smile and allowed Gray's slight pressure to lead him off to a more private spot.

When they were several feet clear of the others, Gray slipped his phone into his pocket and gave Max a solemn look.

"What's wrong?" Max kept his tone low. "Don't try to break it gently. Just tell me."

"Okay." Gray took a breath. "There's been an accident. Penny went white-water rafting this morning. Apparently something went wrong."

"*How* wrong?"

Gray's gaze was careful, which scared the hell out of Max. The man was usually full of glib charm, but right now he looked as guarded as a doctor about to deliver your odds of surviving the night.

"Everyone is alive," he said, getting that out of the way

first. Max was grateful, since of course it was *the* pivotal piece of information.

"I'm not sure what happened. The stretch of river she ran was just a class two. But it sounds as if they hit some rapids that were uncharacteristically rough. Several people got flipped out of the raft, including Penny. Word is, her helmet was knocked off, and she hit her head on a rock."

His heartbeat suddenly drumming in his ears, Max felt in his pocket for his car keys. Olivia would just have to handle the rest of the event. "Where is she now?"

"She was taken to the hospital in Montrose. Bree and Ro are on their way now." Gray put his hand on Max's shoulder again. "But you should know—in case you're planning to race over there. You may not be able to see her."

Max set his jaw and narrowed his eyes, feeling a more like an animal than a man.

"Why not? Does the sheriff of Silverdell get to control what happens in Montrose, too?"

"No." Gray shook his head, and the look in his eyes turned much more sympathetic. "No, not because anyone will try to stop you. Because…Penny's still unconscious."

MAX WENT BY the house first. He wasn't sure when he'd return, and he needed to let Mrs. Biggars know. He needed to be sure she could stay, if he didn't get back by five.

He debated whether to tell Ellen. Everything might turn out fine. Why frighten her? And if everything wasn't fine…

He refused to entertain that possibility. Everything *would* be fine. Penny had been crossing some silly thing off her Risk-it List, that was all. Dancing, juggling, rafting. *A kiss in the ice-cream parlor.*

She asked so little of life. She didn't want riches or fame. She just wanted a life without fear. Life with a little bit of independence, self-respect and room to breathe. Life couldn't possibly respond by sending tragedy instead.

He felt a fury building inside him. It was so unfair. She hadn't been foolhardy. He knew the company she'd chosen—they were on the approved list for guests at Silverdell Hills to use, when they opened. They were licensed, experienced, everything they should be.

White-water rafting could be dangerous, sure, but rarely to people who booked guided float trips with reputable commercial companies. Not to people who appreciated the international scale of river difficulty—and their own abilities. Not to people who brought along helmets and life vests and guides who knew what they were doing.

So everything had to come out fine. And there probably was no need to mention Penny while Ellen was still so angry.

Except that he wasn't ever going to lie to her again, or even mislead her "for her own good." They hadn't found their way to détente, and maybe they never would. But two things had come through loud and clear.

One, his daughter hated being lied to. She hated knowing something was wrong, but being told everything was fine. She hated not being able to trust her parents to tell her the truth.

The other was that she was terrified of being unloved. Maybe she'd been told too many times that she looked like her mother, that she was her mother's "little clone," or a "mini-Lydia." Therefore, any hint that Max hadn't loved Lydia, didn't still love Lydia, must seem exactly the same as his not loving Ellen.

He might have to spend a lifetime proving her wrong about that.

So when he saw her come to her bedroom doorway and

stare out at him, stiff-armed and steely-eyed, he knew he had to tell her the truth.

"I'm glad you're here," he said. "I have to go to Montrose for a while, and I wanted to let you know what's going on."

"Why?" She folded her arms across her chest, obviously forgetting that she had a wet paintbrush in her hand. It left a narrow blue smear across the inside of her elbow. "I thought you had that grand opening thing at the resort all day."

"I did. But something's come up." He remembered how he had dreaded that he might have to endure a long sugar-coating from Gray before he got the facts he needed. So he got to the point. "There's been an accident. Penny was hurt while she was white-water rafting."

Ellen didn't even blink. He wondered whether that should be read as a "who cares?" or an "I care too much to let my feelings show."

"She hit her head on a rock. She's being taken to a hospital in Montrose. I'm heading over there now, to see if she's okay."

"*If* she's okay?" Ellen's voice was still monotone. She just put a little more force on that first *if.* "They don't know for sure?"

"No." He tried not to let his own fear show through, but he wouldn't lie. "She's unconscious, so they can't tell for sure."

He thought perhaps Ellen's face had paled—but she still showed no open reaction, so maybe he was imagining things. However, just in case a helpless anxiety lay beneath that blank facade, the same kind of impotent terror he was trying to cloak, he brought out the best smile he could manage.

"I really believe she'll be fine. I honestly think there's very little reason to be super worried."

"I'm not worried," Ellen said. And with that she turned

around and walked back into her bedroom. At the last minute, she swiveled and gave him that strangely blank look again. "Just so you know, though, I can still tell when you're lying."

BY THE TIME Max got to the hospital Penny was awake. But Rowena met him at the door to Penny's room like the dragon guarding the princess's castle. Before he could say a word, she put her hands lightly against his chest, and backed him up to the waiting area.

He caught only a glimpse of Penny, lying in the center of a crowd of family and flowers, before someone shut the door.

Rowena made a sound under her breath that, if it had been any louder, might be called a growl. She turned to Max.

"She doesn't need any drama," she said without preamble. "She's got a broken wrist, two bruised ribs, sixteen stitches in her calf and a concussion. So I repeat. She doesn't need any drama."

"I've never known anyone who did," Max observed calmly. "Although I've met one or two who seem to enjoy creating it."

Rowena's green eyes narrowed. She had a quick mind, and she knew what he meant. "I don't enjoy drama," she clarified. "But I'm not afraid of it, not if it keeps Penny safe."

"Neither," he said with a terse smile, "am I."

It was a standoff. The man with the magazine hadn't turned a page since they got started, though he'd lifted it up, as if the pages would hide his eavesdropping.

Rowena opened her mouth, ready to retort, but stopped when she saw Dallas come into the room. He went straight to his wife, put his arm around her shoulders and dropped a kiss on her silky black hair.

"Hi, Thorpe," he said pleasantly. Then he looked down at Rowena. "She wants to see him."

Rowena frowned. "But—"

"But nothing." Dallas gave her a one-sided smile. "Not our decision, honey. She said she wants to see him."

That was all Max needed to hear. He turned and headed back toward the little room. Even through the door, he could see that it was filled with a ridiculous number of flower arrangements. They'd probably cleaned out the gift shop entirely.

He knocked, but the minute he heard a voice say, "Come in," he pushed the door and entered. The room was hardly big enough to hold all the flowers, and all the people— Bree, Gray and Barton James circled the bed now, and for the life of him Max couldn't imagine where Dallas and Rowena had found a spot big enough to roost.

But Max's brain acted like a camera lens, zeroing in on the wan figure in the bed and letting the rest of the room fuzz out of focus. "Hi," he said.

She gave him a smile that was almost painful to see, because her upper lip was split.

"Hi," she said. "I told you I was clumsy."

He came closer, and though he still saw only Penny, he sensed that someone melted away to give him room.

"Yeah. You look pretty awful." He took her hand lightly. "What were you juggling this time? Butcher knives? Cannonballs?" He grinned. "Butcher knives *and* cannonballs?"

She started to laugh, then winced, and he felt like an idiot for cracking a joke. Bruised ribs, remember? He'd had a couple of broken ones, himself, and he knew how they hurt.

"She's just being modest," Gray put in. "She was a hero.

A couple of idiots fell out of the raft and decided that was the perfect moment to admit they couldn't swim. The guide had to go in after them, but he couldn't get them both, so Penny went in to get the other one."

She was shaking her head. "I didn't *go* in. Stop romanticizing it. I *fell* in." Her gaze returned to Max, and he was amazed to see that she was truly amused—her eyes were sparkling inside their purpling circles.

"True story. I really fell in."

Gray laughed. "Well, you fell in while you were trying to extend an oar to the person who was drowning. And after you fell in, you kept on trying to save her. And you did." He brushed his hands together smugly, wiping the imaginary dust from his palms. "Adds up to *hero* to me."

"And me," Bree said quietly. Max looked up, and saw that the cool blonde had hot tears in her eyes.

"Did everyone make it home in one piece?" Max looked at the cast on her arm, and the stitches over her eyebrows and beside her ear. "Or…at least in pieces that could be stitched and cast and stapled together again?"

She nodded. "I'm probably in the worst shape. I think I'm the only one who has to stay in the hospital overnight."

He wasn't surprised to hear that—she looked as if one night might not be enough. But he was disappointed. He knew the duplex would feel empty without her gentle presence next door.

"Because of the concussion?"

"Yes," she said. "Apparently they're going to wake me up every hour on the hour and ask me who I am."

Gray laughed. "I know. At midnight, tell them you're Cleopatra. At one o'clock, Madame Pompadour. At two o'clock—"

"Idiot." Bree bumped her husband's arm, but finally she was smiling, and the tears seemed to have ebbed a bit.

"At two o'clock, they'll put her in the psych wing, and then we'll *never* get her home."

"Bree." Penny held out her hand to her sister. "Would you mind giving Max and me a minute alone?"

Hell, yes, she'd mind. Max could see it in Bree's composed face, which, once you knew her better, wasn't quite the ice-queen-calm it seemed at first. Beneath the surface, the Wright women were emotional souls, filled with fiery loyalty toward one another.

"Bree?" Penny smiled, but she clearly wasn't asking permission. She was telling her sister to leave.

"Just a minute, then," Bree said reluctantly. The three of them filed out, each glancing over a shoulder at the very last minute, as if to be sure Max hadn't turned into a three-headed monster while they weren't looking.

Finally, Max and Penny were alone with the flowers.

"I just wanted to say I'm sorry, for what happened at the stables." She held out her hand. He took it without hesitation.

"You have nothing to apologize for." He wanted to tighten his fingers over her hand, but he wasn't sure she didn't have scrapes or bruises or tender places there.

"I do, though. I should have remembered the closed circuit camera was there. I should have warned you we might be observed."

"I'm not sure it would have stopped me."

She looked down. Then, slowly, she nodded. "It will be hard, won't it? But at least not right away. When I leave here, I'm going to Bell River. It'll be a while before I'm 100 percent again, and I honestly think they'll come move in with me if I refuse."

He saw the sense of it. He tried to move past his own disappointment. If she wanted space, if she wanted to get away from any temptation to fall back into bed with him, he was required, by honor, to let her have it.

"I wish…I wish Ellen weren't so insecure," he said. "If she were stronger—"

"But she's not. You're doing the right thing. I want you to know I understand that. Just because we weren't able to…to…"

"To stay out of each other's arms?"

"Yes. We had a plan, and we couldn't quite stick to it. We had a moment of weakness. That doesn't mean we failed. I know it's a cliché, but it's true. You haven't failed until you quit trying. And, with Ellen, you'll never quit trying." She smiled. "I don't want to quit trying, either. I'm really making progress with my list. Did you notice I went straight for the hardest one?"

Of course he'd noticed. He even understood why. She'd needed a challenge, a victory, so that the defeat they'd suffered didn't break her.

Which made this whole disaster his fault.

Somehow, he rallied a smile of his own. "Absolutely. The rafting counts, even if it ends with a hospital stay. So that makes eight out of twelve, right?"

She lifted one shoulder, then winced again. "It's not quite that simple. I took your suggestion, and I made some adjustments. You maybe noticed that I didn't ever get that tattoo."

He let his gaze drop to her hip, where she'd planned to put the tiny bluebird. The bluebird of happiness.

"Yes," he said. "I noticed everything."

Someone knocked on the door.

"One minute," Penny called out, her voice thin. But Max knew their time alone was almost over.

"I'll never forget a single thing about those hours," he said with a sudden urgency, as if he might never see her again. "I don't know how, exactly, but you set me free that night. I haven't had any more dreams about Mexico. And somehow I don't think I ever will."

"That would make me happy," she said. Her eyes welled with tears. "I would like to believe that, when we look back on all this—"

The door swung open. Max turned, feeling as if he might growl right back at Rowena this time, but it wasn't either of Penny's sisters. It was a nurse, rolling a silver stand from which a bag of clear liquid hung, refracting the light from the overhead fixture.

"Sorry, but we're going to need privacy," the nurse said. He was young and chipper and clearly unaware of the tension swirling around the room on perfumed waves of roses and lilies and sweet peas.

Grudgingly, Max let go of Penny's hand.

Her tears had begun to slide down her cheeks. "Friends?" she asked.

"Friends," he said, and as he heard the syllable echo through the sterile room, he wasn't sure that the entire English language possessed a more melancholy word.

CHAPTER FIFTEEN

"WHAT DO YOU mean, you don't know how to get to Montrose?" Ellen sat on the back porch, which had been painted gold by the setting sun, and glared at Alec. "I thought you knew how to do anything."

"Well, I don't know how to get to Montrose. So just forget about it. It's too far."

Alec was in almost as bad a mood as Ellen, but she understood that. Penny was like his aunt, a real member of his family. For Ellen, Penny was just a friend—and not even an old friend. Most people wouldn't understand why she was so upset right now. Even Ellen herself didn't fully understand it.

All she knew was that if anything happened to Penny she wouldn't be able to stand it.

"It sucks not to know what's going on," Alec said. "But they'll let us know when they're sure she's okay." He patted his pocket, frowned, then stood and patted his jeans pockets, too. "Oh, crudbucket! I don't have my phone."

Ellen almost fell off the deck. "You don't have your *phone?* All these hours you've been here, and you don't have your *phone?* She could be dead by now, and we wouldn't even know it!"

He huffed, clearly offended. "Well, you were so panicky when you called. You acted like it was the end of the world if I didn't get here ASAP. So I did. Give me your phone. I'll call Dad and ask."

But, to her horror, Ellen had begun to cry. She had been strung so tightly for about three hours now, and she couldn't take it anymore. She had to see Penny. She had to see her dad. She had to tell them how sorry she was.

"Ellen, don't do that!" Alec's eyes were big. He looked as if he might run away if she didn't stop crying, but she just couldn't.

She plopped down on the deck and put her head in her hands. She still had paint all over them, and her clothes, too, from the little fit she'd thrown when her dad left for Montrose.

Why hadn't she been able to tell him the truth? Why hadn't she been able to say how awful she felt? She should have begged him to take her with him. If Penny died before she could apologize…

"If she dies *at all* I'll die, too!" Ellen wailed, and it was as if she was crying for Penny and her mother, and for the way she'd been mean to her dad, all at the same time. And she was crying for herself, too, because she was so stupid that no one would ever love her again.

Penny maybe could have loved her, someday. She liked her a lot, or she had, before Ellen acted so awful. But now Penny was going to die, just like her mother….

"Noooo! She *can't* die!"

"I'm going to go get Mrs. B." Alec stood, but he hovered nervously next to Ellen. Getting Mrs. B was a major step, and he clearly didn't want to take it. "Come on, stop crying. I've got some Tootsie Rolls."

She didn't let up a bit.

"Come on, Ellen. You're scaring me."

"I don't *care!*" She glared at him, even though he looked like someone she saw from under water. "You said you could sneak away to anywhere. *Anywhere!* But you were just talking big. Just like about the earrings."

"Hey." Alec stiffened huffily, halfway through unwrapping a candy. "We had a deal. You weren't going to mention the earrings anymore."

"I don't *care* about the earrings!" God, why were boys so dense? "Can't you see that if Penny dies, she'll die thinking I hated her?"

"Well, you *were* pretty nasty." Alec shrugged his shoulders. "That's how it works if you say mean things. You always regret it. My dad says, treat everybody like it might be the last time you ever see them."

"I *hate* you," she said, because she knew he was right.

Alec stepped back, widening his eyes and holding up his hands in a way that was all kinds of sarcastic. "There? See what I mean? What if I fell off the deck right now and broke my neck?"

She looked at him, sniffing like crazy because she didn't have a tissue. She hadn't cried this hard ever before, even when her mother died.

"How can you be so calm? Don't you even care whether she dies or not?"

"Of course I'd care, if she were going to die. But she isn't."

Ellen sniffed again. "How do you know that?"

"Dunno. I just do. Maybe because my dad didn't seem scared enough when he left."

Ellen made an angry sound and stood up. "That's not a real reason."

"Yeah?" Alec popped his candy into his mouth. "Just wait and see, then."

Ellen put her forehead against the back wall of the kitchen and just kept crying. She wasn't wailing anymore, but this felt worse. Wailing was like a call out to somebody, like your parents, to come and help you, to come and make things right.

This was the kind of crying you did when there was no one to call. When no one could fix the mess you'd made.

Suddenly the kitchen door opened. She jerked up, not wanting Mrs. Biggars to see her. She couldn't bring herself to explain any of this to Mrs. B.

But it was her dad. He stood in the doorway, looking from her to Alec. Ellen dug her fists against her heart, because it was beating so fast. She hadn't noticed that the shadows were taking over the porch. She couldn't really see his face all that well.

Why didn't he say something? That couldn't be a good sign. Even Alec looked worried, watching Ellen's dad.

Then Ellen remembered what she'd acted like when her dad left. No wonder he wasn't saying anything. He probably didn't know who he was looking at—his nasty, selfish daughter, or Ellen.

"Daddy," she said, and the minute the word was out of her mouth she began to cry again. "Daddy, I'm sorry!"

She hesitated, wondering if it was too late to be forgiven. But her father sank to his knees and held out his arms. She ran into them without even worrying what Alec would think.

"I'm sorry," she said again. And then again. Over and over, into his shirt. She felt as if she could say it a hundred times, and it still wouldn't be enough. She'd done so many mean things over the past year.

He held on to her, his hands patting her hair, the way he used to do when she was a little girl. He was silent, and amazingly, so was Alec. Had he run away?

But she didn't turn around to see. She felt melded to her father's chest. She'd forgotten how strong and solid he was and how safe she felt with his arms around her.

Dad let her go on until her throat was sore from trying

to cry and trying to talk at the same time. Then he nudged her an inch or two away, so that he could look into her face.

His face was so gentle-looking. She thought about Penny's father, throwing her canary against the wall, and wondered how she could ever have taken her nice father for granted. She'd been very angry at him, but she'd never been afraid of him a single day in her life. Not even the day she almost got arrested.

He smiled, using his thumbs to brush away her tears.

"Penny is going to be fine," he said, as if he had known all along why she was really crying. "She got pretty bunged up. Her arm is broken, and she's got stitches everywhere. But she's going to be just fine."

Alec, who apparently had not sneaked away, made a crowing sound. "Told you," he said. But he sounded relieved.

She gave him a dirty look that was really not mad or anything, then turned back to her dad. "Are you completely sure?"

"Completely. I talked to her, and I talked to her family. I even talked to her doctor. She's going to stay in the hospital overnight, and then she's going to stay with her family at Bell River for a while, just till she's all healed up."

A heavy rock seemed to sink through Ellen's chest. "She's not coming back here?"

Dad looked sad, too, as if he knew about the rock. "Not for a while."

"Then how am I going to tell her I'm sorry? How am I going to tell her that I don't hate her?"

Dad put his hands on her shoulders. "Don't you?"

She shook her head, then bowed it. She felt horribly ashamed, and for the first time she understood the expression "hanging your head." She didn't really like to look into Dad's sad eyes right now.

"No," she said. Finally, she looked up. "I love her. You love her, too, don't you?"

He stood, though he kept his hands on her shoulders. He looked at Alec, and then he flicked a quick glance toward Penny's side of the house, which was dark, like a tomb. Ellen shivered, thinking about that expression, and being so glad it wasn't an expression she would ever have to really use.

"Yes," he said, finally, looking back at Ellen. "I love her, too."

"Aw, man." Alec looked at Ellen. "You really made a big cowboy hash out of this one, didn't you? I mean, I screwed things up when I tried to set my dad up with my math teacher, but at least I didn't chase Rowena away."

"Shut up," she said. Then she remembered she was going to try to be nicer to everyone—to treat people as if this might be the last time she ever saw them. Even Alec. "I mean, please don't say things that just make me feel worse. Help me try to fix it."

Alec unwrapped another candy and straddled the railing as if it were a horse. "Well, I guess you could ride over there with your dad, and you could tell her you're sorry you were such a nasty little frog dropping."

Her father made a strange noise, and Ellen put her hands on her hips. "Alec!"

He swallowed his candy and wrinkled his nose. "Sorry. That's what the cowboys say. Dad says I have to be careful, imitating them, because although they're quite colorful they are sometimes inappropriate."

He took on a very precise, lecturing adult tone when he repeated his father's words. "But Rowena says if the shoe fits…."

"Could we, Dad?" Ellen's heart sped up. "Could we go

and let me tell her I'm sorry? I could tell her that I don't hate her, that I really love her. You could tell her, too."

A pair of lights pierced the navy blue evening, and Ellen held her breath. Even though she knew Penny wasn't coming home tonight, seeing a car come up the driveway made her hope.

"I'm leaving, Mr. Thorpe!"

Her heart fell. It was just Mrs. B's ride. Her father called back something polite, and then they stood silently for a minute, watching the headlights back up and pull away again.

"I can't do that," her dad said, as if they were continuing their conversation without any interruption. "I'm very glad you care about her, and I'm glad that you don't mind that I care about her, too. But just because it's okay with us doesn't mean it's okay with her."

A huge void seemed to open up before Ellen's feet. "Do you mean she doesn't love you?"

"I don't know whether she does or not. I couldn't ask her. I wasn't free to, when I thought it would make you very unhappy. What you need always comes first, and she understands that."

The earth steadied a bit beneath Ellen's feet. "I bet she does," she said. "I'm sure she does."

"Don't be so sure," Alec said. "Sometimes ladies only like movie stars, like Brad Pitt."

"That's stupid." Ellen felt as if Alec had insulted her dad. "Why shouldn't Penny love my dad? He's just as handsome as your dad, and Rowena fell in love with him, right?"

"Hey." Her dad looked as if he were caught halfway between wanting to laugh, and wanting to sit down and be really, really sad. "First of all, it's not always about how pretty or handsome a person is. But also, there's an even bigger reason I can't talk to Penny about love right now."

"What reason?"

He took a deep breath, the kind he always started with when he thought he had to explain something that was too grown-up for her to understand. "In a way, she's asked me not to. She wants to have some time being on her own. She wants to learn to live alone, and to find out who she really is and what she wants out of life." He smiled, that same sad smile. "She even has a list—"

"The Risk-it List." Alec nodded. "Yeah. I've seen that. It's like a bucket list, only dumber."

Ellen turned around, making fists. "Alec, if you say mean things about Penny—"

Alec shook his head in a world-weary way he probably picked up from one of the wranglers. "I'm just saying some of the stuff on there is dumb. I mean, come on. Juggling? Would you have juggling on your bucket list?"

"It's not a bucket list. It's a Risk-it List."

"Whatever." Alec swung himself down off the railing. "If the list is the only thing standing in your way, that's easy enough to fix."

Ellen held her breath. This had better not be another of Alec's braggy lies. "How?"

He dug another candy out of his pocket. It must have been the last one, because he practically had to dig down to his shoes.

"How could we fix it?" She was hardly able to stand still while unwrapped it.

"Easy." He filled his mouth with chocolate, then grinned. *Disgusting.*

"Darn it, Alec." She practically stamped her feet. "Easy *how?*"

"Isn't it pretty obvious? We just find a way to help her finish up the things on her list." When no one oohed with impressed delight, he shook his head.

"Listen. Here's how it would go. It would be like…she's got juggling on there, and also 'throw a costume party,' right? So we throw her a circus party, and we all come as juggling clowns, and *wham!* Check, check, check…and *bam,* you're married!"

THE PROBLEM, MAX discovered later, was that none of them was sure exactly what was on Penny's Risk-it List.

He remembered the ones she'd checked off, like the kiss and the hot air balloon, and, of course, the juggling. Alec remembered the costume party. And Ellen remembered something about a sailboat.

"Yeah, but *what* about a sailboat? Sail one? Own one? Rent one? Get someone else to sail her around in one? Just 'sailboat' isn't really all that helpful," Alec said as they sat in Max's kitchen, trying to replicate the list.

Max sat back, enjoying listening to the two kids bicker, both of them caught up in the plan. It felt nice to think the campaign would be a family affair.

He wasn't sure when he decided to go along with the gag and approach Penny this particular way, but he was committed to it now.

Or maybe he meant he should *be* committed.

He couldn't be sure this was the right thing to do. He didn't know if it would work. But he knew that the three of them would always remember the night they plotted to win the heart of Penny Wright.

He stepped outside for privacy, then took out his cell and called Rowena.

"Hi," he said when she answered. "It's Max. Before you hang up, just listen to what I have to say."

The silence at the other end was edgy. "Okay. What do you have to say?"

"I am no threat to Penny," he said, for starters.

She made a disdainful sound. "I know one broken wrist, two bruised ribs and sixteen stitches that say otherwise. And if you're going to say you're not to blame for those—"

"I'm not going to say that. I know I'm to blame."

This time the silence was shock. "Okay," Rowena finally said, very slowly. "I'm listening."

"I'm in love with Penny," he said. "I want to marry her. I want to make her happy, if I can. Right now Alec and Ellen and I are trying to figure out how to make everything on her Risk-it List come true."

Another pause. "You and Ellen...and Alec?"

"Yep. Problem is, we aren't sure what all is on the list. I wondered if you might know."

"No." Rowena spoke slowly, as if she'd just awakened from a deep sleep. "I can't say that I do remember, exactly."

"Then would you be willing to come over, go into the house, and look at the list for us? Penny keeps it on the refrigerator door."

"Umm..." For once Rowena seemed at a loss for words. Finally, she spoke. "The thing is...it's not something I ought to stick my nose into. You see, I promised her I would stay out of this entirely."

"I understand." Max did understand, he thought. Rowena didn't think Max was right for Penny, and she didn't want to cooperate. Well, he'd find a way without her. He'd win Penny first, and then he'd have his whole life to show Rowena how wrong she'd been about him.

"Thanks, anyhow."

He was just about to hang up when she cleared her throat dramatically. "But on an *entirely unrelated* topic, I was wondering whether you might be able to help Penny get that back window fixed."

"Sure," he said absently.

"You know, the one just to the left of the kitchen door,

if you face the house from the back?" Rowena paused a moment, as if to give him time to orient himself. "Well, on that particular window, the lock is broken, and I keep telling her that anyone, I mean *anyone,* could get in the house that way, if they really wanted to."

Max began to laugh. "Oh."

"Yeah." Rowena sniffed. "Oh."

"Yes, of course, I'll look into that." He started to click off, but at the last minute, he decided he might as well be in for a dollar. "You're such a good sister, Rowena." He chose his words as carefully as she'd chosen hers. "I think it's terrific, how you protect her. It's important to be able to tell when there's a danger…and when there's not."

She huffed softly. "As long as you don't prove me wrong, Max Thorpe. I'm a bad enemy to have."

He chuckled softly, then clicked the off button. He slipped his phone back into his pocket and returned to where the children were still arguing about the sailboat.

"Well, that settles it," Max said, sitting down and leaning back in his chair. "I guess we'll have to break in."

Both children turned to look at him, their eyes as wide as saucers.

"Dang, *Ellen!*" Alec's voice was awestruck, and the look he turned on Max was filled with a new, stunned respect. "Your dad is *badass.*"

CHAPTER SIXTEEN

PENNY CAME BACK to Bell River the next day and was welcomed into the arms of her huge, boisterous family—even including Mitch, who had, to everyone's joy, appeared at Bell River the day of her accident. Although, mysteriously, Bonnie was not with him.

She didn't know Mitch well enough to probe any of that, and no one else seemed ready to quiz him, either. So they just made a celebration out of her homecoming, and included Mitch as casually as if he'd never been gone.

It felt strange to be back on Bell River land, but not altogether bad. Especially since she wasn't going to be sleeping in the main house.

Bless Rowena and Bree for that. The River Song cottage had come open, and her sisters had taken it off the "available" list, even on the computer reservation site, because they sensed that Penny might prefer to stay there instead of in the main house.

They were so right. If she stayed in the main house, in what they'd come to call the Sister Suite, she would have to walk past the front staircase, time and again, every single day. She simply couldn't do it.

Someday, she promised herself, she would be strong enough to put that old ghost to rest. But not today.

Today it was all she could do to hold the pieces of her broken, aching body together.

Not to mention her broken heart.

She couldn't allow herself to think of Max. It hurt more than her broken bones, her bruised ribs and her stitches all rolled together. When he'd left the hospital room yesterday, it had been like watching a beautiful, shimmering bubble bursting in thin air.

She had always known the bubble was too fragile to survive. But watching it pop and disappear felt like an act of violence. It felt like a little death.

She would not fall apart, though. She'd promised herself that. She'd gone white-water rafting yesterday to prove to herself that she was still moving forward, in spite of the fact that Ellen's outburst had clearly destroyed all hope of a relationship with Max.

She might have lost the man, but she hadn't lost herself. She hurt, but she was still growing, still risking. She'd looked at her list that day and asked herself, *what is the scariest thing on here?* The answer was the same as it had always been—white-water rafting.

So that was what she did.

And now here she was, twenty-four hours, one broken bone and two bruised ribs later, still missing Max like an amputation.

Maybe it was time to pick out something else to risk.

When the doorbell rang, she assumed it was one of the staff, bringing her lunch.

"Come in," she called, because standing was fairly painful. She'd managed to bathe and dress this morning, but that had taken most of the starch right out of her.

She let her head fall back against the cushioned armchair. Rowena had decorated these cottages so beautifully. She felt at home here already. Maybe later, she'd bring a couple of her paintings over. And of course she'd want her sketchbook....

She opened her eyes, ready with a smile to thank whichever college kid had been recruited to deliver her food. Instead, she thought she must be hallucinating.

Because the person standing in front of her was Max.

She tried to stand, but every muscle protested. He held out his hand. "Don't," he said. "You need to rest."

She felt her head shaking just an inch or so from left to right, like a subconscious expression of denial. Max couldn't really be here....

And what was he holding? It looked like a large white box. Like a box you'd buy a bedspread in.

"Max, what are you doing here?"

"I wanted to see if there were some way I could help you finish up your Risk-it List," he said. He pointed to the chair on the other side of the little, unlit fireplace. "May I? It might take a while."

She nodded carefully. "Max…" She watched him drag the chair closer. He put the large white box between them, on the ottoman. "Max, what's really going on here?"

"Really. It's what I said." He smiled. "I've got some ideas that I hope will get you through your list in record time. Just hear me out, okay?"

She nodded again. Her head was spinning, anyhow, and she wasn't sure she could think straight enough to ask sensible questions even if he let her. She wished, suddenly, that she hadn't taken the doctor's recommended pain pill when she got up this morning. He'd said it might make bathing and dressing easier. But right now she'd rather have a clear head than clean hair.

"Okay, so, as best I can tell you've got only five items left. They are, in no particular order, learn to juggle, get a beautiful tattoo, take a photo of someone famous, host a costume party and something about a sailboat. Is that about right?"

She looked at him, wondering whether she'd actually

fallen asleep in this chair, knocked out by the pain pill, and was dreaming him here. He looked good here, she thought. His suede jacket picked up the browns in the river rock fireplace, and his blue shirt picked up the blue of the carpet. Even in her dreams, she liked a nice color scheme....

"Is that about right?" He narrowed his eyes. "You're listening, aren't you, Penny? Are you feeling all right?"

She smiled. "I'm feeling fantastic," she said. "But if you're a dream, I definitely do not want to wake up."

"I'm not a dream." He leaned forward, and looked carefully into her eyes. "Have you been given some pain medication?"

She nodded, still smiling. "Yes. It was only so-so until a few minutes ago, but it's really kicking in now." She sobered for a second. "Wait. You said you're not a dream."

"No. I'm not. But I tell you what." He stood, and came to sit next to her on the sofa. "How about if you rest your head here." He tilted her very, very slowly toward him, so gently that it didn't even make her ribs cry out in pain. How did he do that? Even talking made them hurt, before.

She let her head sink into the hollow between his shoulder and his neck. It was a perfect fit. She kept her face out, though, so that the stitches about her eyebrows didn't press against anything. They did still hurt, just a bit.

"This is nice," she murmured as she shut her eyes.

"Good. So how about if you sleep here for a little while, until the medication wears…"

And that was all she remembered for a very long time. Later, she woke with a start that made her ribs blaze with pain. The sun was casting long rectangles of light through the great room windows, and the color of the light was clearly an afternoon gold. She glanced at the clock over the fireplace. Three? She'd slept for three hours?

She looked back at the man whose shoulder she'd been

sleeping on. She rubbed at a small round damp spot on the suede. Oops—not just *sleeping* on. Drooling on.

Well, drool was about as unglamorous as you could get. It hadn't been a dream, then. It really had been Max. And there was the white box, on the ottoman.

"Hi, there," he said softly. "Are you feeling better?"

"Actually, I'm feeling physically much worse. But my head is clear, and I know you're real. So that's better." She smiled. "In fact, it's quite wonderful."

"Good." He took her hand. "Do you remember where we were?"

She thought hard. "Oh. You were telling me about the five things left on my Risk-it List."

"Right!" He seemed proud of her, as if she were a student who had just turned in an A paper. "So those were the five things. Juggle, photo of someone famous, tattoo, costume party, sailboat."

She nodded. "Sounds about right. But I'm still not sure where this is going."

"Bear with me. So here's my plan. There's a pro golfer who is behind the Silverdell Hills project. His name is Acton Adams. Ever heard of him?"

She laughed. "Of course. Everyone has."

"Great. That means he definitely qualifies as famous. Which is good, because he'd like to hire you to do his photo shoot for the Silverdell Hills brochure."

"I…" She tilted her head suspiciously. "You arranged this?"

"Of course. Well, I got some help from Ellen and Alec. But the Acton Adams plan was mine."

She wondered whether she'd slipped back into a happy painkiller haze. Had he really said that Ellen had helped him? "Go on," she said cautiously.

"Okay. So that's one. Two, the tattoo. That was Alec's

idea." He felt around in his jacket's outside pocket, and he brought out a small rub-on tattoo. It was a bluebird.

"Nothing on the list says your tattoo has to be permanent. And you said you'd already decided not to get one, so Alec thought one of these rub-on deals would be best."

He grinned. "It took us two hours and seven stores to find one in the right color. Silverdell doesn't exactly have a lot of cutting-edge teen emporia."

"No," she agreed, still bemused. "No, it doesn't."

"Okay. So that's two down. Next comes the costume party. In that white box is a beautiful princess costume that Ellen picked out for you. She says we should have a Halloween party, and you and she can come as princesses. Only two small hitches. One, we have to have an early, early Halloween party, because none of us is willing to wait."

"And the other hitch?"

"Ellen says Alec and I have to come as princes. I'm willing to make the sacrifice, but Alec is standing firm. No prince costume for him. Ellen is very put out."

"I can imagine." She bit her lips so that she wouldn't laugh. Laughing really did hurt. Unfortunately, so did biting her cut lip.

"Okay. So that's three down. Which brings us to the sailboat thing. We were kind of stumped there. None of us had any idea what you really meant by just that one word… *sailboat*. Ellen was sure it meant you wanted to buy one, but then she's a big fan of conspicuous consumption. Alec, who has been brought up frugal, said probably you just want to paint one."

Penny was finally beginning to put the big picture together. And what a lovely, dreamlike picture it was! Alec, Ellen, Max—all conferring together to try to make Penny happy. How she would have loved to see them together like that, heads bent, faces intent, all in harmony. All focused on her—and not with hatred or resentment, but with affection and care.

She felt suddenly so lighthearted she thought she might float up off the sofa. She wondered how a body could be so battered and so aglow with happiness at the same time.

"How about you?" She gave him a teasing glance. "What did you think *sailboat* meant?"

"I thought maybe you just wanted to rent one and sail it somewhere special. Somewhere romantic..."

"Close." She put her hand on his thigh. "I want to make love on one."

His eyes widened, and then so did his smile. "Then I guess I'd better buy one," he said. "It'll be cheaper in the end."

She laughed. "Aren't you getting a little ahead of yourself? I don't remember saying I wanted to make love with *you*...."

"Don't you?" He took her hand and placed it over his heart. "I do. I remember your body telling me that you wanted to make love to me all night long. I told you I'd never forget it, and I never will."

"Yes," she said. "We agreed that we'd be happy memories for each other...."

"That's what I'm here to tell you. I was kidding myself, Penny. I can't be content with being a memory. It's just not enough—not anywhere nearly enough. I love you. I want to make new memories with you every single day for the rest of our lives."

"You do?" She sounded like an idiot. But happiness was like soda fizz spritzing through her veins, making her feel slightly drunk. She could hardly sit still, because everything inside her was bubbling and tickling and doubling over on itself like a hurricane caught in a bottle.

"But what about Ellen?"

"She loves you, too." His face was earnest. "I think we both knew, almost from the first moment we met you, that you were the one we needed in our lives. That you were the one who could teach us to love again. To be happy again. But it was so hard to believe. So hard to trust. We both tried to deny it for far too long."

He touched her face gently. "We're both through denying it, Penny. We love you. I love you. I know you wanted time, time to find yourself, to learn who you are and what you want, and if you still feel that way, we're willing to wait."

It was all she could do not to lean over and kiss that handsome, sensual and yet indescribably gentle face. Good thing her body was a wreck right now, or she wouldn't have been able to stop herself.

And there was still so much to be said.

"I...I don't know," she said thoughtfully. "You haven't told me how you're going to deal with the juggling problem."

He grinned. He knew, the scoundrel. No matter how she tried to tease him, he knew she loved him. He had probably known it from the start.

Or at least from that night—the night she gave him her body, he couldn't have missed that she also offered her heart and her soul.

"Yeah. The juggling. About that..."

She waited.

"We're going to have to remove that from the list. Just cross it off, snip it out, throw it away. Pretend it wasn't ever there. The three of us hashed that out for an hour or more, and we decided you are, indeed, hopeless."

She shook her head. "Fine thing to say to the woman you love."

He leaned over and softly kissed the bandages above each of her eyes. Then he kissed her swollen upper lip, so gently she almost couldn't tell when his lips were gone. Except that her lip tingled, and seemed to heal a little in that very instant.

"I think it's the perfect thing to tell her. I don't love you because I imagine you're perfect. I don't love you just because your body is beautiful and your face is young and sweet. I love you because you're you. I love the parts that are perfect, and I love the parts that are clumsy, or frightened, or sad."

She blinked, willing the silly tears to stay away. This was not a time for tears, not even happy ones.

"So what do you say, Penny? Will you give up that one thing on your list and take a husband and a daughter in its place? We're both slightly used and more than a little damaged, but we love you, and we need you, and I promise we'll work very, very hard to be sure the rest of your life is as happy as we can make it."

She reached up with her good hand and ran her fingertips through his hair. He shut his eyes briefly, absorbing the sensation, and when he opened them she saw that this tiny touch had ignited a fire.

"There's only one problem," she said. She waited to be sure she had his attention. "You see, yesterday I decided that list was absurd. Those weren't the risks I really wanted to take in my life. They weren't the things that mattered. And yet, just because I had put white-water rafting on some arbitrary list, I almost died in the rapids."

She took a deep breath. "So, while I was in the hospital, I made an entirely different list."

His jaw went momentarily slack. "An entirely different list…" He sounded stupefied.

"Yes. Want to see it?"

He nodded, half-dazed.

"It's in the drawer next to my bed." She nodded toward the hall that led to the bedroom. "I'd go get it myself, but…"

"Of course." He stood, went down the hall and within seconds was back, with her notebook in his hand. He extended it, but she shook her head.

"I'd like you to read it, if you will," she said. "It's on the first page."

She knew the list by heart, because, this time, it was the list of her heart. It was shorter, but much harder to achieve. Everything on there was frightening, difficult and very, very real.

He began to read the list out loud.

"One: Learn to separate the Bell River of the present from the Bell River of the past. The stairs are just stairs. Put those ghosts to rest."

He glanced at her, his eyes somber. She didn't speak, so he went on.

"Two: Learn the sound of your own inner voice. It doesn't sound like Dad, or Mom, or even Rowena or Bree. You know it when you hear it. Learn to obey that voice and that voice only."

He hesitated a moment, then sat on the nearest chair, as if he needed to be at rest, so that he could really absorb and understand. He was clearly catching on that this wasn't a list that anyone could "help" her accomplish. And it wasn't a list that would be mastered in a month, or a year, or maybe even in a lifetime. But it was a list to live by.

"Three: Accept that there are no places where no storms come. Don't hide from life. Learn to value the storm as well as the calm."

She closed her eyes, waiting for numbers four and five. They were the ones that really mattered. They were the ones she needed him to hear.

"Four: Tell Max that you love him."

He cleared his throat, as if some emotion had clogged it, making it hard to speak.

He started again, but had to stop. And so she spoke the last one for him.

"Five," she said softly.

"Love is the only risk worth taking."

CHAPTER SEVENTEEN

Three months later

SHE'D BEEN ON a sailboat so long she'd lost her land legs, it seemed. They got off the plane, drove through the bleak gray and white landscape of an approaching Colorado winter, made their way to Silverdell and pulled onto the grounds of Bell River before she really felt that the ground wasn't swaying and swelling beneath her.

The honeymoon had been two weeks on a schooner, sailing around Hawaii, drinking out of coconuts, dancing under the starlight and always, always making love.

It had been two weeks of heaven.

But now they were home, and they could hardly wait to see Ellen, who'd been staying at the ranch while they were gone. They'd talked to her every day, and they'd called on Skype and texted and created Google hangouts...at least they did so whenever Ellen could find the time for them.

Max had pretended to lament the loss of his daughter to her two new loves, horseback riding and photography, but Penny knew that he was deeply grateful to see her so busy, so passionate and so healthy.

She'd shot up about six inches in two months, and was starting to look like a fashion model. Ironically, all that had happened just about the time she stopped believing her looks were the most important thing in her life.

When they arrived, a red-nosed, jacketed welcoming

committee was gathered around the front fountain, so Max parked the car out front. They'd be moving into River Song cottage, and turning the duplex into the art studio Penny had always dreamed of.

They'd spend the first month in the main house, though, while an addition to River Song was finished. Ellen was going to need more privacy than the original two-bedroom floor plan would have allowed. She would be a teenager in a couple of years—and heaven help them then!

Penny was bouncing with excitement as they parked the car. There was Ro, looking…oh, dear heaven, she was looking so very pregnant! And Bree, cuddling under Gray's enveloping arm, and smiling from ear to ear with such warmth it was hard to believe she'd ever been called the Ice Queen.

And there was Ellen, all svelte and elegant in her riding jodhpurs and fur-trimmed jacket. Alec had grown another foot, as well, and would soon be as tall as Dallas. Right now he rode his uncle Mitch's shoulders, but he wouldn't be able to get away with that much longer.

Barton had his guitar out, and was singing "Blue Hawaii" softly in the background, though his hands must be freezing in this crystal-ice air.

The minute Max and Penny emerged from the car, they were swarmed, covered in love and hugs and laughter and kisses like a coating of honey. The men slapped each other on the shoulders, and the women cried and kissed, and the kids just laughed at everyone.

Penny hugged Ro an extralong time. "I can't believe you," she said, putting her hand on her sister's small, but unmistakable, baby bump. "Is everything going well?"

"It's going perfectly," Ro said, and Penny could see that it was true. She was no longer gaunt and bony. Her face had softened with baby weight, until she looked more like a Madonna than a firebrand.

"Is Mitch all right?"

Rowena nodded. "Oh, yes. Thank God. It was killing Dallas, the not knowing. Of course, we still don't know much about Bonnie."

"I wondered whether Dallas would be able to talk him out of going after her," Penny said, her gaze resting thoughtfully on her brother-in-law, the born protector.

When Mitch had returned, he'd told them all that even he didn't know where Bonnie was. He simply had awakened one morning, and she was gone. After Penny's wedding, it had been clear that Mitch had been itching to go back out and try to find her somehow.

"So far, so good," Rowena said, but her voice sounded somber, and Penny knew Mitch's heart wasn't yet resigned to the loss.

Penny nodded. Life was so complex. Amid happiness, fear still had a place at the table. In the middle of security, there was always a kernel of doubt.

But she'd finally stopped dreaming about a day when everything would be sunshine and flowers. She was learning, day by day, to cherish the storm as well as the calm.

Gradually, everyone began to shiver, even with the jackets and gloves. It was mid-December, and far too cold to dawdle outside when the fires indoors called so invitingly. One by one, they began grabbing suitcases and helping to carry them in.

Penny and Max were the last. They stood in the bronzing twilight and let their gazes rest gently on this softly undulating land that was to be their home. The ranch she had left so long ago in agony...

Today she returned in joy.

"You ready?"

Penny nodded. It wasn't strictly true. Fear was knocking at her heart again. *Remember me? Remember me?* But she and Max had talked it over, as they lay in each other's arms under the stars. And they had decided that, today, she would return to Bell River through the front door.

They got all the way to the threshold, and her blood began to run cold. She put her arm on his, and he froze in place. He didn't push. He would never push. She knew he would wait as long as she needed.

"There's always tomorrow, sweetheart," he said softly. "We can go around back today, if you'd rather."

"No." She didn't want to give up. She had thought of this moment so often, and of how triumphant she would feel.... "No. Just give me a minute."

She stared into the foyer. It had been completely renovated, and no remnant of her mother's blood, or her mother's shadow, remained. No remnant, even, of the original structure remained.

So why did she feel so strongly that her mother was waiting for her, just inside the door?

Don't be afraid, Penelope. I love you very much.

Penny turned quickly, and stared, wide-eyed, at Max. He frowned. "Sweetheart, please. Don't let it upset you. It doesn't have to be today."

"Didn't you hear that?" She cast her eyes around the area, to see if anyone else stood nearby. Ro, maybe. It might have been Rowena's voice. She had always sounded a lot like their mother.

But no one was there. And, as Penny looked back into the foyer, she realized that the feeling of her mother's presence was gone. Entirely gone.

There were no ghosts here anymore. There was no lingering pain.

It was, after all, just a staircase.

And a very beautiful one.

"I'm ready," she said. She started to take her husband's

hand, so that they could walk together into their new home, but, before she realized what was happening, he scooped her into his arms.

She laughed, breathlessly, and he gazed down at her with so much love in his eyes that she turned to liquid from the inside out. She lifted her face and accepted his slow, deep kiss, letting her heart fill with the honeyed warmth she'd come to depend on.

Even that didn't frighten her. It was safe to count on Max, because…

Because he was Max. He was a part of her, not some external crutch. He was the other half of her lonely soul, the half she'd been looking for without realizing it, all her life. And she completed him, just as he completed her.

Finally, he lifted his lips. He smiled, and her heart took wings.

"Welcome home, my love."

And then, with his strong arms firm and sure around her, he carried her easily over the threshold and out of the past.

* * * * *

Look for the next book in Kathleen O'Brien's
THE SISTERS OF BELL RIVER RANCH *series!*
Coming in May 2014 from Harlequin Superromance.

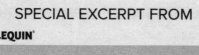
A Promise for the Baby
By Jennifer Lohmann

"I'm sorry to drop in on you like this," Vivian said, gesturing
to the luggage near the door. "I didn't feel I had any choice."

"Were the terms of our divorce not sufficient?" Karl's elbows
rested on the arms of the chair and he'd laced his fingers
together in a bridge over his charcoal-grey suit. Vivian was
certain Karl must have soon-to-be ex-wives drop in on him all
the time, since he managed to remain so self-possessed about
the whole thing.

But his absolute composure was the reason she'd answered
"sure" on that fateful night in Las Vegas when he'd gestured
to the doors of the wedding chapel, and asked, "Shall we?"
with that half-smile on his face. She had wanted to be a part
of his stability then, so she supposed it was unfair of her to
be irritated by it now. And if she also longed for the passion

they'd shared…well, that had gotten her into this mess in the first place.

"Yes. I mean, no, they were fine. I mean, I don't want a divorce—at least not right now."

If she'd shocked him, he didn't let it show. His only reaction was to lean back in the chair and lift his left foot to rest on his knee. Vivian was glad he hadn't sat on the couch next to her. She felt crowded enough by his presence without having to make room for his knees, elbows *and* infinite placidity—which took up far more space than any single lack of reaction should.

"I'm pregnant and I want to keep the baby."

How will Karl react to this news?
And will they stay married?
Find out in A PROMISE FOR THE BABY
by Jennifer Lohmann,
available January 2014
from Harlequin® Superromance®.

REQUEST YOUR FREE BOOKS!
2 FREE NOVELS PLUS 2 FREE GIFTS!

HARLEQUIN

super romance®

More Story...More Romance

This cowboy deserves a second chance...

A Ranch for His Family
by Hope Navarre

Bull riding means everything to Neal Bryant. In his quest for the championships, he's let everything else go—including Robyn Morgan, the woman he loves. Then he has a bull-riding accident that could turn his rodeo dreams to Kansas dust. It's fitting—or maybe it's fate—that she's the nurse at his bedside.

While recuperating on his family's ranch, Neal learns how much he's missed. Robyn is widowed *and* has a son Neal can't seem to resist...especially when he learns *he's* the father. It's a dream he never allowed himself to have. And now he needs to show Robyn he's worth a second chance.

AVAILABLE JANUARY 2014 WHEREVER BOOKS AND EBOOKS ARE SOLD.

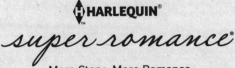

HARLEQUIN®

super romance

More Story...More Romance

www.Harlequin.com

HSR71898